"O'Farrell's sensitive treatment makes *Michael* compelling... She has a keen sense of place and social milieu that sharpens her observations of the characters' psychological conflicts...

A rich, moving exploration of the meaning of family, in all its guises."

—*Kirkus Discoveries Reviews*

Michael

To Marcia
Best Wishes.

Michael

the sequel to *Norah's Children*

Ann O'Farrell

iUniverse, Inc.
New York   Bloomington

Michael
The Sequel to Norah's Children

iUniverse books may be ordered through booksellers or by contacting:

iUniverse
1663 Liberty Drive
Bloomington, IN 47403
www.iuniverse.com
1-800-Authors (1-800-288-4677)

ISBN: 978-1-60528-025-7 (pbk)

Printed in the United States of America

To James Richard,
Jamie,
and Vincent.

Acknowledgments

"Where's Michael?" is the question that has dogged me for some time now. So many readers of *Norah's Children* have taken the time and trouble to write to me telling me how much they enjoyed that story. But, almost without exception, the final sentence in their e-mails and letters has been, "Where's Michael?" So I thank you all for your enthusiasm and patience. I can finally answer. Here he is!

My most sincere and grateful thanks must go again to Tom Coyne, my mentor, editor, and now I am also delighted to call him my friend. His eagle eye, expertise, and support were crucial to the final work.

The Wordsmiths Writer's Group, ably augmented by the Tarpon Springs Writer's Group, also played its part in helping me hone my story. Their fulsome critiques and helpful suggestions kept me focused and on my toes!

The Harbor Authorities in Dun Laoghaire, Dublin, were a most helpful source of information on passenger travel across the Irish Sea during the war years.

My thanks to Jenny Seawright, author of *Irish Wildflowers*, who generously provided so much information on wild flowers, their seasons and possible locations.

To my friends in Spindrift, Georgia Post, Mary Dresser, Michele Ivy Davis, Howard Jones, and Claudia Sodaro—all excellent writers. I thank you all for your encouragement and brainstorming.

A heartfelt thank-you must also go to Pat and Harry McCarthy whose enthusiasm for this project has been infectious.

And so to the first reader of *Michael*, my advisor, best friend, and husband; thank you, John, always. Without you ...

Ann O'Farrell.

The Story So Far...

Michael Kelly, born in Glendarrig, Co. Galway, Ireland, on May 2, 1922, is the youngest of Norah and Brendan Kelly's five children. When Norah dies, soon after Michael's second birthday, his father hastily re-marries to provide a new mother for the children. The morning after the wedding Brendan declares that he has changed his mind and will continue to care for only the eldest son, Pierce. He refuses to give an explanation and further announces that the four other children shall be placed in an orphanage. The children's great-aunt, Bridgie, struggles to prevent this happening. She arranges new homes in England for the three youngest, Colm, Sheelagh, and Michael, but decides to keep the eldest girl, Mary, with her.

Colm goes to a wealthy family, the Sinclairs, in London while Sheelagh and Michael are taken to Bristol by their new guardians, Edith and Jim Porter. As a result of all these traumatic changes in his short life, Michael becomes increasingly silent. Jim Porter feels that this silence hides a slow intellect, intolerable for a potential son and heir of Porter's Haberdashery and Clothing Emporium. He therefore resolves to rid himself of the boy.

Bristol, England
March 25, 1925

Arrival

The man rapped impatiently on the door, stepped back, and almost stumbled over the small child tucked close behind him.

"For heaven's sake, boy, keep out of the way."

Taking a watch from his waistcoat pocket, the man glanced at it, gave a snort of exasperation, and hammered on the door again. A few moments later they heard the slide of a bolt and the door opened slightly. The boy peeked cautiously from behind the man's legs. He saw an old lady peering out. She seemed very cross-looking, he thought. She opened the door a little wider. He saw she wore a long, black dress, neatly fastened at the neck and wrists with shiny black buttons. Her mouth was gathered in a tight purse of disapproval, and the boy could see a small dark moustache across her top lip. Deep frown lines creased her forehead.

Jim Porter turned, caught the boy roughly by the arm, and pushed him toward the entrance.

"Get in, boy. Get in, and stop getting in the damn way."

The surprised woman stood to one side as the man pushed the child into the dark hallway.

"Good morning, Wyn. Sorry to call so early, but I've to open the shop, and I wanted to get this done first."

The woman looked with some confusion from her brother to the young boy standing in front of her.

"Can I come in, woman, or must we conduct our business in front of the whole damn street?"

"That's two curses in almost as many sentences, Jim Porter," the woman said, regaining her composure.

"I'll thank you not to use that kind of language in front of me." She stood further to one side, and her brother stepped past her and briskly walked the length of the short hallway into the kitchen, pushing the child ahead of him.

"Good God, it's as cold as charity in here. Don't you have your range lit?"

She closed the front door and followed him.

"I'm not long out of bed. Why should I have a fire burning down here all night when I'm asleep upstairs?"

"Well, for heaven's sake, light it now. It's March, woman. It's warmer out on the street than it is in here."

"I'll do it when I'm good and ready, thank you. It was you who wanted to be in off the street. I'm not used to having visitors at this hour of the morning."

She looked with distaste at the small boy in the overlarge jacket. Indeed, all his clothes looked too large on him; even his shirt collar was gathered awkwardly at his neck with a thin blue tie.

"Is there a reason why this little urchin is here?"

"Of course there is. He's for you. Say 'good morning', young man."

The child stared up at the woman, but said nothing. She took spectacles from her pocket, put them on, and returned his stare. Her birdlike eyes peered myopically from behind the wire-rimmed lenses.

"What on earth are you talking about, Jim? Is this one of the Irish brats you adopted?"

"He *is* Irish; he's *not* a brat, and I *didn't* adopt him." Jim Porter eased himself into the wooden rocking chair in front of the range. "He is, however, one of the children Edward Sinclair convinced me to take in. He suggested this one might make a possible son and heir. Heaven knows Edith has never been able to provide me with one. I only took the boy because she and Sinclair kept telling me what a good idea it was. Stupid, really."

"And now …?" Wyn Porter moved her steady gaze from the boy to the heavyset, red-faced man occupying her rocking chair.

"I've decided it's far too much for her, having the two children. My wife never seems to be in the best of health anyway, and I don't think she can cope with him *and* his sister. The little girl isn't too bad. She's a bit older and quite a pretty little thing actually." He smiled briefly. "Edith likes dressing her up and fussing with her. However, I think this

8

young man will need more attention. Boys always need discipline, and I just don't believe Edith is up to the task."

He paused, as if to consider what to say next.

"So, Wyn, you're always fretting about what will happen to you in your old age, given that you never found a husband. You're always asking who will care for you, all that sort of nonsense. Well, here's the solution." He gestured toward the child.

"What are you blathering on about, Jim?" She glanced scornfully at the boy who was edging toward the back of the rocking chair. "That," she pointed toward the retreating child, "doesn't look like much more than a baby. And you're suggesting he's supposed to look after *me*?"

"In good time, Wyn, in good time. Of course, he has to grow up a bit first." He held his hand up against a threatened interruption and continued, "But then, you don't exactly need minding right now, do you?"

She sat at the kitchen table and waited.

"Look, Wyn, it's like this. If you take him in, teach him his manners and all that, I will cover the cost of his keep. You won't be out of pocket. Maybe I could even reduce your rent here?" He waited to be sure she fully appreciated this concession. "And before you know it *he* will be able to look after *you*, when you need it, so to speak."

"Have you quite finished?"

"I have."

He looked pleased with his presentation.

"You may have overlooked a few points, in your enthusiasm to dump your unwanted baggage on me, James Porter."

She raised her hand and began to enumerate on her fingers.

"Firstly, I am a single woman, living alone. What on earth will people say if this little stranger suddenly appears?"

"That's quite straightforward; we will explain he is a charity case. Everyone will be most impressed with your kindness and Christianity."

She ignored his interruption and continued making her points.

"Secondly, I don't want a child."

"Don't think of him as a child. He's an investment for your old age, Wyn; an income for when you can't sew anymore!"

"And thirdly, I have no idea how to look after a child."

"Who does, woman? Everyone seems to learn as they go along: look at my Edith! She's looking after the other one. If she can do it, with one anyway, then anyone can. I'm sure you would be very good at it," he said dismissively.

"But, I'd have no idea where to start. I am too old for this kind of hare-brained scheme, Jim. I couldn't possibly cope. I have to earn a living, you know."

"Of course you could cope. Don't talk nonsense. Edith and I are always available. It's not as if we live far away. We would always be here, in an emergency. You can continue to do all your sewing and fixing, even with him here. It's not as if you leave the house to work."

He struggled for a decisive argument. He did *not* want to bring this stupid child back home.

"And I tell you what, Wyn, if you do a half decent job with him, I will even consider bringing him into the business. I could even leave it to him if he shapes up well enough. Let's face it; I don't have anyone else to leave it to."

Wyn narrowed her eyes, looking from her brother to the small boy trying to hide himself behind the rocking chair.

"What about the little girl? What will she get?"

"Well, you don't leave a business to a woman, Wyn; that's for sure. Have sense."

The room was quiet for a moment.

"What's his name?"

"Michael."

"How old is he?"

"He's nearly three, I believe."

"Is he house-trained? I don't want any nasty little messes around the house."

"Yes, of course he is. Martha took care of that."

"Unlike you," she said. "Unlike you," she repeated with emphasis, "I don't have the luxury of a maid. You had better be right."

She paused for a moment and then crooked her finger at the terrified child.

"Come here, boy."

Michael reluctantly left his refuge and came forward. His too-large shoes clacked on the tiled floor. The old woman sat, hands primly clasped in her lap, until he stood in front of her.

"Show me your hands."

He offered them slowly, palms upward. Wyn examined them carefully, turned them over to examine his nails, thrust them away, and turned to her brother.

"We'll see. You will pay for him, you say?"

He nodded.

"And reduce the rent?"

"I barely cover my costs with what you pay me as it is, Wyn." He saw her stiffen and added hastily, "Yes, yes, I'll reduce the rent."

"Good. You know full well I don't earn enough money to feed and clothe a child as well as myself."

"Of course, that's understood. I told you I will cover all his expenses."

She remained silent, looking at the boy. Her brother held his breath. She considered the proposition a moment longer; then gave a curt nod.

"Very well."

Jim Porter exhaled in relief, "Good, that's settled then." He stood. "I'll get his stuff from the car. I've already outfitted him from top to toe, as you can see, so there will be no clothing expenses for a while."

Settling In

Wyn followed her brother to the front door. The boy remained beside the kitchen table, as instructed.

Jim Porter wasted little time retrieving the small Gladstone bag from the back of the car.

"There you are," he said, handing her the bag. He saw the doubtful look on his sister's face and gave a stiff smile of reassurance, "You'll thank me for this one day, Wyn."

She snorted her derision.

He was already returning to his car, calling over his shoulder, "I'll collect the bag when I come over on Sunday. See you then."

He climbed into the car, gave his sister a brief wave, and drove away. Wyn closed the door and walked back to the kitchen.

She glanced at the boy as she dumped the bag on the table. "Well, let's see what you have then." Pushing him slightly to one side, she opened the bag, emptied out the contents, and examined them.

"Hmm, two of everything, a bit like Noah's Ark." She turned to the boy, "Isn't it?"

Michael continued to watch her in silence.

"Are you familiar with the Bible, young man?" she waited for a moment, watching him, then sighed. "Too young, I suppose," she muttered to herself as she repacked the small bundle of clothes. "I must presume it's too much to expect of a three year old and an Irish one at that." She closed the bag and turned to look again at the boy. "I suppose we have to find you somewhere to sleep." She shrugged impatiently and lifted the bag, "Though I don't really have much choice. Follow me."

She strode out into the hall, with Michael trailing behind. Raising the hem of her skirt, she climbed the narrow stairs.

"When the world became full of sinners, God found the only good man left, a man called Noah, and told him to build a boat. An ark they called it. God said he was going to do away with all the sinners, and Noah should collect two of every insect, animal, and bird and take them into the ark with him."

The boy followed her slowly, gripping each banister as he went.

"He took his family too, of course," she added, glancing back at him.

When she reached the top of the stairs she turned to the boy, "So, you see what I mean? Two of everything."

He continued to struggle up the stairs.

There were two doors on the landing, both closed. She opened the first one and stepped inside. Michael stopped at the entrance. He glanced up at the open door, his attention caught by a small brass figure set high in its center, out of his reach. Wyn noticed his gaze.

"It's a monkey, see?" She lifted the monkey's tail. "It's a knocker." She rapped it against the base plate to demonstrate. "You should always knock before you enter a room." She frowned down at him, "Always, do you understand?"

He remained mute.

"Come in, child, come in," she added impatiently.

Michael stepped into the small, overcrowded room. A treadle sewing machine stood in front of a heavily lace-curtained window. A fragile-looking bentwood chair was placed in front of the machine. Beside it was a low table covered with an assortment of pins, threads, bobbins, and scissors. There were also tin boxes, decorated with pictures of flowers, landscapes, and castles. The boxes overflowed with multi-colored lengths of ribbon and lace. To the left of the machine, tucked into the corner of the room, stood a tall, narrow bookcase filled with neatly folded pieces of material in a variety of fabrics and colors. There were more fabric pieces and paper patterns piled on an iron-framed single bed set against the opposite wall. A tailor's dummy stood on its wooden pedestal in the center of the floor.

"This will have to be your room." She put the bag on the bed and indicated the bentwood chair. "Sit there, out of the way, while I see what I can do."

Michael did as he was told, hitching himself awkwardly up onto the fragile chair. He watched as the woman tidied the jumble on the bed, sorting and folding the fabric and paper patterns. She moved the dummy to one side and stacked the folded items on the already overcrowded shelves of the bookcase.

"So, God caused a great deluge," she continued, as if there had been no interruption. She paused in her work to look at the boy. "That's a lot of rain," she clarified. "It rained for forty days and forty nights and all of the sinners were drowned."

She unpacked the bag and placed his clothes neatly in a space she cleared on the bottom shelf. When finished, she stood back to admire her work. She gave a peremptory nod of satisfaction and turned to Michael.

"Right! That will have to do for now. I'm going downstairs to light the range; I have ladies coming later."

She left the room and retraced her steps down the stairs. Michael followed her as far as the top of the stairs and stopped. Reaching the bottom, she turned and saw he had not moved.

"Come on child, what on earth's wrong with you?"

His bottom lip began to tremble.

"Oh, good heavens, don't tell me you can't walk downstairs. You had no problems going up. Come along. I don't have all day." He still didn't move. "Just hold onto the banister, child, and go slowly. Come along I say."

He gripped the rail with both hands. Standing sideways he cautiously tackled the first step, carefully lowered one foot onto it and then the other.

"Good, there you are, just keep doing that."

Michael carefully descended one more step.

"You see! It's perfectly straightforward. Now hurry up."

She continued into the kitchen without looking back again. The boy made his slow descent.

Wyn collected a bucket from the backyard, returned to the kitchen, and spread two sheets of newspaper on the floor in front of the range. She knelt and vigorously raked the cold embers. Fine ash fell through the lower grating. Using a small black shovel she collected the ash and folded it into the newspaper. She lifted out the separate clinkers of spent coal and dropped them into the bucket. Michael finally joined her in the kitchen, and she immediately held the newspaper bundle toward him.

"Here you are, lad, make yourself useful," she said.

He obediently took the package.

Gripping the arm of the rocker, she struggled to stand. "Take those outside and put them in the bin."

He glanced in confusion around the kitchen.

"Out there, boy! Through that door!" She waved her coal and ash-grimed hands toward the back door.

He moved hesitantly, clutching the parcel firmly to his chest with both hands. At the door he carefully transferred the parcel to one hand and fumbled under the heavy lace curtain until he found the door handle. Twisting it awkwardly, he let himself out into the backyard.

Michael stood in the cramped, paved yard. A corrugated metal bin stood under the kitchen window. Beyond it, a low brick wall held back a small mound of coal, still shining from the early morning rain. Michael lifted the bin lid and peered inside. It was half-filled with neat newspaper packages similar to the one he had in his hand. Curious, he replaced the lid and tried to unwrap his own parcel. His cold fingers were clumsy and, in his attempt to explore its contents, he spilled the ash over himself, the bin, and the ground. Throwing a panicky glance at the closed kitchen door, he tried to scoop the fine powder back into the crumpled newspaper. Where it had settled on the paving, in patches of moisture, it congealed into a gray mud that stuck to his hands and clothes. He gathered all that he could, deposited the makeshift parcel into the bin, and replaced the lid carefully. He was reluctant to return to the house, fearful of the woman's reaction to his dirt-streaked clothes. He remembered Aunty Bridgie's scolding when he dirtied his clothing and Mary's ill humor when she had to clean and tidy him up. He decided to continue exploring the yard. As he did so he rubbed his hands on his jacket and pants to remove the dirt.

There was a brick lean-to in the back corner of the yard, its rough wooden door sparsely covered with chipped and peeling blue paint. A half-moon opening, cut high in the door, looked like a tiny window. The door was held closed by a rusty metal latch. Michael lifted the latch and peered inside. A white porcelain toilet stood against the facing wall, patterned with a thousand hair-thin, yellowing, cracks. It was attached by a rusty pipe to a square cast-iron water tank bracketed on the wall above, close to the corrugated tin roof. A knotted rope hung from a lever protruding from the side of the tank. Torn squares of newspaper, threaded on twine, hung on a nail on the side wall. Michael closed the door and continued to explore the yard.

He saw another door set in the back wall. Peering through a convenient knothole he could see a narrow lane. It was clogged with tall, dead grasses and weeds twisted and tangled around a derelict collection of discarded household items, bins and old rags. A thin trace of a mud path was visible along the center of the lane.

Michael turned his attention back to the yard. A large iron mangle stood against the whitewashed wall, its wooden rollers gray-bleached from the constant assault of water and weather. A tin bathtub hung on a nail above it.

The kitchen door opened.

"In heaven's name child, where are you? What are you doing out here?"

She saw the dirty bin lid and the finger-scraped streaks of ash mud on the paving stones. She turned to her left to see the small child standing guiltily beside the towering mangle. His pale face was smudged with dirt; his dark brown eyes round with fright. He quickly stepped behind the mangle, watching the severe-looking woman from under the rollers.

"Get out here this minute, you dirty little urchin."

Michael pressed himself tighter into the wall. In two steps Wyn was beside the mangle. She caught the small boy by the ear and tugged him sideways from his hiding place. Holding him at arm's length, still by the ear, she led him back into the kitchen and over to the sink.

"Stand there and don't move."

She filled an enamel basin with water from the single tap and whipped the wire soap whisk in the cold water in a vain attempt to create suds.

"There's no hot water yet; the range is barely lit. How am I expected to wash off all this dirt with no hot water? What on earth did you do, child? The ashes were well wrapped."

Warm tears began to wash clean runnels down his face.

"Don't start blubbering. I can't stand people who blubber."

She caught a handful of his dark, curly hair and tugged it back so that his face looked up at hers. She scrubbed at it with a rough cloth.

"How can anyone get this dirty this quickly?"

She dried his face with her apron.

"Hands!"

He meekly held out his hands, which she scrubbed with the wood-handled brush. She dried them in her apron too. She used the cloth to scrub at the dirt on his jacket and pants, but finally gave up.

"I suppose it will brush off when it dries."

She pointed to a chair beside the table.

"Sit."

He watched in silence as she emptied the chipped enamel bowl, wiped it with the cloth, and rested it upside down on the ridged wooden draining board. She draped the cloth over it. The old woman then removed her apron, lifting it carefully over her head and tossed it onto the table. She took a fresh one from a drawer in the dresser and put it on. Stepping to the side of the range she unhooked a rope and lowered the wooden drying rack, festooned with clothes, towels, and rags. She hung her apron neatly on one of the rails and raised the rack. The small metal pulleys squealed in protest as she pulled and tied the rope to a peg in the wall.

At last she sat in her rocking chair beside the range and stared hard at the small boy perched on the kitchen chair, his feet dangling awkwardly some distance from the floor.

The Understanding

"If you are going to live here young man, there are a few things you will have to understand. I cannot abide dirt! I will not have dirt in my house. Cleanliness is next to Godliness. Do you understand?"

Michael nodded.

"And I will not tolerate sullenness either. You will answer me properly when I speak to you." She frowned. "Oh, dear, we have to decide what you are going to call me." She thought for a moment, "I don't suppose you can call me Miss Porter." She took a deep breath. "Right then, you will call me Aunty Wyn."

He watched her.

"Well? Say it, child."

"Yes, Aunty Wyn."

"Oh, my!" She looked startled. "You have an Irish accent. That's the first thing we will have to change. You're in England now, young man. We speak English here."

A yellow-gray puff of smoke belched from the fire in the range, and Wyn immediately turned her attention to it. She took the bellows that were lying beside her chair, knelt, and poked its thin nozzle toward the base of the smoking fire.

"Wet coal! I knew I should have brought in a bucketful last night." She pumped the bellows energetically, blowing strong puffs of air into the dying fire. More smoke billowed into the room and Michael began to cough.

"Do something useful, boy. Open the back door and let this smoke out before all my washing is covered in smuts."

Michael clambered down from the chair, hurried to the door, and opened it. The smoke diminished, and the coals began to glow. Wyn sank back on her heels.

"There! That's got it."

She struggled upright and replaced the bellows beside her chair.

"You can close it now, thank you." She smoothed down her apron, removed her soot-covered glasses, and polished them briskly with her handkerchief. Returning them to her nose, she peered down at the child. "Come along, boy, let me show you."

She stepped out into the hall with Michael following. Walking toward the front door, she opened another door and stood to one side so that he could see into the room.

"This is where I bring my ladies, and you will *not* be allowed in here. Is that quite clear?"

He nodded. She raised her eyebrows questioningly.

"Yes, Aunty Wyn."

"Good, that's better."

He stared beyond her into the gloomy room. Thick lace curtains contributed to the darkness, as did a very large potted plant that stood on a table in front of the window. Two overstuffed armchairs in plum red plush velvet stood on either side of the fireplace, which was tiled in dark green. A needlepoint screen fronted the empty grate with a brass coalscuttle and fire tongs beside it. On the mantelpiece were several sepia-toned photographs in heavy, gilt frames. There were also two large, gaudily painted china figurines of crinolined ladies which stood on either side of an ornate brass inlaid clock. At that moment the clock began to chime. The startled boy retreated back into the hallway.

"Haven't you heard a chiming clock before, child? Good heavens, what kind of a home do you come from? Come in and see."

He hesitated.

"Oh, for heaven's sake, boy! You can come in when I *say* you can come in."

He followed her reluctantly into the room as the clock continued to chime, then strike, the hour.

"You see? This is how you tell the time. I assume I will have to teach you that as well. Do you know your numbers?"

He looked at her blankly.

"From your vacant expression I gather you don't." She heaved a sigh. "We have a lot of work to do, you and I, young Michael. I can't imagine how I let my brother talk me into this. Come along."

He cast a final glance around the forbidden room. A red velvet chaise was set against the wall behind the door, with a black-lacquered table in front of it. A floral rug covered most of the polished wooden floor. He followed her out.

She pointed up the narrow stairs. "You know which room is yours, but it is also my workroom so you will *not* use it during the day. I can't imagine why you would want to, anyway. You will remain in the kitchen, especially when I have my ladies in. My bedroom is also upstairs and there will be no need for you to enter that either. Is that clear?"

He watched her face carefully and promptly gave the required response.

"Yes, Aunty Wyn."

"Did you see the WC in the yard?"

He had heard this word, WC, before, during his brief stay in the Porter household. He nodded.

"I trust you will ensure it remains clean and tidy. You do know how to use it, don't you?" He nodded again. Martha, the Porter's maid, had explained how.

"Good! Right! Now let's see how the fire is doing."

They returned to the kitchen.

"There is just one more thing."

After glancing at the now-glowing fire, she crossed to the dresser, opened a drawer, and lifted out a large, leather-bound book.

"This is the most important item I have in this house and you will not touch it, unless I say so." She sat into her chair and beckoned the child to her side. "This is called a Bible. I don't suppose you know anything about it, but this, young man, contains almost everything you need to know. I will teach you to read with this book, and I hope you will learn quickly."

She thumbed through the pages. "Ah, here it is." She pointed to a word at the top of the page, "J-O-B, Job." She looked at the small boy standing beside her, "Say it."

"Job," he repeated obediently.

"Good. Now see here." She indicated the numbers. "That is a one and a seven, together they are seventeen, and that …" she pointed to another number, "… is nine. Repeat!"

He did, and she then traced her fingers across the fine print. "…
and he that hath clean hands shall be stronger and stronger. You see?" she
jabbed her finger at the words. "It says it right here. Remember that."

She closed the book and returned it to the drawer.

"Right! Now I have things to do, and I'm sure I can find ways
you may help. Idle hands make the devil's work. What do idle hands
make?"

"The devil's work?" he responded nervously.

She nodded and gave him a thin smile. For the next two hours
the woman continued working in her kitchen. She washed dishes,
handing him the cutlery to dry. She dusted the china and glassware on
the dresser, giving him a cloth and a small brass bell to polish, and she
prepared their dinner, scraping carrots and potatoes and dropping a
ham hock into a pot on the range. All the while Michael was supervised,
instructed, and admonished by the woman he would call Aunty Wyn.

When they heard the knock on the front door, Wyn hastily removed
her apron and hurried to answer it. In her haste, she left the kitchen
door slightly ajar. Michael watched through the thin crack as Wyn
effusively greeted two women. The younger woman carried a large
parcel wrapped in brown paper.

"So, this is the bride-to-be?" said Wyn, as she ushered them into
the parlor. She caught sight of Michael and closed the kitchen door.
He then heard the parlor door close and the muffled voices of the three
women in animated conversation. He sighed and wandered slowly
around the kitchen. He gently rocked the chair by the fire, but didn't
dare to climb onto it. He peeped out under the back door's lace curtain
into the yard, his breath steaming the window. He rubbed it clean with
his sleeve and returned to his seat at the kitchen table. He waited there,
patiently, swinging his legs.

The two women finally left. Wyn returned to the kitchen. She
showed him how to set the table and ladled the meat and vegetables
from the pot onto two dishes. She placed one in front of Michael and
watched while he ate.

"Well, at least your table manners are not too bad."

After their meal she scrubbed and dried the table and spread a large
white cloth over it. She instructed Michael to pull his chair away from

the table and sit quietly. Then she fetched, and opened, the brown paper package.

"You may sit and watch, but I don't want you near this table or the material. One dirty fingerprint and everything would be ruined. I'll be back in a minute."

He tugged his chair further away from the table and sat again as she left the room. He heard her laboriously climbing the stairs. She returned with tissue-paper patterns, pins, a tape measure, and scissors. Wyn hung the tape measure around her neck and placed the other items on a chair. She reached for the magazine that rested on top of the fabric and turned to a picture of a young woman dressed in an elegant, full-length, white dress. The woman was surrounded by a cloud of white veiling. Propping the magazine open at the page with a spool of thread Aunty Wyn unfolded and spread the intricately embroidered cream material on the table. The excess rested on a chair. Taking the tape measure from around her neck she began adjusting and laying the pattern over the fabric.

Michael watched the process with interest. He watched as she deftly pinned the delicate tissue paper shapes to the embossed brocade. When it was pinned to her satisfaction she straightened for a moment, easing the stiffness in her back. She adjusted the glasses on her nose, took a deep breath, leaned over the work again, and began to cut. He craned to see as, with total concentration, Aunty Wyn cut the first shapes, then turned and draped them carefully over the back of her rocking chair. Michael liked the crunch of the scissors as she cut through the paper and fabric and the quiet of the kitchen as she worked on the next pieces, smoothing and straightening, measuring and pinning, before cutting again. He stuck his thumb into his mouth and sucked contentedly. Wyn, turning to lay skirt pieces over the chair, saw him.

"I don't want to see that nasty habit. Take that thumb out of your mouth this minute or I will sprinkle it with mustard."

He quickly removed his thumb and sat on his hand to make sure he didn't do it again. He didn't know what mustard was, but guessed it was not good.

Finally Aunty Wyn gathered the scraps of leftover fabric, packaged them into the brown paper along with her pin cushion, scissors, and the magazine, and put the bundle on the table. She carefully lifted all the cut pieces from the rocking chair and hung them over her left arm. Collecting the paper bundle in her right hand she struggled to open the kitchen door and went upstairs, leaving Michael to look after himself.

After a while he climbed down from the chair. He listened at the door to the hall, but all he could hear was the rhythmic thudding of the treadle machine, so he crossed the kitchen and cautiously opened the back door. Closing it quietly behind him he continued his exploration of the small yard. He watched a spider weave a fine web across a corner of the wall between two broken bricks. As he watched he thrust his hands deep into his pants pockets to protect them from the cold. He decided he needed to use the WC.

He found the knotted rope was beyond his reach. Fearing the woman's anger, he carefully climbed onto the wooden seat and, balancing precariously astride the bowl, grabbed at the knot. As Michael tugged on the rope he lost his balance, swung off the seat, and tumbled awkwardly to the floor. His elbow took the brunt of his fall and it hurt a lot, but he didn't cry. He had succeeded in operating the flush. He left the privy and looked around the yard. His glance rested on the door to the lane and Michael decided to explore further.

The door was stiff to open. He grasped the handle with both hands and twisted hard, grunting with the effort. It creaked open. He ventured a few steps into the lane, glancing nervously over his shoulder to see if the woman was looking for him. He kicked at a rusty pipe resting against a wall and tugged at an old wheel enmeshed in a tangle of weeds, its spokes broken and bent. The lane was very quiet and he was cold, too. A dog barked in a nearby yard and Michael decided to return to the house. Careful to close the yard and kitchen doors behind him, he returned to his chair and sat there quietly. He watched the fire, almost hypnotized by the flickering flames and the wintry daylight imperceptibly faded beyond the kitchen window. His thumb again stole to his mouth. It had been a long day and he was alone. Hot tears ran down his cheeks, but eventually even these dried.

Several hours later and long after the kitchen had gone dark Wyn came downstairs to prepare supper. Michael was asleep, his head cushioned on his arms which rested on the kitchen table.

Bedtime

Wyn shook the boy awake, raked the dying embers of the fire, added more coal, and coaxed it back to life with the bellows. She prepared a supper of sliced tomato and thinly buttered bread, made a large pot of strong, black tea for herself and a cup of warmed milk for Michael. After supper when she had washed and put away the dishes, she took the Bible from the drawer and settled herself in her rocker. Instructing Michael to pull a chair up beside her, she opened the book, quickly searched for the piece she wanted and began to read aloud.

"Isaiah, chapter one, verse nineteen. *If ye be willing and obedient, ye shall eat the good of the land: But if ye refuse and rebel, ye shall be devoured with the sword.*"

They sat for some time, the woman reading and the boy following her finger's path across the page, his forehead creased in concentration. Every now and then she paused and asked Michael to repeat a particular word to ensure he was paying attention. When he gave the correct reply he also smiled shyly up at the old lady, anxious to earn her approval. She simply nodded and continued reading. Occasionally, after pointing to a number, she would hold up her fingers to demonstrate.

"You see, this is the number four. Now see, these are my four fingers, one, two, three, four."

After a while, as her voice droned on, his eyes began to flicker closed. He yawned, and almost tumbled from the chair. She closed the book with a bang that made him jump.

"Right, young man, it's time for bed. Come along."

Michael slid awkwardly down from the chair.

"There is no water jug in your room, so you will have to wash here in the kitchen."

She looked down at the small boy.

"You will have to stand on a chair, but be sure to take your shoes off before you do."

She put the Bible back in the drawer and turned to see Michael struggling to open his shoelaces. With a martyred sigh she bent down to help him.

"I suppose this is another thing I am going to have to teach you." She tugged roughly at the laces to open them; then stood back. She watched as he loosened them further and removed his shoes.

"Wasn't I the fool that listened to my brother? Mind me indeed! I'll probably be long dead and in my grave before *you're* able to mind me."

She filled the bowl with water as Michael dragged his chair noisily over the tiles to the sink.

"Roll up your sleeves; you don't want to get them wet, do you?" She sighed again as she watched him struggle with the sleeve buttons. "Never mind, I'll do it."

Sleeves rolled, he climbed onto the chair and she handed him a sliver of green soap.

"Don't forget to wash behind your ears."

He poked his wet fingers behind his ears in an unsuccessful attempt to do as he was told. She stood watching as he fumbled with the slippery soap, dropping it into the bowl several times. She reached up and tugged a towel from the hanging rack.

"Obviously, washing was another thing they didn't consider important."

She handed him the towel.

"Now, out you go to the lavatory before I take you up to bed."

He looked down at his stocking feet, then up at the snappish woman.

"Just slip your feet into the shoes," she said impatiently. "I'm not teaching you to tie your laces tonight."

She opened the back door and the cold air brought him fully awake. He peered into the dark; then looked back apprehensively at the woman.

"Go on boy, stop letting the cold in; there's plenty of moonlight."

She gave him a gentle push out of the door and closed it behind him. He hurried across the yard, tripping over his shoelaces, and stumbled against the mangle.

By the time he returned to the warmth of the kitchen he was thoroughly cold and shivering. He stood beside the fire, absorbing its warmth, as Wyn took a brass filigree candle cup from the mantelpiece. Lighting a newspaper taper in the fire she lit the candle stub set in the cup's base.

"Come along then."

The woman led the way from the kitchen. Michael obediently followed her into the dark hallway, fascinated by the flickering lacy light cast on the walls by the candleholder. Wyn climbed the stairs with Michael trailing behind, clutching tightly to each rail of the banister, fearful of losing his footing in the dark.

In the bedroom she took his pajamas from the shelf and, resting the candle cup on the cluttered sewing table, she helped him undress and fasten his pajama buttons and cord.

"Do you know how to say your prayers?"

He nodded.

"Go on then."

He blessed himself, making the sign of the cross, and said the prayer his sister Mary taught him.

"Now I lay me down to sleep.
I pray to God my soul to keep,
And if I die before I wake,
I pray to God my soul to take."

Then he began the familiar litany,

"God Bless Mammy and Daddy,
God Bless Pierce,
God Bless .... "

"Hurry up, child, the candle is nearly out."

The sleepy child looked up startled.

"How many of them are there, for heaven's sake? I think we will just say 'God Bless my family' from now on, shall we?"

"Yes, ma'am," he mumbled sleepily.

"Good, now bless yourself and get in."

As he climbed into bed she picked up the candle-cup and stood by the door, the upward light casting ugly shadows on her face.

"Goodnight, Michael."

There was no response. The boy was already asleep.

The chimes of the clock woke him. His eyes instantly opened wide, his senses alert. He lay perfectly still, his heart pounding, his breathing rapid. As he listened to the clock he began to remember where he was and the cross lady in the black dress.

His heartbeat slowly calmed. He tried stretching his feet down further in the bed, but the sheets were so cold they felt damp and the bedcovers provided little weight or warmth. He drew his feet back up. The sheets smelled faintly of flowers, the same as the old woman.

The clock stopped chiming and the house was breathlessly quiet. Curious, he tugged away the sheets and blankets that were bundled around his shoulders and face and peered into the darkness of the room.

His scream was thin and high and filled with terror. The pale shadowy figure of a headless woman stood in the center of the room, still as a statue, arms by her side. Between short gasping breaths, his screams continued as he edged himself tighter and tighter into the corner of the bed, until the cold iron of the bed head prevented any further retreat. The bedroom door opened and the woman rushed in.

"Stop it, child, stop it this minute. What do you think you are doing? Stop it, I say."

She leaned over the bed and slapped his face, hard.

His screaming stopped as he took a shocked breath. Then he started to cry. She reached over the bed again, caught Michael's shoulders, and shook him roughly.

"Stop it, I say. You will wake the whole street, stop it."

Eventually his crying subsided to heavy, body-wracking sobs.

"What on earth has got into you, child?"

He stared beyond her to where the ghostly figure still stood, motionless, in the center of the room. She followed his gaze to the tailor's dummy draped in the pale cream brocade.

"Oh, for goodness sake, pull yourself together, boy. It's a dummy. Is that what has you disturbing everyone? It's a dummy! You understand? A dressmaker's dummy."

Michael slowly calmed. Wyn stood back watching him. She wore a voluminous white, cotton nightgown that hung loosely on her thin frame. A wispy braid of gray hair hung over one shoulder, and her arms were clenched across her stomach in an attempt to keep warm.

"You have made a complete mess of your bed. Get out and I'll tidy it. Hurry up before we both catch our death of cold."

Michael struggled out of the bedclothes and over the side of the bed until his feet reached the cold linoleum, all the while keeping a wary eye on the dummy. Wyn caught the bottom sheet to tug it back into place and immediately recoiled in disgust.

"It's wet. You've wet the bed, you disgusting child! How dare you?"

She pushed him to one side and yanked and tugged at the sheet. She removed it from the bed, rolled it in a tight ball, and thrust the bundle at Michael.

"Take that down to the kitchen."

He clutched the damp bundle and peered out onto the landing. There was no light. No candlelight, nor any glimmer from the moon, penetrated the interior of the house.

"Go on, child. I'll get my dressing gown and follow you. That will have to be put in soak. I'll not have piss stains on my sheets."

She returned to her room while Michael fumbled and groped his way down the stairs, clutching sheet and banister, his feet catching dangerously in the cumbersome bundle. By the time he reached the downstairs hallway she was bustling past him into the kitchen. She filled the sink with cold water and snatched the sheet from the shivering boy standing beside her.

"Now get back to bed. I don't want to hear one more sound from you tonight, do you understand?"

"Yes, ma'am," he whispered.

"Sleep as you may, you'll get no fresh sheets from me this night. This will have to be soaked overnight. As you make your bed, so shall you lie in it. Go."

He glanced back at the dark hallway but did not move.

"Go, I said."

He stood looking at her for a moment longer before slowly turning and walking toward the door. Reaching it he again turned to look at the woman angrily pounding the sheet into the cold water.

"I will not tell you again."

Michael slowly returned to his room, his eyes straining to pierce the darkness of every corner and shadow on the way. His pajamas clung to him, cold and wet, and he was shivering uncontrollably.

When he reached his bedroom, he quietly closed the door and struggled with the trouser cord knot and the jacket buttons until he was able to remove his pajamas. Leaving them in a sorry bundle on the floor, he climbed up into the bed and found a dry spot. He pulled the disheveled bedcovers around him like a nest and lay there, thumb in his mouth, watching the ghostly figure until he was overcome by exhaustion and he slept.

The Morning

He was startled into wakefulness by the sharp rapping of the monkey knocker.

"Get up child; we have work to do."

He heard her continue down the stairs. Squirming out of the tangle of bedding he struggled to dress himself. For the last few weeks the Porter's maid, Martha, had washed and dressed him in the mornings; before that it had been his sister Mary and, before that, his mother. Now he knew instinctively that he must look after himself. His feet were cold so he began with his socks. They were not too difficult, though the heel of his left sock got twisted to the front of his foot. He struggled with his underwear, then his shirt, pulling it over his head and poking wildly at the garment until he found the armholes. He sat on the floor to tug on his gray flannel short pants and finally stood to hook the suspenders over his shoulders. The fly buttons were impossible, and anyway he heard her calling.

"Michael! Michael! Come along, boy. We don't have all day; what's keeping you up there?"

He snatched up his sweater and fumbled his way into it as he opened the door. Remembering his shoes, he turned back, grabbed them, and hurried out onto the landing. The gray light of a wintry early morning seeped through the leaded glass of the front door, helping him to navigate the stairs safely. When he arrived in the kitchen, Wyn was busy at the sink.

"The next time you do this, it's the orphanage for you. Do you understand?"

He stood just inside the door, watching her in silence as she pummeled and squeezed the sheet in the soapy water.

"I said, do you understand, Michael?"

She glanced over her shoulder at him.

"Yes, Aunty Wyn," he said, his voice quavering.

He didn't really understand the word orphanage, but he did remember his sister Mary saying the word and crying, so he knew it was a bad thing. He brushed a wayward tear from his cheek.

Wyn lifted and lowered the sheet, changing the water several time, until all the soapsuds were gone. Michael remained by the door. She twisted the sheet into a thick coil, squeezed as much water from it as she could, and then dropped it back into the now-empty bowl. She turned to Michael.

"Come along, child, this is your doing; so the least you can do is help me."

Only then did she see his disheveled state.

"Sweet Sacred Heart, what do you look like? Can you not see that your jumper is on backward? Come over here."

He went, sliding his stocking feet reluctantly toward the angry woman.

"And pick up your feet. I don't need to be darning socks if I don't have to."

She snatched his shoes from him and dropped them on the floor. She was not gentle pulling his sweater off either, tugging it roughly over his ears. She buttoned his shirt and pants and replaced the sweater. When he was dressed to her satisfaction she picked up his shoes and pointed to the kitchen chair.

"Sit."

Wyn twisted his crooked sock into position, pushed on his shoes, and tied his laces.

"Come with me."

She lifted the bowl, heavy with the weight of the wet sheet, and opened the back door.

"Don't forget to close the door after you."

Placing the bowl on the ground under the mangle she pushed a corner of the sheet between the rollers.

"You can turn the handle, boy."

He reached up, grasped the handle with both hands and pulled it downward, but he couldn't turn it fully; he was not tall enough. Wyn scanned the yard.

"Fetch that bucket and put it down there. Upside down, child," she sighed with exasperation. "You're going to stand on it."

He did as he was told. Precariously balanced on the upturned bucket, shivering in the morning cold, he struggled to turn the handle while Wyn fed the sheet through the rollers and the water dribbled onto the ground at her feet.

When the sheet had been through the mangle twice and only a little water trickled from its folds, Michael watched her hang the sheet on the rope washing line. She pegged it into place and pushed it up and away from the whitewashed walls with a long wooden prop, to where it might catch the breeze. He had faint memories of his mother doing this same chore.

"Now, let's get the fire done," she said and snatched up the clinker bucket. She returned to the kitchen, followed by the silent child.

"I want you to watch carefully. You should be able to do this job. I'm getting too stiff to be kneeling on this hard floor every morning."

Using the rocking chair to steady herself she knelt in front of the range, spread the newspaper sheets on the floor, raked the cold embers, and lifted out the cinders.

"You see? These are the clinkers." she held out a handful of the spent coal. "When you finish cleaning out the grate you take this bucket of clinkers out into the yard and pour a cup of water over them. That way we can use them again, to save coal, you see. But we can't use them to light the fire, only when it's going well."

She dropped the dusty handful of clinkers into the bucket, shoveled the ashes from the base of the range onto the newspaper, and parceled them, just as she had done the day before. She again thrust the parcel at him.

"You know what to do with these?"

He nodded.

"And don't drop them again."

He meekly took the parcel and did as he was told.

Over the next few weeks Aunty Wyn taught him how to fasten his buttons and tie his shoelaces. She taught him how to comb his unruly, curly hair and wash himself to her satisfaction, and even how to scour his small milk teeth with a dab of bicarbonate of soda on a damp finger.

He didn't like the taste. She bought him a china pot for under his bed, to ensure there would be no more "accidents," and she taught him his special chores, including cleaning out the range. She only helped him if the bucket was too heavy, or if there were still-red embers in the fire. She took him to Mass on Sunday mornings and Benediction on Friday evenings. She introduced him to Father Denton, the parish priest, and she taught him from the Bible.

Every Sunday, after Mass, Jim Porter would call to the house to deliver his old newspapers and collect the rent from his sister. He would record the payment in her rent book and question her on the boy's progress. Once a month he gave her a few shillings toward Michael's keep. He seldom spoke to Michael directly but the child sat at the kitchen table quietly watching the transactions and listening to the conversation, though a great deal of it made no sense to him.

"The little one keeps Edith amused these days. She's a pretty little thing, lively too."

"I can't imagine what got into you both, Jim, taking in a child at your time of life."

"I'm not sure myself, but at least Edith doesn't have to deal with 'you-know-who' as well. You seem to be coping very well."

"I didn't have a great deal of choice, it seems to me. I just hope he doesn't take after his countrymen. I'll have no rambunctious behavior round here."

"Don't be so negative, Wyn. Anyway, he seems like a quiet young man and you know damn well it's a good investment. Besides, it's company for you."

After three years Michael could read almost fluently and he knew his numbers. He could do simple addition and subtraction in his head and could quote several pieces from the Bible. It was a well-ordered life. He had little time for play and rarely ventured out unless it was to accompany Aunty Wyn to the shops. He would help her carry the shopping bags and, when prompted by Wyn, greeted her few friends and clients as she had taught him to do, with a firm handshake and a "how-do-you-do." Over time he forgot his sisters and his brothers and did not remember Aunty Bridgie. His memories of Ireland faded with his accent.

1928

School

Sister Thomas smiled.

"Well, and who have we here?"

Michael clung to Aunty Wyn's hand and stared up at the nun. He'd seen the nuns in church, of course, but he'd never been this close to one before. He couldn't stop staring at her stiffly starched white headdress. It had points, like wings, sticking out on either side of her head. They were even wider than her shoulders. To Michael, it looked like a huge version of the paper boats he saw boys sail down the gutters when it rained. The nun leaned forward and the dark wooden crucifix hanging around her neck swung close in front of his face. He stepped back in fright. She straightened and continued to smile gently at him.

"What is your name, child?"

Aunty Wyn pulled her hand from Michael's vicelike grip and pushed him forward again. "Introduce yourself, boy."

Afraid to look up at the frightening woman with the strange hat, he fixed his gaze straight ahead. He found himself staring at the brown leather belt that cinched her apron at the waist. An outsized, wooden rosary hung from the belt. Michael's eyes slowly followed the rope and wooden beads downward to another black crucifix dangling near her feet. A narrow band of her blue habit could be seen below her stiff, white apron. His aunt nudged him.

"Michael Kelly," he said, so quietly that the nun had to cock her head to one side to hear him better.

"Michael Kelly, you say?" She ran her finger down the names in the open ledger on the desk beside her.

"Ah, yes, the orphan boy, yes. Father Denton told me about you," she said. She turned her attention to Aunty Wyn. "And you, Miss Porter. You must be a very special lady, to take in a little waif like this."

She looked down at Michael and smiled again.

"And *you* are a very lucky little boy to have such a kind benefactor. Now, let me see, who shall we sit you beside?"

She studied the class and Michael followed her gaze around a room already crowded with young boys.

"There's a space over there," she paused and looked back at her register, frowning as she ran her finger down the names. "There are so many new boys for me to remember. Ah, yes." She looked up again. "Harry Winston, put your hand up, please."

A round-faced boy, his hair cut short and slicked down with Brylcreem, put up his hand. "Good, that's right. Go and sit over there, Michael, and introduce yourself."

Michael turned panic-stricken to Aunty Wyn, but she took a step back, out of his reach.

"Go on! Do as you are told and no blubbering, boy. Do as Sister says and I'll be back to collect you later."

Before he could reach for her hand again she turned and walked quickly toward the door. He watched her go, then reluctantly looked back at the nun. She pointed again, to where the round-faced boy sat grinning at them, and gave Michael a gentle push.

"Off you go, Michael."

Considering him dismissed, she looked beyond him, smiling, to the next mother and child.

"And who do we have here?"

With a final desperate glance at the doorway, Michael walked slowly toward his seat and his desk companion. As he did so he could just see his aunt through the grimy, rain-spattered windows. He watched her as she walked briskly across the yard and out of the school gate, then he reluctantly slid onto the wooden bench beside the grinning boy.

"Who are you? I've never seen you before?"

"Michael Kelly."

"I'm Harry Winston. My brother's in this school too, in fourth class. My big brother was here, before he went to big school."

Michael tried very hard not to cry. His eyes felt prickly and his nose began to run. He furtively wiped it on his sleeve; then glanced around the classroom to see if anyone noticed. Most of the boys were sitting in silence, looking as nervous and fearful as he felt. One or two, like

Harry, whispered to each other quietly. They all waited patiently while the remaining boys lined up to meet Sister Thomas. They watched as she ticked names off on the register and assigned them their seats. Michael's stomach was churning. A boy turned from the seat in front and whispered, "My sister says they have all their hair shaved off under those hats."

Michael darted a look over at the nun who was deep in conversation with another parent. He couldn't see any hair; perhaps the boy was right.

The boy had a squint in one eye and Michael was not sure who the boy was speaking to.

"Don't be stupid, Smithy; it would only grow again," said Harry.

"Perhaps they have to go to the barber's every month," said the boy with the squint.

Unsure if the boy was also speaking to him, or not, Michael remembered Aunty Wyn's warning that staring was rude. He decided to ignore the boy, and the comment, and turned his attention to his surroundings.

Although there were windows all along one wall, the classroom was still gloomy. The windowsills were filled with an assortment of religious statues, writing slates, and tired-looking books with faded covers and broken spines. The walls were dark green with small yellow patches where the paint had chipped or flaked off. Michael looked at his classmates; he'd never seen so many boys together like this before. They sat on narrow benches that were fastened by iron frames to dark, wooden, double desks. His and his companion's bench and desk were in the third row.

A blackboard stood on an easel in the corner of the room and yet another large crucifix hung on the wall above the teacher's desk. Sheets of paper, with sums written on them in bold print, were pinned along the wall at the boys' eye level. Michael was pleased to see that he recognized the numbers. A frieze of the alphabet, in big and small letters, was also pinned all around the room close to the ceiling. He recognized them, too.

Some of the smells were familiar from Aunty Wyn's house, like the beeswax from the desks and floors and a faint, musty smell, like the one he sometimes got from the front parlor at home. Other smells were new, like the chalk dust, so dry and fine it made his nose itch, and the metallic smell of dried ink in the china inkwells set into the desks. Several of the boys had leather satchels, unlike Michael's which was made of cloth, and they smelled like new boots.

His companion nudged him hard in his side. Michael winced.

"I'm talking to you."

Michael looked at the boy, but said nothing.

"Oh, great, I'm sitting beside an idiot."

Michael was not sure how to respond to this comment, so, after looking at the boy for a moment longer, he turned his attention back to watching the last few boys meet Sister Thomas and be assigned their seats. One boy in the line was crying, clinging onto his mother's skirt and begging her to take him home. His mother tried to calm him.

"It's only for a few hours, Paul; then I'll be back to collect you. You know Sister Thomas is nice. Didn't your brother George tell you so?"

Nothing the mother could say would comfort the small boy and she finally led him out of the room watched passively by the remaining mothers and boys waiting in line. Harry laughed quietly.

"Big baby!"

Michael heard the boy continue to cry and make a fuss outside, and his mother's soothing voice patiently trying to calm him. When his cries slowly quieted, his mother led him back in. Sister Thomas put him in the desk in front of Michael, beside Smithy.

"Big baby," Harry hissed at him.

Soon every desk was filled and the last parents and guardians were gone. Sister Thomas closed the classroom door and returned to stand behind her desk.

"Good morning, boys."

A few boys around Michael muttered a reply.

"You will answer, 'Good morning, Sister.' Now. Good morning, boys."

"Good morning, Sister."

"Good. Then we will begin."

Michael sat stiffly upright in his seat while the nun spoke. Aunty Wyn always told him to sit up and pay attention and he didn't want to make Sister Thomas cross. The nun seemed strict, but kind, and she spoke gently when she asked the boys questions or told them things.

She taught them the 'Hail Mary' first, though it seemed to Michael that most of the boys were able to say it anyway. She told them it would be the first and last thing they would do in school. Every day they would stand, bless themselves, and recite the prayer aloud before lessons began and again before going home.

At last, when his back ached, and he thought he couldn't pay attention any more, Sister Thomas said there would be a fifteen minute break. She showed her young pupils how she wanted them to line up, two by two. When they were organized to her satisfaction, she led them out of the classroom and into the dismal corridor. Boys' coats and scarves hung on endless rows of wooden coat pegs along one wall and made the corridor smell musty and damp, like the kitchen on wash day. On the other side of the corridor, a line of narrow dirty windows set high in the wall gave little light into the dim space. Below the windows were more classrooms and as the boys passed each classroom door they could hear the pupils chanting their tables, or reading in dull unison from their primers. At the end of the corridor Sister Thomas led them through two heavy oak double doors, scarred and splintered from many years of abuse by young students anxious for their freedom. The doors led out into a playground, already filled with shouting, running boys.

The yard was enclosed on three sides by the tall, gothic-inspired school building. The crocodile of new boys followed the nun in silence as she walked without deviation to the center of the yard. Other boys, who had been released earlier, screeched and yelled as they ran around the newcomers. The newcomers remained in their crocodile and stared around them at their new environment. On the side of the yard not occupied by the granite-stoned school, stood a low, red-brick structure with a grimy, yellow-gray, tiled entrance. Though the tiles might once have been white, age and neglect had long since taken their toll.

"That is the boy's toilet," said Sister Thomas, pointing to the structure's recessed entrance. "You may go there before school, or during breaks. Any boy found there during class will be sent to Sister Josephine. Do you understand?"

A chorus of, "Yes, Sister Thomas," echoed dully down the line.

She looked at the watch pinned to her apron bib. "You have ten more minutes. When I clap my hands you will all line up in front of me as you are now. Understood?"

There was another obedient chorus.

"Right then. Go." She flapped her hands at them, like a farmer's wife shooing geese.

Michael watched as the line erupted. Some boys immediately ran for the tiled entrance, others simply ran. A few looked about them, unsure what to do. Michael remained where he was, watching his classmates and the other boys in the yard. Two of them began to rough house, pushing and shoving each other, then giving chase. Three or four played tag, yelling and shouting as they ran. One boy produced marbles from a drawstring bag in his pocket and soon a small group gathered to play, or to watch the others flick and roll the colored glass balls in one buttressed corner of the school wall. A few boys, like Michael, continued to stand alone watching the activities from a distance.

When Sister Thomas clapped her hands the pupils took their places back in line. Some did so reluctantly and others pushed and jostled for position. A few stragglers ran from the lavatories.

The second half of the morning was taken up with tests. Some of the boys fidgeted nervously as the nun pointed to different letters or numbers around the walls. She taught them how to put up their hands if they knew the answer; how to wait until she called them, then stand to answer. Michael was used to Aunty Wyn questioning him on things that he learned when they read the Bible together, so after an initial shyness, he began to raise his hand for every question and answered correctly every time. Sister Thomas seemed pleased. Michael smiled shyly at her when she praised him; it felt nice. When Sister was looking the other way, Harry called him a creep.

The shrill bell again echoed along the corridor and the first day finally came to an end. The boys stood, the Hail Mary was said, and they were discharged into the waiting cluster of parents and guardians assembled outside the front entrance of the school. Michael saw Aunty Wyn standing apart from the crowd, her black coat buttoned tightly to her throat and her handbag clutched firmly in front of her. They walked home in silence; she asked no questions and he offered no information about his first day.

Over supper that evening Wyn said, "Did Sister Thomas ask you any questions?"

His mouth full of bread and jam, he nodded.

"On what?"

He swallowed. "Letters and numbers."

"Did you answer correctly?"

"Yes, Aunty Wyn."

"Good."

When the dishes were done and with no further discussion about his day, Michael and his aunt sat beside the fire and read the Bible. He was already looking forward to tomorrow and he smiled when he thought of Sister Thomas.

Friends and Enemies

Michael and Paul Howard's friendship began on the second day of school. A few boys, including Harry Winston, asked Michael to join in a game of tag. He shook his head and stepped back away from them.

"Look at him! He doesn't know what we're talking about," jeered Winston. "Don't let's bother with him. I told you he was stupid," he added, and the group wandered away.

"Don't you really know how?" asked Paul who remained standing close by.

Michael shook his head.

"What games can you play?"

"None."

"None? Why not?"

"Aunty Wyn says playing games is a waste of time."

"Who's she?"

Michael shrugged. "She's my Aunty Wyn."

"Don't you have a mother?"

Again Michael shook his head.

"I can teach you, if you like. Games, I mean."

Michael smiled at the freckle-faced boy.

"Yes, please."

And so the friendship began and grew slowly over the following weeks.

Even when they had been sitting beside each other for a full term, Michael and Harry Winston were not friends. Harry constantly called Michael names, like "sissy," and "teacher's pet," because he wouldn't rough house in the playground with the others and because Michael was always ready, with hand raised, to answer any of Sister Thomas' questions. When Sister Thomas wasn't looking, Harry often poked his desk companion in the ribs to make him lower his arm.

"You should poke him back," said Paul.

"Why?"

"To stop him doing it."

"Do you think it will?"

"He won't stop if you don't."

Michael wasn't sure. He was a bit afraid of Harry; he'd seen him and other boys fighting in the yard. Michael didn't know how to fight.

"Teacher's pet, Teacher's pet,
  Lace on your shirttail,
  Nose all wet."

Harry Winston and his cronies trailed behind Michael and Paul chanting their taunt. When they got no response, they tired of the game and one of the group suggested a game of football. Harry and Alan Cook began to pick sides.

"Do you two sissies want to play?"

Michael and Paul shook their heads.

"Cowards! Scaredy cats!" called one boy. "Afraid you might get hurt?"

"Mammy's boy," called another.

A crowd began to gather around.

"Namby pamby," said a third and Michael was pushed from behind. He stumbled into Alan Cook, who roughly shoved him away saying, "Get off me."

Michael lost his balance and fell sideways into Paul. He, in turn, fell into another of the pack.

"Who are you pushing?" said the boy and punched Paul in the arm.

"Leave him alone, that was my fault," said Michael. He could feel his heart pounding faster and his stomach tightening. "Leave us alone."

There was more pushing and shoving, elbows and knees were used, kicks were exchanged and fistfuls of shirt, and sweater, and hair, were grabbed and pulled. Michael stumbled and fell. Shouting, scrapping boys milled over him. He didn't see the boot coming toward his face, only felt it thud into his cheek and rake across his nose. Blinded with rage and pain he flailed indiscriminately at his tormentors as he fought to his feet, clawing at legs and handfuls of clothing to help him upright. He kicked and punched, pulled and dragged, and all the while a thin squeal of fury came from his throat.

He was the last one to hear Sister Thomas' shouts, the last one to drop his arms and try to act as if nothing had happened. All the boys stood, their heavy breathing making a dozen breath clouds on the cold December air. Some were examining hands, elbows, or knees that had been scraped in the fight, while others gave surreptitious thumbs-up to friends for scores settled or targets connected. A few stood with their heads lowered, trying to look contrite.

"Who started this?"

No one caught her eye.

"I *said*, who started this?"

"He did, Sister," said a young boy who had been in the toilet when the fight started. He pointed to Michael. Frank Williams had a score to settle with Michael for getting a better mark than him in the spelling competition and winning the pencil sharpener Sister Thomas offered as a prize. "I saw him."

"Is that true?"

Michael's head was bowed, and he could feel his nose running.

"I'm speaking to you, Michael."

Surprised, he brushed at his nose and raised his head.

"Oh, good heavens, child, let me see. Come on, we have to do something about that."

She took a large white handkerchief from her pocket and handed it to the still-panting Michael.

"Press that, there, to stop the bleeding," she said, pushing his hand and the handkerchief to his bloody nose. She scanned the cluster of boys. "I will deal with the rest of you later. Behave yourselves while I see to Michael. Come along, child."

She guided him back into the school, almost colliding with Sister Josephine at the entrance.

"Good, you have the ringleader."

Sister Thomas looked up at the taller nun. "I'm not sure about that, Sister. He has a nosebleed. I'm taking him to the kitchen to clean him up."

"Send him to my office when you're done. Did you see him? I saw it from my window; like a wild animal he was. Lucky he didn't kill someone. Typical! I'll go and get those other little hooligans back into class for you."

When they got to the kitchen, Sister Thomas lifted down an old biscuit tin from the cupboard. Taking a roll of cotton wool from it, she pulled off two pieces, twisted them into fat tapers, and pushed them up Michael's nostrils. She washed the blood from his face and hands and rubbed at the stains on his shirt and jumper with a damp cloth.

"Your trousers are torn. Your Aunt is not going to be too pleased about that, Michael." She placed her two hands on his shoulders and leaned forward, so that she was on eye level with him.

"I want you to look me in the eye, Michael Kelly, and tell me if it was you who started this."

He was trying not to cry. His cheek and nose hurt. He knew Aunty Wyn would be angry about his clothes, and he had to go and see the headmistress. He shook his head.

"I didn't think so. You have to stand up for yourself, Michael, or those bullies will make your life miserable."

She gently wiped a stray tear from his face.

"Would a cup of milk and a biscuit help you feel better do you think?"

Not waiting for an answer, she took a cup from the cupboard, filled it with milk from the earthenware jug on the table, and placed it in front of him. Opening another cupboard she retrieved another tin and opened it. The nun offered it to Michael who saw it was full of what his aunt called "fancy" biscuits. She allowed him to choose one.

He found it difficult to eat and drink with the cotton wool in his nose, but he nibbled the biscuit and slowly sipped the milk to wash it down. He was in no hurry to leave the kitchen. When both biscuit and milk were finished, Sister Thomas carefully eased the cotton wool from his nostrils.

"There, all fixed. Now you had better run along to Sister Josephine's office. I have to get back to class."

Michael still felt stunned by the fight and puzzled by her kindness. He didn't think Aunty Wyn would have been nice to him if he was in a fight.

They both left the kitchen. Sister Thomas hurried off along the corridor to her classroom, her rosary beads rattling against her skirt as she went. Michael trudged reluctantly in the other direction.

"Come in."

The headmistress' response to Michael's knock was immediate.

He opened the door and stood looking at the formidable Sister Josephine. She was a tall woman, heavyset, with high coloring and a single eyebrow which went straight across her face. It made her look permanently angry, which she usually was.

"Come in and close the door, boy."

Michael did as he was told.

"Why were you fighting?"

He was silent.

"Answer me, boy."

"I don't know, Sister."

"You don't know? Don't talk nonsense. You charity cases are all the same. Breeding will out. We can take you out of the gutter; but you never really leave it, do you? What is your aunt going to think when she sees you like this? You'll be very lucky if she doesn't throw you in the orphanage where you belong, you little ingrate."

She stood and took up the thin bamboo cane from her desk.

"Perhaps we can help you to behave a little better. I will not have ruffians in my school. Put out your hand."

Michael slowly offered his right hand, gripping his elbow to his side. This was his first time to be caned, but he'd heard about it from the other boys. He stretched his palm out as tight as he could; they said it didn't hurt so much then.

"Perhaps this will teach you not to fight."

She raised the cane and brought it down sharply on his palm. He winced and pulled in his hand.

"Put it out, I tell you."

47

She gave him three more strokes of the cane. Michael didn't make a sound and he didn't cry, but he watched her face as she struck him.

"Don't stare at me like that, you insolent little brat. Get back to your class. I don't *ever* want to see you in my office again. Do you understand?"

"Yes, Sister."

Michael left the office, quietly closing the door with his left hand.

The class was very subdued for the rest of the day. Sister Thomas might not be as tall as Sister Josephine, but the boys knew when she was displeased and no one wanted to make her any angrier than she already was.

When school was over and even though Michael took longer than usual to button his coat because of his still-smarting hand, Paul was still waiting at the school door for his friend. They walked across the yard in silence.

"Michael! Michael Kelly."

They turned and saw Sister Thomas hurrying toward them. She still looked cross. The two boys stood and waited until she reached them. She handed Michael a sealed envelope. "Give this to your aunt when you get home, please."

She stood and watched him tuck the cream envelope into his satchel.

"Don't forget, will you?"

"No, Sister."

When she had gone, Paul looked at his friend sympathetically.

"You could pretend to lose it," he said doubtfully. "Are you going to get it from your aunt too?"

Michael shrugged.

"Tell her it wasn't your fault."

Wyn heard the back gate open as she worked at the kitchen sink. She glanced through the window and, seeing the state of him, she hurried to open the back door. As Michael stepped past her into the kitchen her glance ran from the bruise developing under one, swollen eye to the tear in his pants.

"What on earth happened to you? Is that blood on your shirt?"

He nodded miserably.

"Were you fighting, Michael Kelly?"

He nodded again and fumbled in his satchel for the letter. He would be sent to the orphanage; that's what she always threatened and this time she would surely do it. His nose throbbed, and his hand was still hot and stinging from the caning. He also had a pain in his side from a kick in his ribs, and it was making his breathing difficult.

He found the note and handed it to his aunt. The metallic taste of blood in his mouth made his stomach feel sick. The specter of the orphanage was vivid and frightening to him. Boys in school talked about the place where children with no parents went. They told stories about how those children never had enough to eat and how they were beaten regularly and never let out. Maybe, he thought miserably, if I pray hard God will find a way to drown me, like the sinners who weren't allowed in Noah's Ark.

Wyn opened the envelope and read the note. She put it to one side and fetched the Bible. Sitting at the table she placed the book in front of her and told Michael to place his hand on it.

"Michael Kelly, did you start that fight?"

"No, Aunty Wyn."

"You know God is watching you. He knows if you're lying."

He nodded, deciding that he would definitely rather be drowned than live in an orphanage forever.

"Sister Thomas doesn't believe you did either. Did you fight?"

"Yes, Aunty Wyn."

"What have I told you about fighting?"

He said nothing. A flicker of hope made him hold his breath. She didn't seem very, very angry.

"Given what Sister Thomas has written, I will give you the benefit of the doubt; just this once."

He let his breath out slowly.

"But…" She opened the Bible and searched. "You will write out the whole of this," she jabbed her finger onto the page. "Matthew, Chapter five. Write it carefully and take heed of what it says, young man. When you are finished, you may go to bed. A hungry stomach might teach you to behave yourself."

He fetched his satchel and settled himself at the table. He took out his pencil and a copybook and began to write. He wasn't very hungry anyway.

1929

The Communion

It was the day of Sheelagh's Holy Communion. Michael rarely saw his sister except at the annual Christmas dinner at Jim and Edith Porter's house or the occasional church function. Sheelagh never showed interest in her younger brother, and he had long since lost any sense of family with his older sibling. But this was a special occasion, Sheelagh's First Holy Communion, and Wyn and he were invited to attend the Mass and celebration breakfast afterward.

Wyn stood at the bottom of the stairs.

"Michael! Are you ready?"

"Yes, Aunty Wyn, coming."

"Don't run! You'll slip in those new boots. I want you to scuff the soles when you get outside so that you don't slip in them. But only the soles, you understand."

"Yes, Aunty Wyn."

He arrived at the top of the stairs and clattered down, his boots dull-thudding on each step. There were no studs on these boots; these were like rich boys' shoes.

"Let me look at you. They'll be here in a minute."

She fussed with his hair, running her fingers through the thick curls. She licked her thumb and removed an imaginary speck of dirt from his face. He tried to look past her to the door.

"Stop fidgeting, child." She stepped back to inspect him again and nodded her satisfaction, "All right! Now you can go and see if they're coming."

He needed no second bidding. Hurrying to the front door he pressed his nose to the glass and peered into the street.

"Not yet."

He was so excited he could not stay still. He jiggled from foot to foot as he watched his aunt squint myopically into the small hall mirror and adjust her black felt hat. She smoothed imaginary creases from her skirt. He thought that, just maybe, she was as nervous and excited as he was. She had made the skirt and the snug-fitting jacket especially for the occasion. He'd watched her pin the pattern pieces and cut the fabric, though now that he saw the finished items, Michael could see no difference between these and the other black clothes that she usually wore. He suddenly remembered the voluminous pink underdrawers he sometimes saw hanging on the rack over the range. They fascinated him. The thought of Aunty Wyn wearing *anything* pink seemed shocking.

"What are you grinning at, boy?"

He forgot the drawers instantly.

"Can I sit in the front of the car? Please, Aunty Wyn."

"It's may I, not can I. And I very much doubt that, young man. Don't forget we are the poor relations. We will sit where we are told, and *you* will be on your best behavior."

He heard a car horn and peered through the glass again.

"They're here! They've arrived," he said, bouncing up and down on the balls of his feet. "Can we go now?"

"Calm down, Michael. Fetch my missal from the kitchen table, please, and the box."

Michael ran down the narrow hallway skidding into the kitchen on the leather soles of his boots. He snatched the prayer book and Sheelagh's gift from the table and was back before his Aunt stepped out of the front door.

"Make sure the door is closed properly," she called over her shoulder as she walked to the gate.

Michael hurried after her, pulling the door closed behind him and rattling it to check.

Jim Porter sat erect in the driver's seat while his wife sat primly beside him. Michael closed the garden gate; then stopped, startled into stillness by Mrs. Porter's hat. It was enormous and smothered with a mass of feathers. Shimmering black feathers circled the crown, along with the tips of gleaming peacock plumes, their green-blue eyes staring back at him. Even more feathers, long and thin, pointed out over the wide front brim of the hat. They looked like small fishing rods dangling in front of her face, he thought. And she looked like a giant fish. He was grinning again. Edith glowered down at the small boy. Wyn, who had been struggling to open the rear door, turned at that moment. With a swift wave of her gloved hand she boxed his ear and muttered quietly, "Don't stare." Returning to her task, she finally succeeded in opening the door.

"Good morning, Edith. Good morning, Jim. Hello, Sheelagh."

Michael tore his attention away from the amazing hat, rubbing his ear. He waited to follow his aunt into the car.

"Take care as you get in, Wyn. I don't want her to crease her dress," Edith called fretfully. "Don't let him sit beside her, just in case."

Sheelagh carefully slid over to one side. Wyn stepped in and plumped herself down beside the young girl. Edith twisted around in her seat to smooth the child's dress and straighten her veil. Michael squeezed in after his aunt and pulled the door closed. He stared over at his sister. He thought she looked like the fairy he'd seen in a shopwindow last Christmas, except that Sheelagh had no wings.

The little girl wore a full-length white satin dress and a fluffy white bolero jacket. The hem and neck of the dress were edged in fine seed pearls, as was her lace veil. She clutched a satin drawstring bag, adorned with more seed pearls. A small, white prayer book lay in her lap.

"She nearly got it dirty on the gate before we left and then Jim has been driving like a madman. She's been thrown all over the back of the car, poor darling."

"For God's sake, woman, calm down! I haven't been above twenty miles an hour since we left home. She's not bone china, you know!" He raised his voice. "Is everybody settled back there?"

Without waiting for an answer he put the car into gear and set off.

"The clothes fitted him all right then, did they, Wyn?" he shouted over the noise of the engine. As he spoke he reached the street corner and turned the wheel sharply to the right. His passengers tilted precariously to one side. Mrs. Porter clutched her hat and Wyn clutched at Michael to steady herself.

Two days before an errand boy from Porter's Haberdashery and Clothing Emporium delivered a parcel containing a new outfit for Michael, including the new boots.

"Mr. Porter says if they don't fit to let him know," said the delivery boy as he handed Wyn the large parcel wrapped in brown paper and tied with string. He stood, smiling expectantly. Wyn took the parcel, thanked him, and closed the door.

The clothes were a little big. "But then, it will be your first Communion next year. Hopefully they'll still fit," she told him. "We'll be putting them away after today, keep them for best. And I'll be getting the cobbler to put some studs on those boots. No studs indeed! What was he thinking?"

"Yes, thank you, Jim, they're fine." Wyn called back and turned to her charge, "Michael, did you remember to scuff the soles before you got into the car?"

He shook his head and she gave a "Humph" of exasperation, but he was too busy looking at his sister in all her finery to be upset by his aunt's displeasure. He had never seen anyone dressed quite like this before.

Sheelagh glared at him. "What are you staring at?"

Wyn tapped Michael's knee.

"She's quite right, Michael; don't stare. That's the second time I've had to tell you. Do you want to go back and stay at home for the day?"

He shook his head again.

"Say 'hello' to your sister."

"Hello, Sheelagh. You look nice."

His sister smiled at the compliment.

Jim Porter continued to shout a conversation over his shoulder.

"Wyn, did I tell you the Sinclairs are coming down?" he called. "They stayed at The Grand last night."

Wyn nodded at her brother's back and shouted back.

"Are they the people that took the older boy?"

"That's right."

The comment caught Michael's attention. He looked up at his aunt. What older boy? Who was she talking about? He'd never heard of any "older boy" in this small family. He waited to see if anything more was said, but the adults had fallen silent and he quickly forgot the remark in his excitement of the car journey. There was no further conversation

56

for the remainder of the short drive, though Mrs. Porter kept glancing back to make sure Sheelagh was still secure, and her agitation became worse as they neared the church.

"Don't get out of the car until Daddy opens the door for you, sweetheart. And be very careful if there's any mud. Don't catch your veil in anything."

"Edith, you will fuss that child to death," snapped her husband in exasperation. "Here we are."

He drew the car to a halt. Michael looked out and saw a cluster of girls in white dresses and boys in smart suits with white rosettes on their lapels being admired, fussed over and photographed by family, friends and nuns.

Jim Porter parked the car and instructed Wyn and Michael to go ahead into the church. Michael followed his aunt, looking around to see if there was anyone he knew, but there were too many people and he was soon wedged into a pew between his aunt and a portly man with a silver-topped cane and a bandaged foot.

The Mass seemed to go on forever. Even when the boys and girls went up to take their first Communion Michael couldn't see anything. He was bored. He knelt beside his aunt staring up at the lurid pictures of the Stations of the Cross hanging high on the walls. He studied the picture of the soldiers nailing Jesus to the cross and wondered if it hurt more than Sister Josephine's canings.

At last it was over. He heard Mr. Porter explain to Aunty Wyn that, although the nuns had arranged a Communion breakfast for the children in the convent, a few families, including themselves, had chosen to breakfast at the more prestigious Grand Hotel. Michael's excitement returned.

The Breakfast

A young man in a black uniform with two rows of silver buttons on the jacket and wearing a pillbox hat hurried to open the car doors. Sheelagh stood, balanced on the running board, and jumped down.

"Be careful you don't fall, dear," her mother fussed as she stepped gingerly from the front seat.

Aunty Wyn exited next, then Michael. A large man, wearing a shiny black top hat and a bright red coat with gold buttons, was standing at the top of the steps. A row of military ribbons and several bright shining medals were pinned on his chest. He saluted the small group and held the door open for them to enter.

Michael followed the group across the lobby's marble floor, staring in disbelief at his surroundings agleam with gold. Everything seemed to be made of gold. It covered the fluted pillars and decorated the enormous mirrors; it was on the large door frames and even on the intricately carved arms of the furniture. When he looked up at the sparkling glass chandeliers hanging high above the lobby, he felt quite dizzy. They looked like clusters of giant diamonds.

Jim Porter joined the small group just as a smartly dressed couple, accompanied by a young boy, stepped out of the elevator cage. Mr. Porter hurried forward and caught the woman's hand.

"May, my dear, delightful to see you. It has been quite a while." He turned to the man beside her. "And you too, Edward. I didn't see you in the church; quite a crowd, eh? Sorry for the delay in getting here; photographs don't you know."

Edith Porter stepped forward and gave the smart woman a delicate peck on the cheek. "Hello, May! So good of you to come."

"Hello, Edith. It really has been too long, my dear. And where is your gorgeous little girl?"

Michael watched and listened as the elegant woman admired Sheelagh. "Oh my, you look quite beautiful, child." She turned to the sullen-looking boy standing slightly behind her. "Look at your sister, Colm. Isn't she beautiful? Satin is such a flattering fabric for a red head, Edith. She looks just like a young Mary Pickford with those wonderful curls. I wish Colm had curly hair."

She put her hand on the boy's head and smiled affectionately at him. He jerked away impatiently.

"Tell me, Edith dear, is the other one here? The younger one, Michael, isn't it?"

"Yes of course, May. He's here somewhere," said Edith, looking around her. Seeing Wyn and the boy standing nearby she crooked her index finger at Michael.

"Come here please, child."

Michael stared at the other boy. What had the woman said? Look at your *sister*! He stepped forward.

"Oh my goodness, Edith, he's adorable! Look at those brown eyes and that curly hair again. I simply *must* take a photograph of him before we leave, for Colm's album."

She bent down and caught Michael's hands in hers.

"Hello, Michael dear. How are you? I'm so pleased to meet you. I don't suppose you remember me? You spent your first night with us when you came to England." She smiled. "You certainly have grown. What a handsome young man you are. How old is he now, Edith?"

"Oh dear, I'm not quite sure ...."

"He's seven. Say "how do you do," Michael."

Aunty Wyn was standing immediately behind him. The smiling woman stood and extended her gloved hand.

"You must be Jim's sister. I'm May Sinclair, Edward's wife."

His aunt shook the woman's hand, "Pleased to meet you, ma'am."

The woman turned to the boy behind her.

"Colm darling, you and Michael should get to know each other this morning. Michael dear, do you remember your big brother Colm? Colm, this is Michael."

Michael continued to stare at the boy. His big brother! He had a big brother? He glanced up at his aunt for confirmation and she nodded almost imperceptibly. He stared back at the boy. He looked a bit like Harry Winston. His straight, mousy hair was slicked down with Brylcreem, just like Harry Winston's, and he had the same stocky, well-fed frame. The boy was several inches taller than Michael and glared down at him with a kind of sneer on his face, the same way Harry Winston did. *This* was his big brother?

"Let's go in, shall we?" said Jim Porter.

The group followed him into the dining room.

When the breakfast was served Michael accepted everything he was offered. He watched Aunty Wyn, as she had instructed, to make sure he did everything correctly. He ate with his mouth closed and put down his knife and fork between mouthfuls, just as she had taught him, though he thought it made eating take a long time.

While they ate Michael listened to the different conversations at the table. Mrs. Porter and the new lady chattered about hats and shopping and staff. Mr. Porter and Mr. Sinclair spoke very seriously about "The Jewish-Palestinian unrest," and "the first woman in the cabinet." Michael wondered why the lady was in a cabinet and why it seemed to make Mr. Porter so cross. The man's face seemed to get redder as he said things like "labor pandering," and "petticoat politics," but Michael didn't understand. Colm and Sheelagh told jokes and compared notes on the gifts they had received for their Communions.

"I got five pounds for my Communion, and a watch, and a missal with my name on the front in gold!" boasted Colm.

Sheelagh showed off several silver coins she had received from neighbors and other parents at the church. She also had three sets of rosary beads, a small prayer book with a mother-of-pearl cover, a prayer card, and two holy medals from the nuns, and a tiny, silver cross on a hair-thin silver chain that she said Martha had given her.

No one spoke to Aunty Wyn. Michael noticed his aunt sat very stiff and straight, a sure sign she was cross, but she didn't say anything.

When the meal was over, Wyn dabbed at the corners of her mouth with her napkin, folded it carefully, and placed it beside her plate. Michael did the same.

Mrs. Sinclair and Mrs. Porter continued to talk and the two men lit cigarettes. Michael saw Sheelagh tug at her mother's arm.

"Can I leave the table and go and talk to some of my friends, Mummy? I want to see what they got."

"May I dear, not can I! Yes of course, but don't leave the dining room, will you? I don't want to lose you. Take your brothers. I'm sure they will look after you, won't you, boys?"

Michael and Colm nodded and the three siblings left the table. Sheelagh and Colm walked together, with Michael trailing behind them. He was not sure what else to do. He didn't think he liked his brother very much, but he was fascinated by his sister in all her beautiful clothes. Anyway, the grown-ups' talk was boring.

Sheelagh moved from table to table and chattered with her friends. They admired each other's Communion finery and compared gifts. Finally Colm poked her arm.

"Come on. Let's do something else."

She ignored him.

Colm began to tease her friends, tugging at their veils or pretending to step on their shoes. When they continued to ignore him and, having first made sure no adults were watching, he showed them how he could stuff an entire bread roll into his mouth at one go. Michael turned nervously to see if Aunty Wyn had witnessed the behavior. He decided it was time to distance himself from possible trouble and quietly returned to the grown-ups' table, sliding silently into the seat beside his aunt. Once there, he continued to think about Colm. How could he have a brother? During the meal Colm had called him several nasty names, including "a fool." Michael remembered Aunty Wyn saying that *"he who calls his brother or sister a fool is in danger of the fires of hell."* He definitely didn't think he liked his brother.

The two men were smoking more cigarettes, and he saw Wyn watch with ill-concealed disgust. As they both inhaled deeply there was a momentary lull in the conversation. Wyn turned to the young boy.

"Right then! Come along, Michael, I think it's time for us to go." As she bent to gather her gloves and handbag from the floor beside her chair, she added quietly, "I can't waste all day here; I have work to do." She stood, tugging on her gloves. "I hope you have eaten your fill, young man. I'll not be cooking later. Say "thank you" to your hosts, please."

Mr. Sinclair and Mr. Porter stood as she brusquely thanked her brother and his wife for their hospitality and said goodbye to the

Sinclairs. Michael muttered his thanks and followed his aunt as she wove her way stiffly through the crowded dining room to the door.

The man in the black top hat and red coat held open the door as Michael and his aunt left the hotel. They caught the tram home, traveling in silence. Aunty Wyn seemed to be very cross, so he decided not to ask her any questions about the boy they said was his brother.

Michael made his Communion a year later. The Porters and Sheelagh were unable to attend, due to a prior engagement. Michael shared the breakfast prepared by the nuns in the convent and was able to wear the suit provided by Jim Porter the year before. It was a little tight under the arms, but Wyn had lengthened the sleeves and moved the button on the pants so it was not too uncomfortable.

The Porters sent him a small, brown, leather-covered prayer book. Sister Thomas, whom he hadn't seen since first year, was at the breakfast and gave him a picture prayer card of Saint Patrick. Michael studied the picture.

"He's your national patron saint, Michael," she said quietly.

Wyn gave him an altar boy's cassock. She had sewn it herself, and it was made of strong, serviceable, white cotton. It had taken her six months to complete the crocheted lace trim for the hem and sleeve edgings. She worked on it in the evenings, when he was in bed.

"Of course you have to study to be an altar boy before you can wear it," she said, "but I'm sure that won't take too long and I know you will pass the test."

It took another six months before her ambition was fulfilled.

1930

The Letter

As soon as Christmas dinner was over and Martha had cleared away the dishes, Edith, Sheelagh and Michael returned to the dining room. They gathered around the table, emptied out the contents of the box, and began work on the jigsaw puzzle. It was the Porter's Christmas gift to Michael. On the lid was a picture of Admiral Nelson's ship, *HMS Victory*, at the battle of Trafalgar.

At dinner Jim Porter had asked to have a few words with Wyn later, in private. They now retired to his study.

He took the top from a decanter on the drinks tray.
"Sherry?"
"No, thank you."
He poured himself a drink and sank into his chair beside the fire.
"It's about the Kelly family," he said, avoiding Wyn's gaze.
He took a pipe from the rack beside him and filled the bowl from his tobacco pouch. "A while back the older sister sent us a letter to ask if she could write a few lines to Sheelagh on her birthday and perhaps at Christmas. Bloody awkward really, didn't want Sheelagh having anything to do with them."

He took a taper from the pot beside the fire and pushed it into the flames.
"Let's face it; they didn't do a lot for her."
"What did you say to them?" Wyn's voice was tense.
"Oh, Edith got herself all worked up about it to start with. Said she didn't want any contact at all ...." He held the lighted taper to his pipe, "... and then, dammit, a few days later she changed her mind and says 'perhaps it wouldn't do any harm.' I suspect it was probably the letter from May Sinclair that did it."

He blew out the flame, dropped the smoking taper into the fire, and sucked vigorously on the pipe several times. Wyn watched in disapproval.

"That's as may be, but you are the head of this household, Jim, not Edith. What did *you* decide?"

He puffed for a few moments, creating a small cloud of blue-gray smoke; then took the pipe from his mouth and studied the glowing tobacco in the bowl.

"According to Edith, the Sinclairs let their child, Colm—wasn't that the boy's name?—have a letter from the older brother. Edith said that if the Sinclairs approved, then it must be all right. Under the circumstances I didn't see the point in causing a fuss. I *did* say that if Sheelagh was upset *at all* by them I would forbid all letters immediately."

"And?"

"She's just had one so far, on her birthday."

"Did you read it?"

He looked sharply up at his sister. "No, dammit, didn't occur to me." He dismissed the oversight with a wave of his hand. "She told me what was in it anyway. Only bits of nonsense about the old aunt." He cleared his throat. "Now another one has arrived, for Christmas. She doesn't know about it yet. I decided not to give it to her until after you've left, just in case she mentioned it, before I had a word with you."

"I suppose it's up to you. I just hope her family is not going to start scrounging for money or handouts."

"No, no, I don't think it's anything like that. It's just, you know, girlish stuff."

"Is that all then?" The tobacco smoke was making Wyn's eyes sting. She was also offended, as always, by his cursing. She shrugged, "I suppose you know what you're doing. If that's all you wanted to say, I'll get back to help with the jigsaw puzzle."

"Well, not quite." He looked up at her and frowned. "For the love of God, Wyn, will you sit down? You make me nervous standing there."

She sat, stiff-backed.

"The girl asked if she could write to Michael too. Just on his birthday and Christmas you understand …. the same as for Sheelagh," he added hastily, before she could protest. Wyn's back straightened further.

"I don't think that is a good idea. I think it would only unsettle the boy."

Porter puffed hard on his pipe; then cleared his throat.

"Well I'm sorry you feel that way, Wyn. I've already said I thought it would do no harm."

"Did you indeed?"

"Oh, for heaven's sake, Wyn. I told you, Sheelagh didn't seem one bit upset about hers; so where's the harm?"

"I believe you made *me* Michael's guardian, Jim, and *I* certainly don't want him associating with any ragtag Irish folk. As I remember it, even their own father didn't want to keep them! So what does that tell you? I've spent the last five years getting rid of his Irish accent and giving him proper manners and standards. I'll not see that go to waste just because some chit of an Irish beggar wants to send him a letter."

He tapped the stem of the pipe impatiently on his teeth and frowned at his sister over his glasses.

"I've told you. She is *not* a beggar and, dammit, what harm can it do?"

She winced at the curse, took a neat white cotton handkerchief from her pocket and dabbed at her temples.

"What harm? What harm indeed! What if they take a notion to have him back? What if she's only waiting 'til he's old enough to be gainfully employed, so that she'll have access to an easy income? What of *me, then,* Jim Porter? Who will care for *me* when he wants to rush off back to Ireland? You gave him to me so that I would have someone to support me in my old age, not so that he could support some young Irish chit who did nothing to contribute to his upbringing. I have housed him, fed him, and taught him his Bible. I will not have him wooed back to Ireland by any wheedling letters. How could you be so thoughtless?"

She was on her feet, twisting the small handkerchief into a tight knot, her hands quivering in agitation.

"All right, all right, calm yourself, Wyn. There's no call to upset yourself like this. There's no harm done as yet. She doesn't have your address, and I certainly won't give it to her if that's the way you feel."

She was somewhat mollified.

"But you said you gave her permission already."

"The letters come here at the moment, so I can simply ensure he never receives them."

"Oh! … Good. … Fine. Well, that's settled then." She patted her hair, pushing wisps back into place. She pushed her crumpled handkerchief into her sleeve, slowly regaining her composure. "I'm sorry I got so upset, Jim, and in your house too."

"Not at all, Wyn dear, not at all. I quite understand. Why don't you go and ask Martha to make you a nice cup of tea. Don't give this business another thought."

Wyn nodded and turned to leave the study.

"Oh! Just one other thing, Wyn!"

She turned back to her brother.

"Do you want to dispose of this, or will I?"

He held up a small white envelope. She paused for a moment, then stepped forward and took it. It was addressed, in neat round hand, to "Master Michael Kelly, care of Mr. James Porter, Esquire."

"I'll get rid of this one myself," she said. She took the letter, tucked it deep into the pocket of her dress and left the room.

When the jigsaw puzzle was complete everyone admired the picture, except for Edith. As they connected the small wooden pieces she had grown increasingly concerned at its graphic contents. The ship, the *HMS Victory*, occupied the center of a vivid battle scene, aglow in flames of red, orange and yellow. Billows of gray and white smoke swirled around the warring ships with their cannon-shredded sails and rigging. While that part of the scene was lurid enough, what upset Edith most were the dead and injured sailors floating in the blue-black water in the foreground of the painting, illuminated by the ships' fires.

"Dear me, I hadn't realized how gruesome it was, the picture on the box is so small. I don't think it is really suitable for a little boy."

"Stuff and nonsense, Edith," said her husband. "It's all part of our heritage. Mr. Turner did a fine job."

He pointed to the line of flags hung from the main mast of the damaged ship.

"Do you know what they say, boy?"

Michael shook his head. "No, sir."

The man indicated the flags as he spoke.

"England expects that every man will do his duty. You remember that, boy! *That's* a code to live by! Admiral Nelson lived and died by that code. He *died* for England that day."

Having admired the completed picture briefly, the rest of the family retired to the Porter's sitting room to play I Spy and Hide the Thimble. Michael carefully disassembled the puzzle and packed it back into the box. When he joined the others, he saw that Martha was closing the heavy, red velvet curtains against the December cold, though the heat from the log fire already made the sitting room hot and stuffy. Aunty Wyn never had a room this hot at home.

Michael took his turn at hiding the thimble. When everyone had closed their eyes, he pushed it between the branches of the small Christmas tree in the corner. A shower of pine needles fell to the floor leaving a bare patch in the tree. He tried to brush the needles out of sight, but the more he brushed, the more they stuck into the carpet and pricked his hand.

"Come along, boy, hurry up, I can't keep my eyes closed all day."

Michael gave up and said, "I'm ready."

As soon as Jim Porter opened his eyes he glanced around the room and saw the fallen needles. He immediately turned on his wife.

"I told you the fire was too damned hot. Blasted tree will catch fire before we're finished. Look what the boy has done! Stupid damned game anyway."

The family was subdued after his outburst. The games finished and everyone was relieved when, at five o'clock precisely, Martha announced tea.

Michael watched the maid carry in a heavily laden tray. As she placed it on the side table he eyed the egg and watercress sandwiches, the mince pies, and the finger slices of dark brown fruitcake topped with marzipan and snow-white royal icing. He still felt very full after his Christmas dinner, but decided he would try and find room for some of the mouthwatering food. Aunty Wyn rarely made dessert and *never* made dainty-looking sandwiches with the crusts cut off.

Martha left and quickly returned pushing a small tea trolley, its contents gently rattling. On top was a fine, bone china teapot, milk jug, and sugar bowl all decorated with delicately painted flowers. The fragile cups, saucers and plates were set out in an orderly line, cup handles meticulously aligned. On the bottom shelf of the trolley was a dish filled with cream. Highly polished silverware lay beside neatly folded white linen napkins.

Edith poured the tea and Martha handed out plates, napkins and cutlery. She offered the contents of the tray to each family member, beginning with Mr. Porter and finishing with Michael. With his plate balanced precariously on his knees Michael ate quickly, fearful of dropping something. Wyn frowned at him.

The family ate without speaking; only the clink of cup on saucer and knife on plate occasionally broke the silence. When Edith gave a short stifled scream and clutched her cheek, everyone was startled.

"I think I may have broken a tooth on the icing," she said, taking a lace-edged handkerchief from her pocket and holding it to her mouth. She excused herself and hurried out of the room. She did not return until tea was over and Martha notified her that Wyn and Michael were leaving. She apologized for her absence, gave Wyn a perfunctory peck on the cheek, nodded to Michael, and returned to her room.

Jim Porter drove them home. Sitting in the back of the car, Michael held the jigsaw box carefully, afraid he would be jostled and spill the pieces. He also held onto the other gifts he had received. There were three monogrammed handkerchiefs and a new tie from Wyn and a strange toy from Sheelagh. On opening it he found two sticks joined by a thin waxed cord and an odd wooden object which looked like a hollow hourglass. He had no idea what to do with them.

"It's a Diabolo," his sister explained. "I bought it in Hamley's in London when we were visiting Colm and his family. The man in the shop could spin it up and down the string, *and* he could throw it in the air and catch it too. He made it look so easy."

Michael looked at the strange toy and decided he would have to ask his friend Paul about it. *He* would know how it worked.

By the time they arrived home he was very tired. As soon as he'd filled the coal bucket and polished Wyn's shoes and his own, ready for the morning, he was content to go to bed.

Once Wyn heard Michael's bedroom door close, she retrieved the small, white envelope from her pocket and sat at the table to read.

> *Main Street,*
> *Doonbeg,*
> *Co. Galway.*
> *December 1, 1930*

Dear Michael,

How are you? I am so glad that I can write to you now. I am very grateful to Mr. Porter and you can tell him so. Aunty Bridgie and me miss you very much, but we know your going to England was for the best. It is hard to believe you are eight years old, nearly nine, I still remember you as a baby with big brown eyes and such a serious face.

Mrs. Sinclair sent us the photographs of Colm and Sheelagh in their Communion clothes and one of you, not in Communion clothes, or I don't think they are anyway. So have you made your Communion yet? In the picture you look very sad, but I expect that is just the picture. I suppose you are at school now and I hope your reading is good enough so that you can read this. I am making the letters big for you, just in case. Maybe the lady who is caring for you can help.

I am well and so is Aunty Bridgie. I am fourteen now and have finished school so I work with her in the shop. She is a bit stiff and says it is the roomatics, so she is happy I am here, I think.

Pierce is nearly eighteen and still works with Da on the horse and cart. He has just got a second horse and says he will hire it out. I hope that will make him a bit happier. He comes over to visit sometimes, but Da never does. I don't want to see him anyway.

Do you see Sheelagh a lot? And what about Colm? I
know he lives in London, but is that far from you?

Well Michael, it will soon be Christmas and we are
thinking of you, as always. We are killing one of our
chickens for Christmas dinner and hope Pierce will come
and be with us. I will write again on your birthday. I
hope you are very happy and that the lady is nice. We
remember you in our prayers and hope you remember us
in yours. I miss you very much.

Your sister,
Mary

Wyn snorted her disgust. Horse traders and rag and bone men; that's what they were, and just what she'd expected. Gypsies! A shop indeed! Tinkers' gewgaws sold on a market stall more like! And no man in the household, that's exactly what she expected too. No wonder they were ready to lure young Michael back. The chit didn't want anything to do with her own father, so of course she wanted her brother back. Well, not if she, Wyn, could help it. He had prospects here. If she reared him right and he learned well enough, he could inherit Porter's Haberdashery and Clothing Emporium. They had no need of Irish riffraff and hangers-on.

She carefully refolded the letter, slipped it back into the envelope and threw it into the fire. She watched as it caught alight and burned with a yellow and blue flame. Only when soft white ash was all that remained on top of the dying fire did she fetch her Bible from the drawer and read again the story of Christmas.

1931

Best Friends

Margaret Howard, Paul's mother, liked Michael. He was a quiet lad and well mannered. She'd learned much of his story from her son during the three years the boys had been friends, although she considered his story strange and was not initially convinced her son had all his facts right. After a while she made it her business to enquire among friends about Miss Porter. She learned that the older woman was a very private person who earned a living dressmaking and doing clothing alterations. No one was exactly sure why the spinster had taken in the boy.

"She must be fifty-five, if she's a day," said one friend, "and he's not even a relation, as I understand it."

"Not even a by-blow from a female relative," added another woman.

From her friends' accounts Mrs. Howard understood the woman took good care of the young boy, though her overall impression was that Michael received little love in Miss Porter's house.

When Paul and Michael became altar boys, Margaret Howard suggested that perhaps, on early-morning Mass days, Paul's friend would like to come back to their house for breakfast, before they went on to school. Michael, having asked Aunty Wyn's permission, shyly accepted the invitation and was quickly absorbed into the arguments and banter which flew between the five Howard children as they breakfasted and prepared for school.

Even when he was not present, Michael was often the focus of the breakfast conversations. Margaret noticed that it was her youngest daughter, Beth, normally a shy and reserved child, who often pressed her brother for information. She seemed concerned for the orphan boy who was only a year older than herself.

"Does he *really* have no mother and father, Paul, just that horrible Aunty Wyn?"

"Now, Beth, don't be rude," chided her mother. "Miss Porter is obviously a very kind lady, or she wouldn't have taken him in, in the first place,"

"She just wanted a slave," muttered Paul.

"That's quite uncalled for, young man. If you can't say anything nice about the lady, don't say anything at all!"

"But she *is* a dragon, Mum," he protested. "He always has chores to do, and he's not allowed out after school or to have anyone in the house. Not even me!"

"Why not?" asked Beth. "What does he do on his own all the time?"

"He says they read the Bible every evening."

"He must be very lonely," said Beth. "Couldn't we adopt him, Mum?"

Margaret smiled fondly at her youngest daughter. "He's adopted already, love."

"Sounds like a really horrible life to me," said Evelyn, Beth's older sister. "I'd hate to be an only child."

"He says he has a sister," Paul corrected, "called Sheelagh, but they don't live together and he's only seen her a few times."

Evelyn pushed her empty plate away. "That's weird." She eased her chair away from the table. "There's a girl in my class called Sheelagh, but she spells it a really funny way."

"Pass me those plates, will you, Maggie dear?" Margaret Howard took the dirty dishes from her eldest daughter. "I'll start on the washing up. You go and finish getting ready for school."

"Thanks, Mum." Maggie kissed her mother before leaving the kitchen.

Margaret put the dishes beside the sink, and whisked the small soap cage into the hot water. A few rainbow bubbles floated on the surface and she lowered the dishes into the milky water.

"Right, then, I'm off." George, the eldest son, finished drinking his tea and stood from the table.

"See you tonight, Mum." He gave her a quick peck on the cheek before leaving.

"Is she cruel to him?" asked Beth. She'd finished her breakfast but remained at the table, her chin cupped in her hands, frowning at her brother.

"Who? Oh! You mean his Aunty Wyn. Well, he has to go to bed with a candle, which I think is pretty awful. They only have electric light downstairs. And they don't have a wireless *at all*, not even a crystal set! They don't even have a toaster!"

"They probably don't have that much money, Paul," said his mother. "We're very lucky your father has such a good job."

Her husband, Tom, had been an engineering manager at the Bristol Aeroplane Company for fifteen years now.

Evelyn snatched the last slice of toast from the toast rack and stood.

"Evelyn, you stop right there. Where do you think you're going, young lady? Finish your breakfast before you leave the table. And for the love of Heaven, would you please straighten your ribbon? You're an untidy scatterbrain who'll forget her own head one of these days." Margaret straightened the bow.

"That's fine, Mum, it'll fall apart in five minutes anyway." Evelyn pulled away from her mother's fussing and made a mock-serious face. "Evelyn Howard, dear child, you are as unkempt as a vagabond! Have you no sense of decorum, child?"

Paul and Beth laughed at her very accurate imitation of Sister Francis, her class teacher.

Though she smiled, Mrs. Howard warned. "Don't you let any of the nuns catch you at that, young lady, or you will be writing lines for a month. "Now," she caught Evelyn by the shoulders, turned her toward the door and gave her a gentle push. "Go to school, all of you, and give me some peace."

"Bye, Mum, love you." The girl called over her shoulder.

"Love you too, now go!"

Beth, still smiling, took her plate to the sink, kissed her mother and left. Only Paul remained.

"You know, Mum, I'm glad everyone likes Mike. He never laughs much at school and he's always laughing like crazy here."

She gave her son a hug. "I think that young friend of yours could do with a few fun times. I hope we make him laugh lots more. You know he's always welcome here, Paul."

Paul smiled. "Thanks, Mum, see you later."

Margaret watched him leave the kitchen. Suddenly it was very quiet. She turned to wash the dishes and thought about the breakfast conversation.

"Poor little mite," she said aloud.

The following year, when Paul joined the church choir, no one was surprised when Michael joined too.

1936

Connections

After nearly twenty years as the Porter's maid, the optimism of Martha's youth had long since faded into mute resignation at being in service. Jim Porter's bombast and intolerance made her seethe with anger, and she had no respect for Edith's inability to run her own household. The only reason she remained with the family was Sheelagh. From the moment the little girl with the mass of curly red hair and cornflower blue eyes arrived in the house, Martha devoted herself to the care of the child. Edith, prone to headaches and "weak spells," was content to allow the little girl spend a great deal of time in the maid's company. The maidservant and her young charge soon became firm friends and remained so, though Sheelagh was now a young woman. Sheelagh kept no secrets from Martha.

Mary's letters arrived regularly for Michael and Sheelagh, one each at Christmas, and another on their birthdays. Martha, as instructed, delivered Michael's to Jim Porter, who promptly disposed of them and made it clear to Martha that she should not mention their arrival to anyone else. The maidservant kept her word, not even mentioning them to Sheelagh.

Martha knew her young mistress enjoyed Mary's letters and looked forward to their arrival. They were always full of village gossip and stories about the aunt's shop and its customers. The girl read them aloud to Martha as the maidservant worked preparing meals in the kitchen, or brushing Sheelagh's hair before bed. The young girl confided in the maid that she felt she almost knew all the people her sister wrote about. When Mary mentioned an Aunty Bridgie, Sheelagh said she thought she remembered the old woman who always wore black and smiled a lot. She also remembered chickens in a backyard and a tiny bedroom with all the children sleeping crowded in one bed, head to toe. As she grew older Sheelagh often compared her own life with her older sister's. She told Martha she was glad that *she* didn't have to cook her own meals, wash her own clothes, or clean her own room, as Mary did. Martha laughed.

"You would do it if you had to, Miss Sheelagh."

Sheelagh shook her head and gave Martha a big hug.

"I could never cope without you, Martha. I don't know how Mary manages without help."

The flustered maid felt herself blushing.

"You know I enjoy looking after you, miss."

The two letters that arrived in October were unexpected. It was neither Christmas, nor Sheelagh or Michael's birthdays. Martha dutifully handed Michael's to her employer. He tore it up and threw the fragments into the fire, as usual. Martha delivered Sheelagh's letter to her on her breakfast tray. The young woman read it aloud as the maid busied herself preparing Sheelagh's clothes for the day.

> *Main Street,*
> *Doonbeg,*
> *Co. Galway.*
> *October 21, 1936.*

> *Dear Sheelagh,*
> *I know it is not your birthday or Christmas, but I had to write and tell you that Aunty Bridgie died a week last Tuesday. It was very peaceful. Dr. Taaffe said it was her heart and that her rheumatism was so bad it was probably a blessed relief anyway. She was buried beside her mother and father and is near Mammy.*
> *There were a lot of people at the wake and at the funeral. Even Mrs. Kelly came, though I didn't speak to her. Canon Finnegan gave a lovely sermon on how good Aunty Bridgie was, and kind and generous, and didn't press people for money when they didn't have it. I told him that bit.*
> *A lot of people offered to carry her coffin, but Da and Pierce, and Uncle Pat and his two sons and Joe*

did it. There is no one left from her family. Uncle Liam could not get back in time, though I sent him a telegram the same day she died.

Aunty Bridgie's solicitor, a Mr. Maguire, wrote and told me to come and see him after the funeral, and when I did, he told me that the house was now mine. Her and Uncle Liam decided that that was for the best, and anyway he said he will not come back and live here now that she is gone.

It is very quiet in the house, and it feels strange to be here on my own. Joe says if I want to get wed we can, and then I would not be on my own, and we have somewhere to live so that's not a problem. I might.

I am sorry to give you this sad news. She loved you very much and hoped you were all happy in England. I hope to hear from you soon,

Love,
Mary.

Sheelagh put down the letter. "Oh, how sad." She looked bleakly at the maid. "Mary always said she was a kind old lady."

Martha put her arm around the girl's shoulders.

"I think you will have to tell Master Michael about this, Miss Sheelagh."

"Mary says she writes to him as well; he probably got his own letter."

The maid knew this was untrue, but what could she say?

"If he's never mentioned them, maybe he doesn't actually get them, miss," she said.

"Why on earth wouldn't he?"

"Well." Martha paused. "You know what Miss Porter can be like. Maybe she doesn't want him to know about your other family."

"That wouldn't surprise me, with that nasty woman."

She wondered how she should write back to her sister.

"Don't you think you should mention it to him, miss?" the maid persisted. "Just to make sure. She was his aunt too."

The girl stared thoughtfully at the maid for a moment before shaking her head. Sheelagh was acutely aware of being an adopted child. Jim Porter frequently reminded her. Whenever she misbehaved, or asked for things, he would admonish her by pointing out how fortunate she was; how she had been saved from a life of poverty and need by being taken in by himself and his wife. Even now, after so many years, she harbored a fear that the Porters might send her back to Ireland if she displeased them. Especially if she displeased her adoptive father! She studiously obeyed his instructions never to mention Mary's letters, or their contents, to Michael. She couldn't really understand what harm it would do, but her father imposed the rule and she did as she was told.

"Why wouldn't you tell him, miss?"

"What if Aunty Wyn found out? She'd kill me. Daddy would be very angry too."

"You could tell young Master Michael not to mention it to her, if you like. I think he has a right to know about this, Miss Sheelagh. It's his kin after all."

Martha was close to her own family. She visited them whenever she could and wrote to them regularly when Jim Porter was disinclined to honor her monthly day off. It upset her when her employer tore up Michael's letters, keeping the boy in ignorance of his family, especially when they clearly loved and missed him. It was not as if that old biddy, Wyn Porter, showed any concern for him, she thought, except to use him as an unpaid servant and nag him about his manners and his speech and anything else she could find fault with.

As Sheelagh chewed slowly on her toast and sipped her tea, Martha tried once more.

"He's fourteen years old, Miss Sheelagh. He's almost a young man. He's entitled to know about his real family. You don't have to actually *tell* him about the letters if you don't want to disobey your father. Just tell Master Michael that you've heard that your Aunty Bridgie died and explain that she was the one who took you all in, after your mother passed away."

"But what if he doesn't know about her, or Mary, or Pierce? *I* can't be the one to tell him."

"All right. Then you don't have to mention any of *them* if you don't want to. But the old lady should be remembered. She did her best for you all. He deserves to know that *somebody* cared about him."

Martha saw Sheelagh's lips purse and a small frown crease her forehead. She knew there was no point in trying to discuss the matter any further that morning. Sometimes her young charge was as obdurate as Mr. Porter. She decided to let the subject drop, for the moment, but she knew the boy would be visiting the house with his aunt on Christmas day. It would be an opportunity for Sheelagh to speak to her brother and the maid determined she would make one last attempt.

"Good morning, Miss Sheelagh." Martha set the tray beside the bed and tugged open the curtains. "Happy Christmas, miss, though a pretty gloomy Christmas morning it is. It's drizzling rain."

Sheelagh woke slowly, blinking at the melancholy daylight. She reluctantly sat up in the bed, pulled the eiderdown up to her chin, and shivered. Martha wrapped a pink fluffy bed jacket around the girl's shoulders and plumped up the pillows; then put the breakfast tray on the bed.

"Well, miss, did you give any more thought to telling Michael about your Aunty Bridgie today?"

Sheelagh lifted a small triangle of buttered toast.

"Martha, I've told you before. Daddy told me never to mention the letters to Michael. If he's not getting the ones from Mary, then I can't tell him. And if he *is* getting them, he knows already, and if he isn't saying anything after all that, then he doesn't care anyway."

Martha had to smile at the girl's logic, but she knew the truth and remained determined. "I understand Miss Sheelagh, but why don't you just mention it, and see what he says?"

"I'll see," said the girl, shrugging her shoulders and continuing to eat her breakfast.

Telling

Sheelagh fidgeted all through dinner. Though fearful at the thought of defying her father, Martha's persistence had won. If, for some reason, Michael really didn't know about his Irish family, then he should be told *something*. She was still arguing with herself when dessert was served. It wasn't as if she actually *knew* her brother very well, she thought. They only met occasionally.

When dinner was over, the family retired to the sitting room while Martha cleared away the dishes.

"Then we can do the jig-saw," said Edith, eager to maintain the rituals of their Christmas day.

"We have to listen to His Majesty's Christmas address first, Edith."

"Oh, yes, of course, dear," said his wife.

She sat meekly into her armchair. Her husband turned on the wireless and twiddled the knobs, impatiently trying to tune it in, though he knew from experience that it took several minutes for the tubes to warm up and the instrument to come to life.

Sheelagh was too agitated to sit still.

"Martha will be finished clearing away soon, Mummy. Michael and I will get the jig-saw ready while you do that, Daddy."

She indicated to her brother to follow as she returned to the dining room. Seeing them enter, Martha quickly scooped up the remaining dishes and the tablecloth. She smiled encouragingly at Sheelagh and retreated to the kitchen.

As he opened the jig-saw box and tipped out its contents Sheelagh cleared her throat. "Michael… Martha thinks I should mention something to you."

He stopped turning the pieces up and looked at his sister.

"It's not very important, but she thinks I should tell you anyway. But if Daddy found out," she continued, her words tumbling over each other, "he would probably be awfully cross, so please don't tell him I told you, all right?"

He nodded.

" ... Or Aunty Wyn," she added.

"All right."

"Well ... Aunty Bridgie died."

He looked at her blankly.

"The old lady who looked after us ..." she continued.

He clearly had no idea what she was talking about.

"... before we were adopted. The one who took us in and arranged for us to come over here," she persisted, trying to jog his memory.

"From where?"

"From Ireland."

"I thought I was Irish somehow, with Kelly as my surname, but Aunty Wyn never said anything." He frowned. "She doesn't even like the Irish."

"Yes, well, she doesn't like anyone. Anyway we *were* Irish, but we're English now." She paused. "Anyway, she's dead."

Jim Porter's voice boomed from the sitting room, "Sheelagh, Michael! Call Martha from the kitchen quickly. His Majesty is about to speak."

"All right, Daddy." She lowered her voice and hissed, "Why don't you ask Aunty Wyn about your other family. Then you'd know what I'm talking about. Just don't say I said anything."

Their private talk was over and Sheelagh was relieved that Michael hadn't asked his sister how she knew. She went to the kitchen door, called to Martha, and she and Michael returned to the sitting room.

All six listeners clustered around the wireless, Martha slightly to the rear, straining to hear the new king's Christmas speech to his people. The monarch's voice could only be faintly heard over the crackle and static of the radio. Jim continued to fiddle with the knobs.

"I wonder when the coronation will be?" asked Edith.

"Shhhhh," hissed her husband.

She waited until the speech was over before returning to her topic.

"I was only wondering, dear, what with all the fuss and the abdication and everything."

"Well, I'm hardly privy to the government's decisions, am I?" he snapped as he turned off the wireless.

Michael thought about Sheelagh's news for the rest of the day, but mentioned it to no one. He continued to think about it occasionally in the days following and wondered if he should mention it to Aunty Wyn. But that was a problem. He'd promised his sister he wouldn't get her into trouble. Aunty Wyn always told him that lying was a sin punishable by hell's fire ... and she was sure to ask him how he knew about the aunt. Breaking his promise to his sister was lying, wasn't it? So how could he bring up the subject?

After the Christmas holidays he returned to school and his studies. Any curiosity he had about the old Irish woman who died soon faded. He knew nothing about her and she was dead now anyway. He knew Aunty Wyn wasn't his mother, but she *was* the one who took him in, so he'd always presumed she was some kind of distant relative.

Years ago, in junior school, some boys had called him a "get." He looked it up in a dictionary and after that he *never* wanted to find out that he really *was* a bastard. If he asked Aunty Wyn about where he came from, she would probably tell him and he wasn't sure he wanted to know. He preferred to think that he and Sheelagh and Colm were orphans. When he was younger he remembered Wyn often threatening to send him to an orphanage. That meant he was an orphan, didn't it? He was grateful to her for continuing to keep him and *especially* for not putting him into the dreaded orphanage.

While she'd always been a strict woman, Wyn rarely struck him. She preferred to cite the teachings of the Bible to reinforce her argument. If he was slow to do as she asked, she would tell him, "*The wrath of God comes upon the sons of disobedience*, Michael Kelly, and don't you forget it. He sees everything, even if I don't."

Michael was actually more afraid of the wrath of Aunty Wyn. When she was displeased, her icy coldness made him more miserable than any beatings, though her occasional ranting lectures, listing all his mistakes and shortcoming, were definitely to be avoided too. He constantly tried to earn her thin smile of approval.

In time he simply dismissed the conversation with his sister. His life was full, his household chores and school studies kept him busy. He was fourteen now and attended the Christian Brothers school, where the leather strap replaced Sister Josephine's cane. He continued to study hard to avoid the displeasure of his teachers and Aunty Wyn. He still served Mass twice a week, practiced with the choir on Fridays after Benediction, and sang at High Mass every Sunday with his friend, Paul. He also continued to enjoy the warm hospitality of his friend's family, despite the teasing he often received from Paul's middle sister, Evelyn, about himself and their younger sister, Beth.

1937

Decisions

Evelyn clattered down the stairs as Paul and Michael pushed open the front door.

"Well, good morning, Errol Flynn. Who has all the girls swooning when he serves Mass then, Michael Kelly?"

Michael smiled, but a faint blush colored his face.

"Lay off Ev," said her brother. "It's too early in the morning."

She laughed and went ahead into the kitchen. The two boys threw their jackets under the coat stand and followed her.

"Just ignore her, Mike," said Paul.

"I try," said his friend, smiling ruefully.

Mrs. Howard stood at the stove frying bacon.

"Evelyn, your breakfast is on the table. Put some more bread in the toaster, please, before you sit down. Beth, have you nearly finished? Lay two places for the boys will you, love? Wash your hands, lads, and sit down, your breakfast will be ready in a minute. Michael, I declare, you get taller every time I see you."

He smiled and straightened his shoulders. He knew he was growing fast. He was already taller than his aunt.

As Evelyn sliced the bread she teased, "Paul, make sure Mike is sitting beside Beth, or she'll be all upset."

"Shut up, Ev," Beth wailed. "Mum! Ev's teasing again."

"Evelyn Howard, I keep telling you, leave your sister alone *and* poor Michael. Sit down all of you and finish your breakfast." She put two plates, stacked with bacon and sausage, in front of the boys. "And you should have more sense than to listen to her, Beth."

Evelyn pulled a face at her younger sister.

"Stop it, Ev! Mum! Stop her!"

"Evelyn, stop it, act your age. You're sixteen, not six!"

Michael ate his breakfast, trying to ignore the bickering, but he did glance sideways, sneaking a look at Beth. He saw unshed tears sparkling in her eyes, and he too became angry with Evelyn. He thought Beth was the nicest of the Howard girls and the prettiest. He was fascinated at how her hair and eyes were almost exactly the same color, a soft, pale brown. She was just fourteen years old, but Michael though she would probably be very beautiful when she grew up.

Evelyn fluttered her eyes at her sister and clutched at her heart. Beth pushed back her chair, scowled at her sister, and left the kitchen.

Mrs. Howard saw Beth's departure and turned to Evelyn, "Now look what you've done; she hasn't even finished her breakfast. Don't tease her like that, Ev," she added, with exasperation. "And get ready for school, or you'll be late again."

"I hate school anyway, and the nuns all hate me."

Mrs. Howard often said that Ev's departure from school would probably be as much of a relief to the nuns as it would be to her daughter.

"Go."

"All right, all right, I'm going."

Ev kissed her mother, waved at her brother and his friend, and left.

Mrs. Howard looked back to the boys. "Come on, lads. You'll be late too if you don't hurry."

They shoveled down the rest of their food, snatched their coats and satchels from the hall floor, called their goodbyes, and set out for school.

On their walk Paul returned to his favorite topic, what they would do when they left school.

"Imagine, Michael, if you were a pilot, flying over the tops of houses. Imagine being able to dive-bomb the school and frighten the daylights out of Brother Pius." He turned and walked backward in front of Michael, laughing. "Or flying over Harry Winston's house and dropping dog crud down his chimney."

Michael laughed too. Paul turned to walk beside his friend again.

"When I'm good enough, I'm going to be a test pilot for the planes that Dad and George build."

His older brother, George, was now an apprentice aircraft engineer at the same firm as their father.

"Or maybe I'll join the RAF or work with a big commercial company."

One way or another he was determined to be a pilot. Michael envied him his dreams. He'll probably do it too, he thought.

"Have *you* decided what you're going to be yet, Mike? Why don't you join the RAF with me? We could travel all over the world together."

Michael usually shrugged when his friend questioned him like this. He knew what Aunty Wyn wanted to happen, but her brother had never mentioned that he might inherit the shop. Michael wasn't really sure if Aunty Wyn's plan was going to work.

"You must have some idea, Mike."

He decided to share his aunt's plans with his friend.

"Aunty Wyn says if I study well and mind my manners I might get to inherit Mr. Porter's business."

"Mr. Porter? Your aunt's brother?"

"Yes."

"The one who owns the buttons and bows shop?"

Michael smiled. "It's not a button shop; it's a haberdashery."

"Same thing. Why do you call him Mr. Porter, not uncle?"

Michael shrugged, "I always have. He never said I could call him uncle."

"Weird. Anyway, is he ancient? If he's not, you can't just hang around waiting for him to die. What are you going to do straight after you finish school?"

"I don't know, but I know I have to earn enough to keep us both. Aunty Wyn says she's getting too old to keep on sewing. She says it hurts her eyes."

"What if you get married?"

Michael snorted at the idea.

"I'm not getting married. Aunty Wyn says wives just spend your money for you."

"Don't tell our Beth that; she has her cap set at you."

Michael swiftly picked up a small pebble and threw it at his friend.

"Don't you start; I get enough of that from Ev."

But he did wonder what he was going to do. Paul was right; it didn't seem likely that the man was going to die any time soon. His friend was lucky; he knew just what he wanted to be when he left school *and* his family would probably let him do it. Michael hoped his aunt was right. He decided he'd have to talk to her about it.

Jealousy

Jim Porter scribbled his signature in the rent book. Wyn watched over his shoulder, glasses perched on the end of her nose, squinting at the page to make sure he filled in the correct amount.

"Did I mention Sheelagh was coming to work in the shop?"

Wyn stiffened at his words and rounded the rocking chair to stand in front of him.

"She'll be working with you?"

He blew on his signature, drying the ink, and glanced up at his sister.

"Well, not with me exactly. You know I leave the everyday running of the place to Ramsey. I prefer to supervise, keep an eye on everything, not to be stuck behind the counter."

"But will she be working there full time?"

"Yes. Yes, of course she will. Did you think I was going to let her sit around the house doing nothing when she finished school?"

Wyn pulled out a chair from the kitchen table and sat facing her brother. Michael, his head bent over his schoolbooks, pretended to ignore the conversation. He flicked the pages of his math book, as if searching for something, while furtively eavesdropping at the same time.

"She'll be working behind the counter then?"

Jim looked a little uncomfortable. His older sister glared at him as he handed the rent book back to her.

"Well, no. Miss Dewey is getting on a bit, so I thought Sheelagh could help her in the office, learn the accounts. Lord knows I paid enough for her education."

"But you said that Michael could learn the business. You promised me."

"Come come, now, Wyn, don't start making a fuss about nothing. I didn't exactly promise you. I said I would consider it, *if* he proved himself."

Michael scribbled a few numbers in his copy. He was used to being ignored at these Sunday-morning meetings, but the conversation was rarely about him.

"But you can see for yourself he studies very hard." She gestured to Michael who tried to look as if he were engrossed in a problem. "And he is a good boy. Ask the Brothers; ask Father Denton."

"I have no doubt he is, Wyn, and when the time comes we will discuss it further. He has to finish his schooling first. He has another year to go, don't you, boy?"

Michael looked up, feigning surprise. "Sorry, sir? I didn't hear what you said."

Wyn cut across him.

"But you *will* consider him, then? He has to earn a living, and you said you would never leave the business to a girl."

Jim snorted, "Quite right too. Now, stop fretting yourself, Wyn. I just want her to earn her keep 'til she finds herself a decent husband. Then she'll be too busy rearing children to be interested in any business. Yes, I will consider him. But there's many a slip, woman, remember that! There's many a slip! I'll not leave my business to any lazy, disrespectful, popinjay. I'd leave it to a woman first."

He stood and frowned down at the boy, his face and neck turkey red above his collar.

"Make no mistake, young man. I keep a very close eye on you. You just play your cards right; do as you're told, and continue to get good reports from school and your prospects could be very good. Very good, indeed!"

He fumbled in his waistcoat pocket and drew out his watch. Wyn also stood, beaming her pleasure.

"Now! Do you hear that, Michael? Just like I've been telling you, virtue is its own reward."

Her brother tapped the watch face impatiently.

"Well, I won't keep you, Jim. I'm sure Edith will have your dinner on the table. I will see you next week, God willing."

She accompanied him to the front door, waited as he drove away, then returned to the kitchen. Michael remained at the table, bent intently over his books. As Wyn prepared the Sunday dinner, his head buzzed with the overheard conversation. He *would* be going to work for Mr. Porter. Aunty Wyn had been right. Was she right about his inheritance too? Would the shop be his one day? And the house too? Maybe? He thought of the Porter's large house and their maid, Martha. He pictured himself driving Porter's big car and wearing the same kind of smart suits as Mr. Porter, with a gold watch chain and a striped shirt with a white starched collar and gold cufflinks and studs. He couldn't wait to tell Paul. He was going to be rich, own a big store, and drive a huge car.

Christmas

"What's it like working in the shop, Sheelagh?"

Brother and sister sat at the dining-room table halfheartedly sorting the jigsaw pieces. This year it was a picture of the coronation. George VI had finally been crowned the previous May. Edith was delighted to find the puzzle and pointed out to Michael what a collector's item it would become in future years. He thanked her politely, but the annual jigsaw gift had long since lost its appeal, and he cared little about the royal family, or the coronation.

"It's not too bad," said his sister. "Miss Dewey is very nice, but she is a bit of a fusspot. She made me add up one column of figures four times because I was a farthing out! I've only been there a few months for goodness' sake. I told her she could take it out of my wages if it was that important, but she was determined to make me get it right."

"But is it easy to learn? You know, all the prices and where everything is?" he persisted. "What are the people who work there like? I've only been in there twice, ages ago. What's Ramsey like; is he as old as Mr. Porter?"

"Why do you care?" she said dismissively, then added, "He's all right, I suppose, a stuffy old stick, but everyone in there is as old as Methuselah."

She threw down the jigsaw piece impatiently and went to examine her reflection in the mirror over the fireplace. She was a striking-looking young woman, tall, slim with a crown of red hair, cut short, and coaxed into soft waves. A fine dusting of pink-white powder softened her many freckles and highlighted her vivid blue eyes.

"Do you like my hair like this? Mummy says it's too short. I hate how it goes all curly."

"It's nice. How many people work there?"

"Seven," she said distracted by a tiny smudge of her lipstick. "And a woman who only comes in on Saturdays." She turned to her brother, "Did you know Mary got married?"

"Who's Mary? Is she the Saturday girl?"

"No idiot, *sister* Mary." She turned back to the mirror, delicately moistened her finger with her tongue and smoothed her fashionably arched eyebrows.

Michael was puzzled. He hoped that this Christmas visit to the Porters would give him the opportunity to question his sister about the shop, *his* shop, and here she was fussing with her hair and talking about some nun who was getting married. He looked at her blankly. She saw his expression in the mirror and turned.

"Don't tell me you don't know about Mary?" she asked incredulously. "Michael, didn't you ever talk to Aunty Wyn? Don't you have *any* interest in your family? I'm sure I told you to talk to her *last* Christmas, for heaven's sake."

He continued to look at her, frowning. Sheelagh returned to the table and sat opposite him. She thought for a moment about whether she should say anything more, but decided she'd better give him some explanation, now that she'd said this much. After all, she decided, she wasn't a schoolgirl anymore. She was nearly seventeen years old now *and* earning her own living. She could make her own decisions. Glancing over her shoulder to make sure the double doors to the sitting room were fully closed, she leaned toward Michael and spoke in a low voice.

"Don't you know anything about the Irish family? Colm isn't our only brother, you know. There's another one, in Ireland, in a place called Glendarrig. And there's a sister as well, that's Mary. *She's* the one who got married, to Joe, Joe Daly. His father owns the local pub. Aunty Bridgie left her the shop and then Joe proposed and they were married. I want to go and visit them one day, but Mummy says Daddy wouldn't approve, so I'll wait a while. But Mary says I can come any time."

Michael stared at her, trying to understand everything she was saying. She said he had another brother and another sister! He remembered his meeting with his brother Colm years ago. If the other brother was like him, he was not much interested, but another sister? And *she* had a shop too?

101

"Didn't you ask her? Oh, Mike, you're impossible. Not even after I told you about Aunty Bridgie dying?" she paused, remembering what Martha had said.

"Mary says she writes to you, but you never write back," she said tentatively.

"I never got any letters."

"Why not?"

"I don't know, do I?"

"She thought you just didn't care."

Michael sat quietly toying with one of the jigsaw pieces. He looked across at his sister. "Why wouldn't I care? Of course I'd care."

"Why don't you ask Aunty Wyn about them now, when you go home?"

He nodded, but his thoughts were elsewhere. Was his sister telling the truth? Would Aunty Wyn *really* not have told him if there were letters? He would have seen them surely. The postman often delivered mail before he left for school. But then, why on earth would his sister lie to him?

Sheelagh was tired of the subject.

"Come on, we'd better finish this puzzle or Mummy will be all upset and think you don't like it."

He gave her a brief glance, pulling a funny face. She laughed and they returned to the puzzle. She chattered on about a recent film she'd seen, and Michael pretty much ignored her while he considered all this new information about his family and the missing letters. He couldn't wait to get home and ask Aunty Wyn. The old bat, he thought. He surprised himself at just how angry he began to feel.

As Jim Porter drove away and Michael followed Wyn up the pathway to the house his stomach was tense, but he had made up his mind. He was determined to ask his aunt about the letters. He'd never received a letter in his whole life. To find out that a sister he knew nothing about had been writing to him for years and that his aunt might be taking those letters, made him angry. She was always telling him what he could and couldn't do; always quoting the Bible at him. Surely she couldn't do something like this? The more he thought about it, the more angry and frustrated he felt. She was constantly telling him, "You get what you deserve." Is this what he deserved? To be treated like a fool? Lied to? He *didn't* deserve to have letters kept from him! He *didn't* deserve to be kept in ignorance of his other brother and sister, even if they *were* like Colm.

As soon as they were in the kitchen he took a deep breath and began.

"Aunty Wyn."

She turned and peered over her glasses looking up at his angry young face.

"Yes?"

"Did any letters come for me?"

Anger

Wyn slowly tugged off her gloves, pulling at the tips of the finger seams to loosen them from her fingers. She placed the gloves on the kitchen table; then reached up to pull out a long, silver hatpin, before removing her hat and placing it carefully on top of the gloves. She methodically undid the buttons of her coat. Michael remained standing in front of her, teeth clenched, arms stiff at his side, his balled fists pressing against his thighs.

"Aren't you going to help me off with my coat, Michael?"

Instinctively, as his aunt turned, he stepped forward and eased the coat from her shoulders. He draped it briskly over his arm. She turned again and handed him the hat and gloves.

"Hall stand, please."

Years of obedience conditioned his response as he took her coat, gloves, and hat and left the kitchen. When he returned she was putting her hatpin box back in the dresser drawer. He watched as she slowly walked to her chair, turned, and sat.

"Now then, is there something you want to say to me?"

His mouth felt dry, his stomach was still churning.

"Did any letters come for me?" he repeated.

"Not that I know of," she said, her voice terse. "There have been no letters arriving here."

"But Sheelagh said there were letters for me, from my sister."

"From Sheelagh?" she sounded faintly surprised.

"No. My other sister, Mary."

"And Sheelagh told you this, did she?"

"Yes, she did," he said defiantly, his voice rising slightly.

"Don't you take that tone of voice with me, young man."

"Well, she did," he said more quietly.

"Then I will have to have a word with my brother about that young lady."

"I don't want to get her into any trouble."

Michael knew that Jim Porter had a bad temper, a bit like Aunty Wyn. He didn't want to be responsible for Sheelagh getting told off.

"Well, perhaps you ought to have thought of that before she and you accuse me of having hidden mail from you."

"I didn't, I only asked."

He was beginning to doubt his sister's story more and more.

"Of course, now I think of it, I don't suppose Mr. Porter is going to be very happy about your accusations either. You only have a few months left at school, you know. How old are you now, fifteen? Sixteen in May I believe? And you want him to employ you when you leave school?"

"I only wanted to know," he said with some defiance.

"Don't you have studying to do?" She stared back at him, her gaze hard and cold.

He couldn't hold her stare any longer. His eyes fell, he was defeated. His stomach still felt sick, but the small knot of anger at its core remained. He'd only asked. He had believed Sheelagh. Why should she lie to him about something like this? But then, he couldn't believe his aunt would lie either, though he had a feeling she was not telling the whole truth. She wasn't shouting at him, or quoting passages from the Bible like she usually did. She was very quiet.

Michael left the kitchen and trudged slowly up to his bedroom. Had he destroyed his future employment at the shop? Would Aunty Wyn tell her brother what he, Michael, had said? He closed the bedroom door and threw himself on the bed. He began punching the pillow with his balled fist, hot tears of anger and humiliation blurring his vision.

He did not see the old woman get up from her chair so angrily that the rocker almost tip tilted. Neither did he see her pace the small kitchen in fury.

He did hear the front door slam about five minutes later. And then he was afraid.

Martha hurried from the kitchen to answer the insistent clamor of the Porter's doorbell. She answered it just as Jim Porter stepped out of his study to see what the noise was all about. Wyn strode into the hallway.

"Out of the way, girl, I want to have a word with my brother."

She pushed past the startled maid, who hastily closed the front door and followed her.

"Good God, Wyn, what's got into you? I dropped you home less than an hour ago. What on earth is wrong? Has something happened to the boy?"

Wyn was breathing hard; she had walked the two miles to her brother's home at a rapid pace, fueled by her anger.

"You could say that. I told you those letters would cause trouble."

Jim Porter cast a quick glance beyond her to where the maid was standing.

"That will do, Martha, thank you. You may get back to your work. Come into the study, Wyn, you don't want to upset the whole household. Edith and Sheelagh have already gone upstairs."

"Will I take Miss Porter's coat, sir?"

"No, I said that will do, Martha. You can leave us now."

Wyn strode into his study, and he hastily followed, careful to close the door behind him. His sister stood in the middle of the room, foot tapping, tugging angrily at her gloves.

"Right then, Wyn, sit down and tell me what this is all about. Would you like a drop of brandy?"

"I would not, thank you very much," she said sharply. She opened the buttons of her coat and sat, pointing an accusing finger at her brother. "You promised me there would be no letters. You told me it would not be a problem."

"What on earth are you talking about, Wyn?"

"The letters to Michael! He knows about them. He knows about the chit of a sister in Ireland. You promised me!"

"But he's received none of the letters. I've destroyed them immediately."

"But you didn't stop her sending them, did you?"

He hadn't. It had seemed easier at the time to let the Irish girl send them, then just dispose of them.

"How would he have found out," he protested. "No one knew except …" he stopped abruptly and held up his hand to prevent Wyn from further comment, "Just one minute, Wyn." He tugged at the bellpull beside the fireplace. In a few moments Martha knocked on the door and entered.

"You rang, Mr. Porter?"

"Come in, girl, and close the door."

She did as she was told, glancing anxiously from her employer to his sister.

"The boy was here today," he waved his hand at Wyn.

"You mean Mr. Michael, sir? Yes, sir."

"And you told him about the letters."

"Letters, sir? No, sir. You have always told me not to mention them, sir, and I haven't."

"No, Jim, it wasn't …"

"I will handle my own staff, thank you, Wyn."

He looked back at the maid, standing stiffly in the center of the room.

"I will not have liars in my household. You may pack your bags and leave this house immediately, young woman. And rest assured you will not be receiving a reference from me. Damned if you'll find an employer who will take in an untrustworthy piece of baggage like you. Now get out, do you hear? I want you packed and gone within the hour!"

Martha's face was burning with anger. "But I didn't …."

"Out, I say."

Wyn leaned forward and raised her voice to match his, "It wasn't her, Jim. It was your daughter. It was Sheelagh."

The room became very quiet. For a moment Jim Porter stood as if frozen in position, staring at the maid. "Fetch Miss Sheelagh please, Martha," he said, very quietly.

"But she's in bed, sir, she's probably asleep," Martha's anger had quickly turned to concern for her young charge.

"Then wake her."

Brother and sister stared unblinking at the maid.

"Perhaps it was me, sir, after all. Perhaps I said it without thinking."

Wyn turned to her brother, "Michael was quite clear that it was Sheelagh who told him."

"Fetch her, Martha." Porter's face was deep red and she could see a vein pulsing at his temple. She didn't dare disobey.

"Yes, sir. Should I still be packing my bags then, sir?"

He ignored her question, fumbling in his pocket for his tobacco pouch. The maid waited.

He dismissed her with the wave of a hand, "We'll talk about that later. Now do as I say and wake Miss Sheelagh."

When Martha left the room, Wyn watched her brother select a pipe for the rack beside him. He teased out a small tangle of yellow-brown tobacco threads from his pouch and slowly pressed them into the bowl of the pipe.

Wyn sighed audibly, "Do you have to smoke that now? It's very stuffy in here already."

He slammed the pipe down onto the side table.

She ignored his display of temper.

"He could decide to go back to them, you know," she said, determined to make her point. "He's nearly finished school. If that sister of his asks him, he might just go back to Ireland and work for her. And then where will I be? He was supposed to look after me! Remember your promise? I'm getting old. That's why I took him in, that's why you gave him to me. And now look what's happened! I told you no good would come of those letters." She dabbed at a stray tear. "Everything ruined, after all my work."

"Yes, yes, you've said that already."

Her voice rose, "As for your Sheelagh, is this the thanks you get for taking her in, giving her a good home, for trusting her? Is this the young woman you have put in a position of trust in your shop?"

"She's always been perfectly trustworthy, Wyn. I will not have a word said against her until I hear what she has to say for herself."

Wyn was silent for a moment, choosing her words carefully before she continued. "I'm just saying that it seems to me she lacked judgment, which seems to me to be a very poor trait for someone put in a position of responsibility."

Jim Porter looked shrewdly at his sister.

"So, that's what's behind all of this? It's not just the letters. You don't like Sheelagh working in the store, do you? I've already told you that Sheelagh will not be taking over the business." He leaned forward in his chair. "Don't try to turn me against my daughter, Wyn. That would be most unwise."

There was a light tap on the door.

"Come."

Martha opened the door and let Sheelagh step past her, into the room.

"Miss Sheelagh, sir. Will I go now, sir?"

Sheelagh only glanced briefly at Wyn; she was far more concerned about her father's anger. Martha had already warned her, telling her the reason for the summons. She hugged her robe tight around her body.

"Yes, that will be all."

Jim Porter watched the maid leave the room and then turned his attention to his daughter.

"You know what this is about, young lady?"

"Yes, Daddy."

"Did I, or did I not, make it quite plain that Michael was not to know about the letters you received?"

"Yes, Daddy."

"And so …?"

She took a small handkerchief from her pocket and twisted it nervously in her fingers.

"I didn't tell him about them."

"Don't lie to me, girl."

"I'm not lying, Daddy. I just mentioned about Mary getting married. I thought he already knew."

"And why did you think that?"

"Because Mary told me she wrote to him as well."

Wyn gave a snort and nodded her head triumphantly at her brother. He ignored her.

"So you took it upon yourself to make sure he knew?"

"No, Daddy. I was just happy for Mary. It just slipped out. I didn't think it would do any harm."

Jim Porter turned and picked up the pipe from the side table, lit a taper from the fire, and held the flame to the bowl. The room was again very quiet. He sucked on the ebony stem.

"You may go back to bed now, young lady. You will not discuss this with your brother again. Do you understand?"

"Yes, Daddy."

She turned and left the room.

"So where does that leave me?" said Wyn. "She can't take it back. He knows now. What am I supposed to do?"

"You will do nothing. I will have a word with the boy myself, when I collect the rent tomorrow. Meanwhile, you will say nothing."

Wyn knew their conversation was over. She stood, buttoned her coat, and put on her gloves. He did not call Martha to see her to the door and he did not offer to drive her home.

She left, closing the front door quietly behind her.

Sunday

Michael didn't sleep well. He lay listening and waiting for Wyn's return, dreading another confrontation. When she did come home and he heard her pass his room and close her own bedroom door, he began to worry about what would happen in the morning, Sunday morning, the day for Jim Porter's weekly rent-book visit. The clock in the parlor chimed three before he finally fell into a fitful sleep. When he was woken early the next morning by Wyn's rapping on his door, she didn't speak. Her icy silence continued on their long walk to and from the church for Mass and during breakfast.

He was sitting at his usual place at the kitchen table, studying, when he heard the familiar, impatient knocking on the front door. It made him jump, even though he was expecting it. His heart hammered faster, and he felt a thin bead of perspiration form on the wisps of downy hair across his top lip. Wyn went to answer it. He heard no sound of voices when she opened the door, or as she and her brother returned to the kitchen. Michael kept his head bowed and tried to appear as if he was reading, though he watched their every move from the corner of his eye. Jim Porter grunted as he took his customary seat in the rocking chair beside the fire. The rent ritual continued as it did every Sunday. Wyn fetched the rent book from the drawer and handed it to her brother, along with the six shillings rent money. Porter took the silver coins, checked them, and tucked them into his waistcoat pocket. He signed the book, waved it for a moment to ensure the ink was dry, then closed it and handed it back to his sister. Still there was silence. Michael cast a furtive glance toward the rocking chair, and his gaze was instantly trapped by the hard stares of the large man and the thin, dark-clad woman standing behind him.

"I understand you are unhappy with your life here?"

Jim Porter's eyes were a pale, watery blue. They also protruded slightly and were faintly bloodshot, but they did not waver from Michael's face.

"No, sir, I didn't say that...."

"And that you called your aunt a liar."

"No, sir, I only asked her ..."

"And that you would prefer to return to your riffraff Irish family?"

"No, sir, I don't. I ..."

"Well, that's certainly how it sounded to me. After all that she's done for you? This is the gratitude you show? After all I *intended* to do for you. You choose to throw it all away for some Irish beggars trying to benefit from your more fortunate circumstances?"

"No, sir, really I didn't. I really want to stay here. I want to come and work with you and learn."

"Do you indeed? And do you expect me to take you on after this?"

"I'm very sorry, sir. I didn't mean to ..."

"And is there any reason in the world why your aunt should allow you to remain under her roof after what you have said and done to her?"

"Please Mr. Porter, please give me another chance. I am very sorry. I promise ..."

Jim Porter raised his hand to stop Michael and allowed a long silence to weigh in the air.

"I don't think the choice is mine, young man. I think the choice lies with your aunt. It is to her you must direct your pleas and promises. It is she who has cared for you all these years, with little thought for herself." He paused and twisted in his chair to look at Wyn who stood behind him, her gnarled fingers clutching the back of the chair, pressed tight against the polished wood, her knuckles white. "What do you think, Wyn? Do you still want this ingrate in your house? Do you think you could find the Christian charity to let him stay here?"

Michael stood slowly and stared at her.

"Please, Aunty Wyn."

She returned his stare for a long time; then looked down at her brother.

"Perhaps I could try and forget this, though I'm not sure how." She looked back at Michael. "I will give you one more chance, young man, but if you *ever* challenge me again, it will be the last time. Do you understand?"

"Yes, Aunty Wyn."

Jim Porter rose from his seat. "I hope you do, young man. Let this be a lesson to you."

He tugged his watch from his pocket and flipped it open. "I must be off. Time's wasting. I will see you next Sunday, Wyn." He turned again to Michael. "We will say no more of this unfortunate incident, young man." He looked back at his sister, "And get him a razor, Wyn. It's time he removed that damned fuzz."

Jim Porter left. Wyn returned to preparing dinner and Michael returned to his studies. It was several more days before an uneasy civility was reached between them. Meanwhile Michael worked hard at home, and at school, to prove he had learned his lesson.

1938

Endings and Beginnings

"Thank God, that's finished," said Paul. "I thought that miserable old bugger was actually going to cry when the last bell went."

"I think he was genuinely sorry to see us go," said Michael, kicking a pebble out of his way.

Paul swung his satchel over his head. "And we never have to put up with that fat bastard Harry Winston any more, or any of his cronies. We're free."

He threw the worn and battered bag into the air. Its contents began to spill and fly everywhere. Scraps of paper spiraled upward on the summer breeze and drifted across the street. A tattered copy of Virgil broke loose from its cover and fell in the gutter.

"We're free," he shouted again at the top of his voice as he snatched at his satchel and kicked the book along the gutter.

"Won't your mum be mad at you for doing that with the book," said Michael, watching him doubtfully.

"I don't need it anymore, and Beth is certainly never going to study Latin. Come on, Mike, I'll race you to my house and we'll see what's for dinner."

"I can't. Aunty Wyn said I was to come straight home. Are you serving Benediction this evening?"

"No, I told Father Denton I was finished this week. I have to go out and get a job. I'm not a schoolboy any more.

"I thought you were going to wait until you found work before you quit serving Mass and Benediction."

Paul stopped kicking the tattered remains of the book and turned to his friend.

"I'm going to be an aircraftsman, Mike."

"But you're too young to be a pilot. You said that already."

"I know, but Dad says there's going to be a war. He says I should choose where I want to go before they start calling us up. I can start as an aircraftsman on the ground, learn all about the planes; then, when I'm old enough, I can be a pilot. Dad says he doesn't want to see me in the trenches like his dad was."

"Mr. Porter said that Hitler wouldn't dare start a war. He said the Hun knows they would only get beaten again, like the last time."

Paul shrugged. "I'm going to be a pilot anyway, so I don't care."

"I think he's going to take me into the shop, Paul; let me work there."

"What if a war does start? You can't work in a button shop then."

It was Michael's turn to shrug. He had tried so hard this last six months to get back into Porter's good books, as well as his aunt's. He never mentioned Sheelagh's name, or the letters, and he tried not to think about the "other family." Getting work in Porter's Haberdashery and Clothing Emporium was far more important, especially if he wanted to inherit it one day.

They walked in silence for a while.

"I suppose I'll stop serving Mass too, and the choir. I'll have to see what Aunty Wyn says."

Paul looked with sympathy at his friend. He'd long since stopped wondering why Michael put up with the old she-dragon.

"Right! I have to go, Mike. See you Sunday. Hey," he added, looking a little awkward, "Will you be coming to the church dance on Saturday night?"

Paul had wanted to go to the dance for some time, but it took him a while to work up the courage to ask his sister Evelyn to teach him to dance. He'd been learning the waltz and the quickstep for weeks now. He was ready.

"Dance? Me?" Michael laughed. "Are you out of your mind, Paul Howard? I can't dance. And when did *you* learn anyway?"

Paul looked a little abashed. He hadn't told his friend. He wanted to make sure he wasn't going to make a fool of himself first. "It's easy. I just watched Ev and Beth doing it. They dance to the music on the gramophone all the time. Will you come?"

"Why would I want to go dancing, for goodness' sake?"

"Cos you get to dance with the girls; and you can hold them tight. Well, Arthur Willis says you can, as long as old Mrs. Walters isn't looking at you. She's in charge. I'm going to ask Winnie Luscomb to dance."

"Winnie Luscomb, but she's ugly."

"Yeah, but she's got big thingies. Will you come? You can dance with her too if you like."

"I don't know how."

"Ev will teach you, or Beth will."

Michael wondered what his aunt would say. Beth might teach him? Perhaps he *should* learn to dance, just in case he had to, some time, for something. It might be interesting.

"I'll see. I'll call over to you tonight, after Benediction."

"Alright. See you then."

Paul swung his satchel on his shoulder and ran in the direction of his house. Michael walked slowly the rest of the way home, thinking about dancing, war, Beth, Mr. Porter, and finishing school.

The Interview

Wyn was sitting at the kitchen table when Michael arrived home, her hat and handbag on the table in front of her.

"Where have you been? I've been waiting for you for half an hour."

"Sorry, Aunty Wyn, we had to clean out our desks before they let us leave."

"Well, put your bag in your room; we're going into town."

"What for?" But he felt a clutch of excitement in his stomach. *This was it. It was going to happen.*

"Mr. Porter wants to see you," she said, standing.

He flew up the stairs, two at a time, opened his bedroom door, and threw his bag on the bed. He was back downstairs before she had buttoned her coat.

"Wash your hands and comb your hair before we go."

He did, and continued running his fingers through his hair as they hurried to the tram stop.

Wyn walked through the store like a ship in full sail. Michael followed. They passed the cashier's desk where Sheelagh sat. He'd seen her as soon as they entered the store, but Michael carefully avoided catching her eye as he passed her desk. She didn't seem to have seen him and was busily occupied counting coins. Beside her sat a tiny old lady wearing a dark blue dress with a white lace collar. Black-framed pince-nez were perched on the end of her small, pointed nose, and her snow white hair was piled high on her head and held in place by delicate silver combs.

Half-hidden at one side, at the rear of the cashier's desk, a short staircase led up to a dark wood door emblazoned with a large sign in gold lettering which read "Mr. J. Porter. Proprietor." Wyn climbed the five steps and knocked on the door. Porter's voice bellowed.

"In!"

She turned, gave a peremptory jerk of her head to indicate that Michael should follow her, and opened the door. As they entered, Michael gave a quick glance around the room. He saw that a wide window beside Porter's desk gave him a clear view of the entire shop, as well as the cashier's desk just below him.

Porter waved his visitors to two wooden, upright chairs in front of his desk. Barely waiting for them to sit, he spoke.

"So, you have finally finished school, young man. Brother Pius says you have been a good student, particularly over the last six months."

"Yes, sir."

"Do you think you have earned a place here?"

"I hope so, sir."

Porter leaned toward the window and tapped it hard. Sheelagh looked up. Porter waved at her, and she stood and left her desk. Michael wondered if she was coming into the office. A few moments later there was a light tap on the door.

"In," said Porter, again straightening the papers on his desk.

An elderly man, wearing a brown, knee-length cotton coat, walked stiffly into the office.

"Miss Sheelagh said you wanted to see me, sir?"

"Yes, Swinton, this is the young man I mentioned to you. Michael, this is Mr. Swinton, in stores. You will be working with him from tomorrow morning, starting at eight o'clock sharp. Swinton, take no nonsense from him."

Michael stood and shook hands with the man.

"Pleased to meet you, sir."

"And you, young sir."

Porter tapped his desk impatiently.

"Well, I'm sure you have work to do, man, so I won't keep you."

"Indeed, sir. That'll be all then, Mr. Porter?"

"Yes, yes, you can go now. And make sure he gets a store-man's coat tomorrow, I don't want him ruining his clothes back there."

"Yes, I will, sir. Good day, madam, sir." Mr. Swinton gave a slight bow to Wyn and left. When the door closed behind him, Porter continued.

"You will receive ten shillings a week young man; you will have one break, at twelve thirty, and you will be back in the storeroom by one fifteen. I expect you to hand up most of your money to your aunt, for your keep, but you may retain a little for your personal expenses so that you may learn thrift and budget management. Do you agree, Wyn?"

She nodded; then leaned forward in her seat. "Will he be eligible for an increase when he proves satisfactory?" she enquired.

"Good God! Of course he will, woman. I treat all my staff fairly."

"I don't doubt it; no need to take the Lord's name in vain. I only asked. Better to have these things clear from the start. Is that all we need to do?"

He nodded.

"Right, we will be off then." Wyn stood and Michael followed suit. "Thank you, Jim. What do you say, Michael?"

"Thank you very much, sir."

"One more thing, boy," Porter held up an index finger, as if in warning. "You needn't bother giving the staff your history. Don't want it to seem like I'm setting a spy among them. Understand?"

Michael nodded.

Porter dismissed them with a wave. He did not get up from his seat. As they left the office Michael still avoided looking directly at Sheelagh. Somewhere, deep inside, he felt a small kernel of resentment that she got to work in the cashier's office straight away, whilst he had to start in the storeroom. Still, he was IN! He had a job in Porter's Haberdashery and Clothing Emporium.

He and Wyn caught the tram home and almost arrived at their front gate before Michael remembered the dance.

"Aunty Wyn. May I go to the dance on Saturday?"

She stopped and looked at him surprised. "Where? What dance? Why?"

"The church dance. In St. Nick's, I mean St. Nicholas. In the church hall. Paul asked me to go with him; his mother said he could go. Mrs. Walters supervises."

"How much is it?"

"Threepence."

"Can you afford it?"

"No."

"Then, I suppose you must wait until you can."

He expected her to say no; at least this was a maybe. She was obviously in good humor.

Awkwardness

Michael checked the time on the clock over the jeweler's shop at the end of Castle Street. Determined not to be late on his first day, he saw that he was now half an hour early. That's all right, he thought to himself, slowing his pace for the last hundred yards. He didn't want to be all hot and sweaty when he arrived. His neat and tidy appearance was a little marred by the small squares of paper stuck to his bloodied face. His early morning encounter with a new blade had not been a complete success. Arriving at the shop entrance, he stood in the warm June sun and watched a road sweeper brushing dust and debris along the gutter. The man smiled and winked at Michael.

"Morning, son."

The cigarette that dangled in the corner of the man's mouth wobbled as he spoke. Michael smiled back at him. Everything somehow seemed brighter and more alive to him today. He felt nervous and excited too.

Two women joined him at the recessed entrance to the shop. They were about the same age as Mrs. Howard and both gave him a friendly smile.

"Hello, son. Cut yourself then, did you?"

"Those razors can give you a nasty little cut if you're not careful."

Michael felt his face flush. He wanted to make a good impression on his first day, and here were these two women laughing at him, even before he got inside.

"You know, you could probably take them bits of paper off, lad. I'd say you've finished bleeding by now. What d'you think, Doris?"

"I'd say so. Just do it a bit gentle, son, or it'll start up bleeding again."

Michael tugged at each of the makeshift dressings, wincing as he did so.

"Put a bit of spit on yer finger, love, that'll help."

"Are you the new lad to work with Mr. Swinton?"

He nodded, concentrating on his task.

"You missed one there, love."

The woman called Doris touched a spot just below his ear. He gripped at the paper and pulled sharply.

"Now look what you've done. I told you to use spit." She licked her thumb and rubbed at the spot. "There you are, right as rain. No one would ever know you'd cut yourself."

She stepped back to admire her work as a tall, sallow-skinned man with a thin, graying moustache arrived in the doorway. Michael continued to rub at his face to make sure there were no other signs of his inexpert shaving. He studied the man as he did so. He was very smartly dressed, thought Michael, like Mr. Porter, but much thinner. He wore a dark gray, pin-striped suit and shoes that were polished to a glassy shine. His gray and white striped shirt had a stiff, white, starched collar which almost seemed to be holding his head in place. His silky, blue tie matched the handkerchief pointing neatly from his top pocket, and he carried a tightly rolled, black umbrella. He glanced briefly at Michael then tipped the brim of his gray fedora in acknowledgment of the two women.

"Good morning, Mr. Ramsey."

"Good morning, Mr. Ramsey. Expecting rain, are we?"

He ignored the question.

"Good morning, Miss Wall, Miss Williams."

He turned back to Michael.

"You must be the new boy. Mr. Kelly, isn't it?"

"Yes, sir."

"Good." He waved Michael aside. "Excuse me please, young man."

Fumbling in his pocket, he drew out a bunch of keys and sorted through them. He bent to insert a large brass key into the lock set low in the door, turned it with some difficulty, and pushed the door open. Once inside the shop he flicked on a panel of switches, lighting the interior of the shop, section by section. He removed his hat and Michael was surprised to see that the man was almost completely bald. Somehow he had expected him to have dark shiny hair, neatly parted in the center. Ramsey strode to the back of the store near Porter's office and unlocked a second door which had a small sign on it saying, STAFF ONLY. The two women followed, removing their light summer jackets as they went. Michael stood inside the store entrance, unsure what to do. The women quickly returned and began to roll back the cloths that covered the glass counters and showcases. They seemed to have forgotten him.

"Good morning, Mr. Kelly."

Michael jumped and turned to see Mr. Swinton standing beside him.

"Good morning, Mr. Swinton, sir."

The elderly man put his hand on Michael's shoulder. "Come on, lad. Let's get to work." The man's eyes flickered to the large, white-faced clock which hung over Porter's window. "Mr. Porter likes to see us working when he gets in, and he should be here any minute."

He walked past Michael to the rear of the store, beside the staff room, and unlocked large double doors. Michael followed him. He peered over the old man's shoulder into the dark, musty-smelling space. It seemed to be filled with clothes racks, high stacks of cardboard boxes, and rows of overcrowded wooden shelves which stretched back into the darkness. Mr. Swinton ran his hand over several brass-covered switches set to the left of the door. The lights came on, one by one, but their dim glow did little to illuminate the darkness. The old man lifted his brown, store-man's coat from a nail beside the door and handed Michael a second one that was folded on a box nearby.

They spent the morning checking invoices against stock. Over the day several lists were delivered to the storeroom by Mr. Ramsey. Swinton and Michael studied the lists, located the items on the shelves, boxes and rails, and loaded them into enormous baskets that looked like giant hampers on wheels. As each basket filled, Mr. Swinton delivered it out through the double doors and into the store, to restock showcases and shelves. He didn't ask Michael to accompany him, but left him sorting and counting boxes of fasteners, ribbons, needles, and buttons. Michael thought of Paul calling it a button shop and he smiled.

He was glad when the older man said it was time for the lunch break. Mr. Swinton unlocked another door, almost hidden behind racks and boxes, at the side of the storeroom. The door opened onto a back lane. An empty packing case sat neatly just outside the door.

"Find an empty one for yourself, lad, while I make the tea. There should be two or three back there."

When Michael returned from the storeroom with his improvised seat, Swinton already had two tannin-stained cups and a couple of small brown-paper bags sitting open beside him on his packing case, alongside a blue china tea pot with a chipped spout. A blackened and battered kettle sat on a precarious-looking primus stove set near his feet.

"Tea will be ready in a minute, lad. Hope you don't take milk."

He tipped a little hot water into the pot, swirled it around, then tossed it in an arc across the alley. Shaking tea leaves from one of the paper bags into the pot, he added the now-boiling water, returned the lid, and rotated the pot gently with his right hand.

The old man and the boy ate their lunch in companionable silence, enjoying the bright sunlight, a pleasant change from the gloomy storeroom. After a while Swinton poured the tea and tipped a drizzle of sugar into each cup from the second bag. He stirred the tea with the yellow pencil he usually kept tucked behind his ear.

Michael didn't leave the storeroom again until the evening. He didn't meet any other members of staff and didn't even see Mr. Porter, or Sheelagh. He was just as well pleased. He had not spoken to her since Christmas and was still nervous about speaking to her again.

Surprises

Michael soon got into his new routine. He did his home chores before leaving for work; then walked to Porter's shop on Castle Street. It was only about three miles and Aunty Wyn said if he wanted to ride the tram he would have to find the fare from the shilling pocket money she allowed him every week.

He used some of his first week's allowance to go with Paul to the church dance at St. Nick's, but didn't enjoy it. He'd hoped to ask Beth to teach him some steps, but she wasn't there. Paul said she was too young to come to the dance; she wouldn't be fifteen until nearly Christmas. For most of the evening Michael stood at the side of the dance floor with the other boys, feeling awkward and out of place.

After Mass the following Sunday he called in to the Howard house and asked Beth if she would teach him some dance steps. She agreed, and they began the next evening. The lessons took place in the Howard's kitchen, after supper. Michael was relieved that Evelyn wasn't there to tease them.

"We hardly ever see her, since she started work," said Paul. "She's always off with her friends, at dances or going to the pictures. I think she has a boyfriend too, but she won't tell us, and she hasn't brought him home yet. Even Maggie doesn't go out as often as she does."

"You know Maggie and James are saving up to get married, Paul. That's why they stay in so much."

"Yeah! And hogging the front room when Dad's out!" Paul responded, raising his eyebrows suggestively, and they all laughed.

Paul was in charge of the music, putting the records on the turntable and keeping the gramophone properly wound, so that the music didn't change speed. If the sound got too scratchy, he would carefully change the fine steel needle from a small dish set in the corner of the gramophone box. He hummed or sang along with the music as he watched Mike and his sister shuffle and twirl around the cramped space, bumping into chairs, the table, and the sink while still trying to keep the count. Michael muttered "*one* two three, *one* two three," over and over as he tried to guide Beth around the small room in his stiff rendition of waltz steps.

At first Beth had been shy and they spoke little, except when she was explaining the steps. As the weeks went by they relaxed more and eventually both of them were able to laugh at his awkwardness. If Michael stepped on her toes, he apologized and she would reassure him.

"It's all right, Mike. You're doing fine."

Anytime she compared Michael's attempts to Paul's, saying things like; "Paul was much worse than you when he started," or "He nearly broke my foot; he was so clumsy for the first few weeks." Paul would throw whatever missile was to hand, a tea towel, a napkin, or the tea cozy at the two dancers. Beth ignored him.

"You're doing very well, Mike, really! Don't mind him."

Michael enjoyed the evenings spent with Paul and Beth. It was very different from the Bible reading he had done with his aunt in the evenings when he was younger, or the homework every night when he was in senior school. Aunty Wyn didn't seem so cross these days either, now that he was actually working in the shop. She didn't seem to mind him visiting his friend's house in the evenings, though Michael decided not to mention Beth or the dance lessons.

More and more there was talk of war. Often, Michael sat on the kitchen floor and read the old newspapers Porter gave Wyn before he used them to wrap the ashes from the fire. He read about Mr. Hitler and how dangerous he was becoming. Sometimes he spoke about what he read with Wyn. In September she surprised him by buying a wireless. She said she didn't want to be caught off guard if a war did happen. After that they listened to the news every evening, her head bowed, straining to hear, because she kept the volume low. She thought the louder the sound, the more they would have to pay for the electricity, just like the brighter the light bulb, the more money it cost. Michael could not convince her otherwise.

On the 30th of September they both listened in rapt attention as the prime minister, Mr. Chamberlain, announced the agreement with Mr. Hitler; that peace was assured. Wyn complained that she needn't have bought a wireless after all, but they were both relieved.

At work, Michael had become bored in the storeroom, though he liked Mr. Swinton. He was a kind old man who brought in biscuits and slices of his wife's home-baked cakes, to have with their cups of tea. Michael brought a wrapped lunch from home, but it was usually bread and cheese and the sweet biscuits and cake were a nice treat. Early on, Mr. Swinton swore him to secrecy about the primus stove.

"I don't think Mr. Porter would be too happy if he thought I had a primus stove back here, though I only ever light it out in the alley."

Michael promised he would say nothing. He also kept his word to Porter not to tell anyone, even Mr. Swinton, about his relationship with the Porters. That was sometimes a difficult secret to keep, when the two store-men sat in the alley and chatted, at lunchtime.

Though he never mixed with them during the day, Michael often met the other members of the staff as they waited in the shop entrance for Mr. Ramsey to open the doors. Mr. Porter usually arrived a little later with Sheelagh, so Michael rarely saw them. There was another young woman who worked in the shop; Miss Wall introduced her as Mabel, Miss Butterworth. She always seemed to be giggling and talking about her boyfriends. On the second day she had asked Michael how old he was and barely spoke to him afterward. He didn't care. He thought she was very loud and what Aunty Wyn would call "brassy." A young man worked in the shop too, in Gentlemen's Apparel. His name was Mr. Higgins. He had a very bad case of acne, and his hair was always smarmed down with Brylcreem. Michael watched Mr. Higgins try very hard to get Mabel's attention, telling jokes or messing around, but she tried just as hard to ignore him. Michael took an instant dislike to Higgins and suspected the feeling was mutual.

Michael liked the two other ladies, Miss Wall and Miss Williams. They explained that, actually, they were both married and should be called Mrs., but Mr. Ramsey and Mr. Porter said that, in quality establishments, the ladies were always called miss. He'd met Miss

Dewey, the cashier, a few times too, as they waited at the store front for Mr. Ramsey, but she was a *real* miss. She was a frail-looking old lady, with a squint in one eye, and he heard Mr. Higgins say he didn't know how she kept the accounts straight when she couldn't even see straight. Despite the joking, even Mr. Ramsey deferred to her as if she, and not he, was the manager. She hardly spoke to Michael, only nodded when he said "good morning" and looked him up and down as if examining, and not liking, his clothes. On the rare occasion when he did see Sheelagh they would smile an acknowledgment, or pass the time of day, but there was no conversation. No one in the shop seemed to know they were brother and sister. Michael supposed that was hardly surprising really, as her surname was Porter and he was still Michael Kelly. They didn't look much alike either, he thought, except for the curly hair, but hers was red and his was almost black. He was certain *he* was never going to mention their relationship to the rest of the staff after Mr. Porter had instructed him not to. Sheelagh didn't seem to have said anything either, or the two ladies would surely have mentioned it. Anyway, he thought, it wasn't as if they were a real brother and sister, not like the Howard family.

Because of the distance maintained between the two of them, Michael was surprised when, toward the end of November, she came into the storeroom. He hadn't seen her for over a week, and he'd heard Doris say she thought Miss Sheelagh had gone on holidays on her own. The two ladies were very surprised that Mr. Porter had allowed it.

"Mr. Swinton, could I have a word with Mike for a moment? I won't keep him long, I promise."

"Well, Miss Porter, you know your father doesn't allow shop personnel back here. What if he catches you?"

"He won't, Mr. Swinton. He's just gone to the bank; he'll be gone for at least half an hour. I promise I won't tell."

"Perhaps if you go out in the back alley, then you can't really be said to be in the store, can you, miss?"

He smiled at her and called Michael from the back of the storeroom.

"Mr. Kelly, you have a visitor. Why don't you show her out to the back alley for a few minutes, but don't be long. I don't want Mr. Porter firing me, especially at my age."

When Michael saw Sheelagh, he was surprised. What was she doing here? Was she going to cause trouble again? Was she going to get *him* into trouble again? He'd still not forgotten the confrontation after last Christmas day and he never wanted another scene like that, especially as he was now actually working for Mr. Porter.

"What is it?" he said, standing a wary distance from his sister. Mr. Swinton frowned.

"That's a bit ungracious, young man. Now take Miss Porter out the back and mind your manners when you are speaking to the boss's daughter."

They left the storeroom in silence. Michael pulled the door closed behind him.

"What do you want, Sheelagh?"

She pulled her cardigan tightly around her. She had not expected to go outside and had not brought a coat. A cold wind blew down the alley, carrying a damp promise of rain to come. Still, she smiled at her brother.

"I've seen them, Michael. I've seen both of them, and Joe, and the baby."

"You've seen who?"

"Our other sister and brother, Mary and Pierce, and Mary's husband, and their new baby. They called her Norah, after our mother."

He sank onto the tea chest and looked up at her in astonishment.

"Really? You really went? The ladies said you were on holiday, but I didn't know you'd gone to Ireland."

"Daddy told me not to mention it in front of them. He said they don't need to know. It would cause too many questions. I don't think they know I'm adopted."

"They don't know about me either, do they?"

She shook her head.

"I'm the poor relation, that's what it is, isn't it?" He knew he sounded childish, but he was envious of his sister. "Don't ever tell them about the cave dweller who lives in the storeroom. Oh, dear, no. That wouldn't do, would it?"

"Look, Michael, I didn't come out here to listen to you feeling sorry for yourself. I thought you might like to hear about them. But if you don't, that's fine too. I can go back in the warm."

She turned to open the door, and he stood quickly, putting his hand out to stop her.

"No! Sorry, Sheelagh, I know it's not your fault. Yes, of course I want to hear about them, tell me."

He indicated the other packing case and they both sat. She told him the story of her trip on the train and the boat and a second train to a place called Ballyfin. She described meeting Pierce and how he drove her to Mary's shop in a village called Doonbeg in his lorry. She laughed as she told about nearly smothering the baby because she didn't know it was wrapped in Mary's shawl, and she told of the little shop and the tiny living room at the back.

And she told him how their father had had a stroke.

At that point Michael jumped up, shouting at her, "Father! What father? Bloody hell, Sheelagh, what are you telling me now?"

She paused; she'd forgotten he didn't know about their father either.

"Dammit, Michael, don't shout at me 'cos you didn't know!"

"What are you talking about? What father?" he persisted, lowering his voice to a harsh whisper.

So she told him about their father and their stepmother and how Mary wouldn't talk to them or have them at the christening and then how their father had a stroke when he found out about it.

Michael sat, stunned into silence. Sheelagh looked nervously toward the storeroom door. She didn't want to start another row.

"I have to go, Mike. He'll be back soon."

"Yes, all right." He stood and absentmindedly opened the door for his sister. She stood, walked to the door, then stopped and looked up at her brother.

"Mary said to tell you that they still miss you."

She stepped inside and had returned to the shop before he came in himself and closed and locked the door.

Mr. Swinton watched the boy as, silently, he went back to work.

"Everything all right then, son?"

Michael knew the man was curious, but he simply nodded, and his silence discouraged further enquiry.

He couldn't stop thinking about it for the rest of the day. They missed him! All the years he didn't even know his family existed, and they had missed him. All that time! And he had a father, a real father. He walked home, his mind a confusion of thoughts. He wanted to see them, to see his father especially. The more he thought about it, the more questions he wanted to ask, questions that he hadn't thought to ask Sheelagh. Why had they all been split up? What had happened to his mother? What were they like?

By the time he reached home Michael had made several decisions. He would not discuss this with Aunty Wyn, not this time, nor Mr. Porter or even Sheelagh. He'd been saving his money to buy a bicycle, but now he was going to save his money and go and visit them, just like Sheelagh had done. She said they missed him, so he was sure they wouldn't mind, but he would keep his plan a secret. He knew, from listening to the other staff, that when he'd worked in the shop for a year he would be able to take five days holidays. All the others did it. Ramsey and Miss Dewey got ten days, because they were senior staff. If he kept his plans for the visit secret then Mr. Porter couldn't get angry and call him an ingrate. What had he called them? Riff-raff? And beggars? Sheelagh hadn't seemed to think they were like that. She was smiling all the time that she spoke about them.

Yes! He would save up his money and go and meet his father. How strange that sounded, he said it again, in his head. His father! But he still wanted to stay working in the shop. He wanted to inherit it, like Aunty Wyn said he would, so he must be very careful not to make her, or her brother, angry. He must say nothing.

He walked up the lane and opened the back door into the yard. Wyn was gathering in washing from the line.

"Can I help you, Aunty Wyn?" he said, reaching for the laundry basket.

She handed it to him.

"Why have you got that stupid smile on your face?" she snapped.

He looked at the old woman in her long, black dress. He didn't think he'd ever seen her smile, not a real, happy smile, only the false smiles she gave to the ladies whose dresses she made or mended, or when Father Denton called on one of his parish visits.

"No reason, I'm just happy."

He opened the kitchen door and carried in the basket of washing.

Bad News

Sheelagh again arrived in the storeroom as Michael helped Mr. Swinton put a large box of undergarments into the hamper ready to be delivered to the ladies department. When Swinton saw her, he hurried from the back of the stores.

"You know, miss, this really is most irregular. This is the second time in only a few weeks. I can't have you breaking Mr. Porter's rules like this."

As he got nearer and saw her face more closely, he realized she had been crying.

"Is everything all right, miss?"

"I need to talk to Mike for a minute. Mr. Porter said I could come."

She dabbed at her eyes with her handkerchief. Michael watched from the gloom at the back of the storeroom, but didn't come forward until Mr. Swinton called him.

"Miss Sheelagh would like a word with you, Michael, and you can bring up that hamper. I know the ladies department is waiting for it."

He took the basket from Michael and wheeled it out through the double doors into the shop. Michael stood watching his sister, not sure what he should say or do. She glanced around to ensure Swinton had gone, then burst into tears.

"He's dead. I got the telegram last night. I never heard him speak."

Michael got that sick feeling in his stomach, like when Aunty Wyn was really cross with him, or when he was going to get the strap in school.

"Who is?" he asked. But he knew.

"Our father, he had another stroke. I knew he wasn't very well, but I promised him I would go and visit him again when he was better, so that we could talk. I know Mary didn't like him, but I felt so sorry for him, lying in the hospital, not able to move or talk. Now I'll never know what he was really like."

She sobbed into her handkerchief, and Michael continued to stand, watching her. Eventually her sobs quieted. She wiped her eyes; then blew her nose. There was silence for a moment. Sheelagh looked at her brother standing impassively in front of her. She took a deep breath, then shrugged.

"I just wanted to tell you. I don't suppose it means much to you. You never met him or anything."

She sounded awkward.

"That's why I came in today. Daddy said I could come and tell you."

She looked at Michael again, as if she was waiting for him to say something, anything, but he stood, silent and unblinking.

"He said I didn't have to stay in the shop today if I didn't want to. I suppose everyone will only want to know why my eyes are all red." She glanced around the storeroom. "Is there a mirror in here anywhere?"

He shook his head.

She fumbled in her pocket and retrieved a delicate silver compact. Opening it, and holding the mirror close to her face, she used the puff to dab powder around her eyes. She examined the result and, content with what she saw, closed the compact and returned it to her pocket.

"Do I look like I've been crying?"

He shook his head again.

She took another deep breath.

"Well, anyway, that's it. I said I'd tell you. I'm not going to the funeral; we'll be too busy here. It's too near Christmas."

She turned and left the storeroom. Mr. Swinton had obviously been waiting for her departure and pushed the empty hamper back through the doors before they had stopped swinging.

Michael still had not moved.

"Are you all right, lad?"

"I'm fine." He turned to go to the back of the storeroom. "I've to finish the rest of that list, Mr. Swinton; you took it out half-finished."

"That's all right, lad, there's no rush." He watched the boy walk away from him and raised his voice. "They have enough to be getting on with. Why don't you take a break for a minute?" Michael continued to walk. "Is there anything I can do?"

The boy stopped and turned. "No thanks, Mr. Swinton. I'm fine."

He consulted the list and began to fill a new hamper.

Michael knew the old man must be wondering what was going on, but how could he explain? He didn't want to either. In fact, he didn't know what he wanted. He only knew he was disappointed. He knew he was very, very disappointed; and he felt sad.

For the rest of the morning Michael went about his work and Mr. Swinton asked no more questions. Later in the morning Mr. Higgins put his head around the storeroom door to say that Mr. Porter wanted Michael in the office. Swinton tut-tutted and frowned as he summoned Michael from the back of the store.

"I knew there was going to be trouble. I told Miss Sheelagh she shouldn't have been in here. What have you two been up to, young man?"

Michael looked at him miserably. "Nothing, but I suppose she's managed to get me into trouble again."

"It takes two to tango, Michael lad, and I don't know why Miss Sheelagh would want to get you into trouble. It seems to me she was very upset herself when she came in here earlier."

Michael was tempted to tell the old man why his sister was upset, that she *was* his sister, but it would all be too complicated to explain, and it would really put the cap on his chances in the shop, if Sheelagh hadn't done that already.

"You'd better get going, young man. Mr. Porter doesn't like to be kept waiting."

Michael gloomily pushed open the double doors into the store and walked the short distance to the office. He noticed Sheelagh wasn't at the cashier's desk. He trudged up the shallow flight of stairs and knocked on Porter's door.

"In."

Michael opened the door and waited for Porter to look up from his desk.

"Come in, for God's sake, boy, and close the door after you."

Porter waved his hand toward the chairs in front of his desk.

"Sit, sit."

He continued to write for a moment and finally blotted the page, replaced the cap on his pen, and returned it to his inside pocket.

"Well, young man, I gather my daughter told you the news."

"Yes, sir."

"Can't imagine it means a great deal to you. I don't know why *she's* blubbering like a baby. It's not like he gave a jot for either of you."

Michael sat, his head down, waiting for whatever reprimand was to come.

"Just wanted to make sure you had no fool idea of going over for the funeral or anything."

Michael looked up, surprised; he hadn't even thought of it.

"No, well, of course you didn't. Why would you? Damn fool journey; shouldn't have let *her* go on that visit. Then we wouldn't have all these dramatics."

He paused, and Michael wasn't sure if Porter was addressing him, or not, so he waited.

"Swinton says you are doing very well. He says you learn quickly. Maybe in a while we can see if you can work out on the floor, learn how to deal with customers, that sort of thing." He paused again, staring at the boy, but Michael showed no reaction. "Right then, just wanted to make sure. Don't want any problems with you and that Irish bunch. My sister would be none too happy. Off you go, boy. I suppose we'll see you at the house on Christmas day?"

"Yes, sir."

Michael left the office, aware that some of the staff were watching. Swinton was waiting for him.

"Well, lad? Is everything all right?"

"Fine."

"Are you in trouble?"

"No."

The old man stood watching the boy.

"How about I put the kettle on and we have our lunch?"

"Fine."

Swinton put his hand on Michael's shoulder, "Come on, son, cheer up. Nothing is as bad as all that."

When he arrived home, Michael said nothing to Wyn about his father's death. He ate his evening meal in silence and was washing the dishes when he heard the familiar rat-tat-tat of Paul's knock on the front door.

"That sounds like that young friend of yours. Tell him you've to finish the dishes before you can go out."

Michael answered the door. Paul stood there, a big grin on his face.

"Well, what do you think? Does the color suit me?"

Michael couldn't help but smile at his friend, standing in a mock pose to show off his new uniform.

"Wow, it looks good. When did you get back?"

It was two months since Paul left for basic training and Michael had missed his friend.

"A couple of hours ago. Are you coming over to the house?"

Michael glanced over his shoulder. "I have to finish the dishes. Will you wait for me, I won't be long."

"Fine, I'll wait out here; see if I can impress any passing women."

Michael hoped his aunt hadn't heard that remark.

"I'll be out in a minute."

Paul caught him up on his adventures at the air base on the walk to the Howard house.

"It's even better than I thought it would be, Mike. I can't wait to make sergeant, then I can apply to be an airman, but an aircraftsman is fine. I'm learning all about the engines and how the aircraft work. It really is terrific, Michael, and all the girls love the uniform."

Michael laughed at his friend as he explained about torque, cylinder head temperatures, oil pressures and all the different aircraft. Though Michael had little idea what he was talking about, it was good to have his friend back. Paul's enthusiasm was infectious and his job certainly seemed more interesting than Michael's.

"How long are you home for?"

"Just for the long weekend. Will you come to the dance at St. Nick's tomorrow? I want to see if Winnie Luscomb is still around."

Michael hadn't been to the dance since his first visit in the summer; though he still visited the Howard household occasionally and practiced dancing with Beth.

Paul glanced slyly at his friend.

"We could bring Beth. She's fifteen now and I know she can't wait to go."

Michael blushed and grinned at the same time. He knew she was old enough to go to the church dance, but he'd felt too awkward to ask her.

"Right then," said Paul, laughing at his friend's discomfort. "That's settled, will you tell her, or will I?"

"You can if you like," said Michael, trying to sound casual. They walked up the pathway to the Howard house, and Paul continued laughing as took his front door key from his pocket and inserted it in the lock.

"Don't ever play poker, will you, Mike?" he added, as he pushed open the door.

In the buzz and banter of the evening, Michael's thoughts of his father's death receded. By the time he left to go home he'd reasoned that he could hardly get too upset about someone he'd never known. Mr. Porter must be right too; his father couldn't really have cared about his family, or he wouldn't have let them be taken away.

The Dance and After

Paul, Michael, and Beth paid their entrance money at the door, gave their coats into the cloakroom, and stepped into the large church hall. It was as dingy as Michael remembered it, despite the Christmas decorations and colored light bulbs that now embellished it. The walls were stained nicotine yellow and grimed with several years of greasy dust and dirt. Wooden chairs edged the side walls of the room. The raised stage at the far end was framed by tired, red velvet curtains. They were ripped in places and trimmed with tattered gold braid and fringing.

Michael glanced down at a smiling Beth. Her eyes seemed to reflect every colored light that hung from the low ceiling. She caught his glance and her smile widened. He returned her smile and Paul caught the exchange.

"All right, all right! I'm leaving you two for a bit; I don't think you need me to be a gooseberry." He winked at Michael. "Anyway, I can see Winnie Luscomb over there, and nobody's asked her to dance yet."

He gave Michael an encouraging pat on the back and walked off down the hall to where a cluster of girls were standing around a radiator.

Now that he was alone with Beth, Michael suddenly felt very uncomfortable. He stared intently at the three-piece band, already methodically playing their way through a waltz. The drummer squinted with disinterest at the dancers from behind the smoke haze of a home-rolled cigarette that dangled from his lips. The pianist gazed vacantly offstage as he played and the violinist kept his eyes closed as he sawed on his instrument.

"Come along, young people, don't block the doorway, please. Move down the hall, more people want to come in, you know."

Mrs. Walters, "the dance dragon" as Evelyn called her, was glowering down at them from her high stool perch against the back wall. Michael looked around and saw a group of girls standing behind them. He looked at Beth again.

"Do you want to dance?"

She smiled and nodded.

The drummer's heavy emphasis on the rhythm kept the young dancers' faltering steps fairly well synchronized, but, despite all his practicing, Michael stepped on Beth's toes several times, then lost count when he tried to apologize. She said she didn't mind, and he finally relaxed and began to enjoy himself. It was nice to have his arm around her waist, her hand in his. Her hair smelled good, like flowers and fresh air and sunshine.

When the music stopped, they stayed on the dance floor with a few of the other dancers. They were unsure where else to go. It looked as if all the boys were gathered on one side of the hall, near the refreshment table, and all the girls huddled around radiators on the other side.

The pianist announced the next dance, a quickstep, and Beth looked up at Michael hopefully. He shrugged.

"I'll do my best, mind your feet."

She laughed. "You can do it, we've practiced enough."

This time he only stepped on her toes once.

They danced together all evening, stopping at the interval to get lemonade from the soft drinks table near the restroom. During the evening Paul occasionally glided past them on the dance floor, clutching Winnie Luscomb close to him and winking at Michael as he passed.

Michael remembered the previous time he came to the dance and how he'd wondered if it would ever end. Now he wished it would go on forever. He and Beth didn't talk much, but as he saw the clock over the stage nearing ten, he began to wonder what he should do when the dance did finish. Should he take her home, or would Paul? Should he try and kiss her before she left? What would he do if she wouldn't let him? What was he supposed to do if she *did*? He'd heard the boys at school talking about French kissing and how you were supposed to put your tongue in the girl's mouth, but he thought mixing spit sounded pretty disgusting. The more he thought about it, the less he concentrated on the dancing. He bumped them into another couple so that they nearly fell over, then he stood on Beth's toes, twice. He began to wish he'd never come after all.

The pianist announced the last dance and Paul arrived at Michael's side.

"Will you make sure Beth gets home safely, Michael? I'm going to walk Winnie home." He leaned in to whisper in Michael's ear, "See, I told you they loved the uniform. She says the blue brings out the blue in my eyes!" He laughed and turned to his sister, "Tell Mum I'll be home later." Then he was gone, his arm squeezed tight around his partner's waist.

Michael looked at Beth, who seemed to be blushing, though the multi-colored lighting made it difficult to tell.

"Is that all right with you, Beth?"

She shrugged, "If you don't mind."

"No, I don't mind at all."

And his worried thoughts got worse. What if Mrs. Howard was waiting for them, and he did try and kiss her? Or worse, what if it was Mr. Howard? What if they were mad at him for bringing her home alone? Damn Paul anyway, it was all his fault.

"Don't look so worried. I don't bite," she said grinning up at him.

"Sorry."

He decided to concentrate on the waltz steps and worry about what might happen later, when they left the dance.

They said little walking home. He opened the gate and Beth walked in front of him up the path. The sitting room light was on, and they could hear Mr. Bing Crosby singing "Ain't Misbehavin" on the wireless in the front room.

"Do you want to come in for a cup of tea?" she asked, half whispering.

"No, thanks. Aunty Wyn will be wondering where I am if I don't get home soon."

They stood in the shadow of the porch. Her hands were thrust deep into her coat pockets.

"Thank you for letting me come with you."

He shrugged. "That's all right. It was Paul's idea."

"I enjoyed it," she said shyly.

143

"I did too."

There was an awkward silence. Michael shuffled from one foot to the other. They both began to speak at the same time.

"Sorry, you go first."

"No, it's OK, you go first."

"It was nice, you know, dancing," she said, and he thought she was blushing again, but couldn't see in the darkness.

"Yes." He paused. "Would you like to go again next week?"

"Yes, please."

"Great." He glanced down the road, nervous that Paul might arrive any minute. "I have to go; she'll be worried."

She nodded, "I have to go in too."

"Alright."

"OK."

She took her hands out of her pocket, stood on tiptoe, and turned her face up to his, her eyes closed. After another hasty glance over his shoulder he bent and gave her a swift kiss, bumping noses as he did so.

"Have to go," he said, stepping back, and she nodded. He turned and hurried for the gate.

"Goodnight," he whispered as he closed it behind him.

"Goodnight."

At the corner he turned back for a last glimpse. She was still where he had left her, and gave a small wave. He waved in return and continued home, smiling.

Another Christmas

It didn't feel like a jigsaw. The parcel was bigger and thinner, and he didn't hear the rattle of jigsaw pieces. Jim Porter watched as Michael opened his gift.

"I told her this would be more useful to you than a damned jigsaw. You need to know about these places."

Michael ripped off the last of the wrapping paper to reveal a world atlas, with a picture of a globe on the front cover. He flicked through the pages and saw all kinds of maps. Some showed the locations of mountains and valleys, rivers and seas, others had charts on population, rainfall, and major crop distribution.

"Can you see where Germany is? And Austria?"

Although Michael had studied geography in school, it held little interest for him. It was Paul who wanted to know about all the different places in the world. He hastily flicked through the book again, but couldn't see the two countries Mr. Porter mentioned.

"Part of the map of Europe, boy; don't tell me you don't know what part of the world they're in!"

Michael found Europe and searched for Germany. Porter looked over his shoulder.

"There, there it is," he said, jabbing at the page with his finger. "And there's Austria. That's what he's taken now, but he won't stop there, mark my words. Can't trust Hitler for a minute; can't trust any of those bloody Huns."

"Jim dear, I don't think we need that kind of language, especially on Christmas day."

"Don't tell me what I can and can't do in my own house, woman. That man has to be stopped."

Edith Porter adjusted her glasses nervously and turned to Wyn. "Did you hear the news on the wireless about all the refugees that are leaving Germany?"

"And where are they all going to go?" her husband blustered, now jabbing his finger in his wife's direction. "Here, that's where! Here! We're going to be flooded with bloody foreigners. As if there aren't enough of them here already!"

"Oh, no, dear. I believe they are going to Palestine. At least that's where a lot of them say they want to go."

He snorted. "Bloody map will be useless in a couple of months if they start partitioning the damn place. That's what they're talking about, you know. Partitioning Palestine!"

He turned his attention back to Michael.

"Let's see if you can find that then, boy, Palestine."

Michael hastily thumbed through the book. Despite Porter's irritability, this Christmas day was becoming more interesting, what with the atlas to look through *and* no jigsaw to make. He found the Middle East section of the map and held it up for Porter to see. The man nodded.

"See, see, they're talking about partitioning all this. Our boys are being killed over there already. And it's all that bloody Hitler's fault, driving out refugees. Germany's armed to the teeth; there's all this talk of emergency powers and that bloody fool Chamberlain is trying to tell us everything's under control."

Edith Porter rang the small silver bell on the table beside her. "I think it's time for a cup of tea. Don't you, Wyn?"

His aunt had been sitting in silence, wincing at each of her brother's swear words, but now her back stiffened and she ignored her sister-in-law's question.

"I don't know why they let the Arabs and Jews live in the Holy Land anyway; it's not like they're Christians," she said. Michael recognized that hard edge to her voice which meant she was trying to control her anger. He saw that her fists were clenched in her lap, their thin purple-blue veins standing out even more than they usually did, and the skin on her knuckles was bone white. "I think the Great War was quite enough for our lifetime. I don't intend to see Michael going off to fight some needless war between heathens."

"Who's asking him to? If he has to go to war, it won't be to fight the Jews and Arabs. It will be to fight that bloody upstart in Germany."

Martha tapped on the door and wheeled in the tea trolley. Edith then busied herself pouring tea and Jim Porter sat back in his chair breathing heavily.

"Thank you very much, sir," said Michael, breaking the tense silence. "For the atlas, I mean. It's very interesting. My friend Paul says he's going to be an airman and fly all over the world. Now I'll be able to see where he goes."

"Dear me," said Edith, "I can't imagine why anyone would want to be an airman in dangerous times like these, what with all this talk of war."

"Patriotic duty woman; any young man would want to fight for his country."

Wyn glared at her brother, and Michael tried to deflect her anger.

"Did you fight in the Great War, sir?"

"No, no. Too old, boy. Would have had to though, if it had gone on much longer. Running out of good men they were."

Wyn sniffed. "I'll thank you not to fill his head with notions like that, Jim. I didn't rear him all these years for him to be killed or maimed just when he's started to earn his keep."

"We will have to get rid of that Hitler blighter one way or the other. We're going to need all the soldiers we can muster."

"I'm sure he's far too young to be a soldier, Wyn,' said Edith reassuringly. "How old are you, Michael dear?"

"Sixteen."

"There you are then. Even if there was a war, it would be over before he was old enough. They wouldn't take sixteen-year-olds."

Her husband snorted his derision. "There were fourteen-year-olds fought in the last war. Fourteen! Fighting for God and country!"

"They were not supposed to," snapped his sister. "They lied about their ages, more fool them." Wyn glanced at Martha and pointedly changed the subject. "I believe he's doing very well in the Emporium?"

Jim nodded as he took a cup and saucer from the maid.

"So, there's no reason for him to consider going into the army, is there?" she concluded triumphantly. "I think he has far better prospects with you, than in any army."

"Do you *want* to go into the army?" asked Sheelagh who had been listening to the conversation as she tried on the soft pink wool cardigan her mother gave her for Christmas.

Michael thought of all the beatings he had taken in the school yard from Harry Winton and his cronies. He'd learned to defend himself and fight back, but he didn't enjoy fighting, not like some of them seemed to.

"No. I like working in the shop."

She pulled a derisory face as she examined herself in the mirror over the fireplace.

"In that dingy old storeroom?"

"Your brother is only starting there, dear," Wyn retorted sniffily. "I understand your father intends to teach him every aspect of the shop before he can take over."

She took her cup from Martha, declining the proffered sugar.

"Let's not be too hasty, Wyn," cautioned her brother. "He's only been there a few months yet. I have to see how he does. He has a long way to go before he can fill my shoes." He turned his attention to Sheelagh. "And don't you be pulling faces, young lady. That shop keeps you in fine style."

The group fell silent as they drank their tea. When they finished, it was time for the king's speech on the wireless, and any talk of the possible war and Michael's future, was forgotten.

Michael was still thinking about war when they arrived home.

"Does every man *have* to fight?" he asked as Wyn handed him her hat, gloves, and coat. "No, there are volunteers. I remember when the Great War was declared; we saw hundreds of them marching down through Old Market, all volunteers."

"So you don't *have* to fight?"

He'd seen the beggars in town with no legs, or blind, with scraps of cardboard hung around their necks on pieces of string. Some held scrawled signs saying things like "war veteran," or "injured at the

Somme." Most of them were old men, but he still didn't want to end up like that.

"If I remember rightly, they introduced a call-up of young men in 1916. They ran out of volunteers after the first two years. Too many killed and injured. But I think they had to be eighteen years old."

Michael took her things out to the coat stand in the hall. He returned and spread a sheet of newspaper on the kitchen table, then took the polish and rags from the cupboard under the sink. Meanwhile Wyn fetched her Bible from the drawer. She sat into her rocking chair, removed her shoes, and rubbed at the bunion on her right foot. Michael took her shoes, placed them with his own on the newspaper, and began to polish them, ready for the morning. He was still thinking about the afternoon's conversation.

"I don't think I want to be a soldier."

"There has to be a war first. Mr. Chamberlain will make sure that doesn't happen. Anyway, for once I agree with my sister-in-law. You are too young right now, and I'm quite confident it will all have blown over before you are old enough. Even if it doesn't, there will be plenty enough volunteers this time. No, you'll be staying where you are, young man, and learning all about the clothing and haberdashery business."

She opened the book and began to read. Michael buffed the shoes to a high shine, then tidied the table. He lit a candle and picked up the atlas.

"I'm off to bed then, goodnight."

Wyn nodded, as she continued to read.

1939

Changing Times

Michael's shirt collar felt uncomfortably tight. Mr. Howard was in his favorite armchair, the wireless within arms' reach on the sideboard, and his abandoned newspaper on his lap.

"You know she's only fifteen?"

"Yes, sir."

"I'm sixteen this year, Dad."

"Not 'til November, miss." Beth's father glanced down at his newspaper then back up at his daughter, "And according to this, it's only February."

"It's only to the dance, Dad, and you know Mrs. Walters supervises. I went to it before."

"That was with your brother. Let your dad speak, Beth."

Michael called to the house earlier in the evening to ask Beth to the Valentine's Day dance in the church hall. Beth asked her mother who said, "You'll have to ask your dad, young lady; he's in the sitting room reading the paper."

Mrs. Howard followed the two of them across the hallway and stayed by the door to hear the outcome of the conversation.

"What do *you* think, mother?" asked Mr. Howard peering over his glasses at his wife.

"Pleeeease, Mum. Evelyn was going to them when she was my age."

Margaret Howard smiled at her daughter. "I suppose it will be all right. You're not going to run away with her, are you, Michael?"

"No, Mrs. Howard."

He was too nervous to know if she was serious or not.

"She's only joking, Michael, don't mind her," Beth said, as if she could read his mind.

Mr. Howard harrumphed.

"That's a fine way to speak to your mother, especially when you're looking for a favor."

"Please Dad, don't tease. You *know* Michael; you *know* I'll be all right."

"And you'll come straight home?"

"Of course we will."

Tom Howard turned to Michael with a stern look on his face, "And no dawdling on the porch when you get here?"

Michael's collar felt even tighter and he couldn't swallow properly. How did he know?

"No, sir."

"All right then. But you just remember, Michael Kelly; she's our youngest daughter, and we're quite fond of her, despite all her faults." He smiled at Beth, gave his wife a wink, then looked back at Michael and said sternly. "You take care of her, or you'll have me to answer to, young man."

"Yes, sir, I will, sir. Thank you, sir."

"Right then, get out of here, all of you, and let me read my paper in peace and quiet."

Beth threw her arms around her father's neck and gave him a kiss.

"Thanks, Dad! You're the best Dad in all the world."

He pretended to fight her off. "Yes, yes, I know. You're crushing my paper, miss. Get out before I change my mind."

After that Michael took Beth to the dance every Saturday night. They held hands on the way home and kissed goodnight in the shadowed privacy of the Howard's porch, even though Michael had the uncomfortable feeling that Mr. Howard knew what they were doing.

Often, on the walk home, Michael would tell Beth about things that happened at the shop. How Mr. Swinton's wife would send in homemade cakes and pies for them to have after their sandwiches, and how Mr. Higgins was sweet on Miss Butterworth but how she didn't like him back. He told her about Mr. Ramsey and how Mr. Swinton said he'd been an officer in the Great War, and about Miss Dewey, the cashier, and her funny eye. And, after a while, he told her about his other family. He told her about Sheelagh and her visit to Ireland and how he found out he had another brother besides Colm and another sister who was married with a new baby.

"So you are an uncle, too?"

He'd stopped in the middle of crossing the road when she said that.

"I hadn't thought about it." He smiled, "Yes, I suppose I am."

He told her about his father and how he'd started saving his money to go to Ireland because Sheelagh said they missed him. He wanted to see them as well, and especially meet his father, and then the man had died three weeks later, before Michael had hardly any money saved.

"But you're still going to go, aren't you?"

"Yes, I think so, but I expect it will be a year before I've saved enough."

Michael didn't mention his dates with Beth to Wyn. He only told his aunt he was going over to the Howard house and she asked no questions. After all, he'd been visiting Paul's home for many years.

In March Hitler occupied Bohemia and Moravia. Michael found the countries in his atlas and shaded them in with a pencil. He'd already filled in Austria, and he heard Mr. Ramsey tell Mr. Swinton that Czechoslovakia was only a puppet state, so he filled that in too, but lighter.

In late April he asked Beth if she would like to go to the pictures. She asked her mother who said yes, but it would have to be a matinee, not an evening one.

Michael had a half day on Wednesdays so he waited for Beth after she finished school and they went to the Odeon to see *You Can't Take It With You*. Beth said Jimmy Stewart was one of her favorite film stars and that Michael looked quite like him because he was tall and thin, too, with dark, curly hair and a nice smile.

They arrived in the cinema just in time for the Pathe News. There was one piece of news about the possibility of a war and how everyone had to have gas masks. Then, while they showed grainy black-and-white pictures of a group of young men getting off a train and an army officer waiting for them, a man announced that the government was introducing a Military Training Act and that all men aged twenty and twenty-one had to do six months military training.

"Does that mean George will have to do it?" whispered Michael.

"I don't think so. Dad says his job means that he won't have to go into the army or anything. If there's a war, they'll need people like him to build the aeroplanes," then she added, even more quietly, "and people like our Paul to fly them."

In June, a year since he had started work in the stores, Michael was again called into Jim Porter's office.

"So, young man, I think it's time we gave you a chance to learn more about the business. How would you like to work on the floor? As a trainee, you understand, no wage increase. You could do six months as a trainee and then we'll see."

Michael smiled and stood a little taller. "That would be very good, sir. When do you want me to start?"

"Well, we can't have you out there dressed like that, can we? I've asked Mr. Ramsey to outfit you with a suit and an appropriate tie. We can take the money from your wages each week 'til they're paid for. You had better buy yourself a couple of new shirts too." He gestured at the shirt Michael wore. "Those are all very well for the storeroom, but not on the shop floor. We'll start you next Monday."

Porter waved his hand in dismissal. Michael returned to the store, excited to tell Mr. Swinton the good news. The elderly store man was waiting for him, smiling broadly.

"He told you, then?"

Michael was disappointed that the old man already knew, but he was still excited.

"Yes, I'm moving out into the shop."

Mr. Swinton looked a little concerned. "But only for a while, temporary like, while Mr. Higgins is away doing his military training. He did explain that to you, didn't he? It's temporary, just for the six months Higgins is away."

"Then what?" said Michael, a small knot of anger in his chest.

"Then, I expect he'll want you back in the store, helping me."

"So, it's not really a promotion! I'm just filling in." Michael sank onto a packing crate.

"No, no, lad. I'm sure he means to put you out there, properlike, just not right now. It's an excellent opportunity for you. You'll be able to learn a great deal in six months. Besides," he added, and Michael knew the man was trying to find some consolation, "how could I manage without you for any longer than that. I don't even know how I'll manage for the six months. I'll miss our tea breaks too. Don't forget you'll be eating in the staff-room now, with all the floor staff."

On his way home, the anger inside him grew. "Mean bastard," Michael muttered kicking a stone into the road which nearly hit a passing cyclist. He carried the brown paper parcel tied with string, containing his new suit, two shirts, and a tie. Three pounds, two shillings, and seven pence! It would take him *years* to pay it off on his wages, and he wasn't *even* being promoted, just filling in! He decided he didn't like Mr. Porter at all; he decided he was nothing but a pompous, bullying tightwad. He felt better just admitting it to himself. Maybe he *would* one day inherit the business, like Aunty Wyn said, but would it be worth it?

Once he thought about Aunty Wyn he knew he didn't have much choice. He kicked another stone. *She* would be pleased with the news, even if it *was* only a temporary promotion. *And* she'd like it that he had a new suit, especially as she wouldn't have to pay for it. As long as she got her housekeeping every week, she didn't care if he had no money. He decided he didn't like her much either.

War

Michael and Wyn hurried home from church. The priest had said it was a sad day for England. He said he hoped all his parishioners would pray for peace, but he also gave a shorter sermon than usual so they could get back in time to hear Mr. Chamberlain's speech.

As soon as they arrived in the house Michael turned on the wireless and tuned it in to the Home Service. They waited in silence.

"This is the BBC Home Service. It is eleven o'clock, September the third, nineteen thirty nine. Here, in a special broadcast from Number Ten Downing Street, is the prime minister, Mr. Neville Chamberlain."

Michael and Wyn huddled closer to the wireless set on the shelf beside Wyn's chair. She turned up the volume.

> *"I am speaking to you from the Cabinet Room at 10 Downing Street. This morning the British Ambassador in Berlin handed the German Government an official note, stating that unless we heard from them by eleven o'clock, that they were prepared at once to withdraw their troops from Poland, a state of war would exist between us.*
>
> *I have to tell you now, that no such undertaking has been received and consequently this country is at war with Germany."*

Michael caught Wyn's eye; she quickly put her finger to her lips to keep him quiet and leaned closer to hear the rest of the speech.

When the Prime Minister finished, she turned off the wireless, stood and slowly paced the kitchen. Michael watched her.

"What do we have to do now?" he said, finding it hard to understand exactly what the news meant.

"They'll tell us when they know, boy."

A loud wail broke the silence. To Michael it sounded a bit like the Thristle Engineering factory siren he heard on his way home from work every evening, except that this sound kept going up and down in pitch. Anyway, it couldn't be the factory, it was Sunday, and the factory was closed on Sundays. The noise seemed to go on forever, and Michael wanted to put his hands over his ears to block it out.

"What is it, Aunty Wyn?"

"I don't know," said his aunt. Her voice was quiet, and she looked as if she was standing very stiff. "Have a look out the front door and see what's happening."

All the neighbors were out in the street, trying to talk to each other over the ear-piercing noise. When it finally stopped, one man, who lived two doors down and was a policeman, told anyone who would listen that it was an air raid siren. He said the police had helped set them up on tall buildings and on factory chimneys weeks before, just in case. Mrs. Johnston, from across the street, began to cry, and her husband put his arm around her shoulder and held her close. Another neighbor asked what they were supposed to do.

"Get into the cupboard under your stairs or under the table, until the all clear is sounded."

"How the bloody hell are we supposed to know what that sounds like?" said the policeman's exasperated wife as she tried to control their three small children who were chasing each other up and down the road. At that moment the siren began again, but this time it wound up to one long, high-pitched, steady sound. The children stopped playing, frozen like statues. They looked fearfully toward their parents.

"That's it," the man said, when the siren eventually went silent again. "They were probably just testing them."

Michael turned to see Wyn standing in the shadows, just inside the hall door.

"Come in, boy."

He glanced back at the street. Many of the neighbors were now gathering in small groups. They all had worried faces and spoke quietly together. He went in.

They listened to the wireless for the rest of the day. The broadcaster said that the air raid sirens would all be tested that day and that everyone who did not already have a gas mask, should collect one from their local distribution center and everyone should carry them with them at all times. Rationing books would also be distributed, he said, and everyone was to stay calm and listen to the wireless, or read the newspapers, to ensure they knew what to do. In between the different announcements and speeches by the King and different politicians the station played somber music. Now that the war was really happening, Michael had more interest in the gas masks; the government messages never explained what kind of gas they expected or exactly what it would do. Aunty Wyn explained to him about the mustard gas that had burned so many soldiers in the Great War and how it had even blinded people.

One of the announcements repeated the instructions, given two days previously, about blackout curtains and how everyone must now use them. The announcer said to make sure no light from houses could be seen from outside, as that would be a guide for enemy bombers. The blackouts would have to fit better than ordinary curtains, she said, which let light out at the top and the sides.

"Do I go to work tomorrow, or do we have to stay home now?" Michael asked his aunt.

"You go to work, of course. Life doesn't stop, just because there's a war. Just be careful and find shelter somewhere if you hear that siren."

"Will you be all right on your own?"

"Of course I will, boy. I have to find out about these rationing books and I must get the material and make the blackout curtains. I may be able to earn some extra money, if people need them made."

He felt frightened and excited. He wanted to talk to Beth about it all, but decided he would stay in with his aunt this evening. It didn't seem right to leave her on her own on the first day of the war. Then he started to worry about Paul.

When Michael arrived at the shop the following morning the two older ladies were already there, in deep conversation.

"My Tommy said he's going down to the recruiting office this morning to sign up," said Doris wiping her eyes. "I didn't know what to say to him. I'm worried sick."

Ethel, Mrs. Wall, patted her friend's hand. "Don't cry, love, maybe he's got flat feet or something. My Bert says flat feet will get you out of serving, and being deaf. I didn't suppose he's deaf, is he, love?" she asked hopefully.

Doris shook her head and cried some more. Michael felt awkward. He wished Mr. Ramsey would hurry up and arrive with the keys. He was grateful when he heard the clack of Mabel's high heels on the pavement; at least it would be someone else to talk to. The young woman stepped into the doorway and saw Doris crying into her handkerchief and Ethel patting her hand. She glanced at Michael and mouthed, "What's wrong with her?"

Michael shrugged. He felt he couldn't explain with Doris standing right there.

"Her boy's signing up," said Ethel, just as Mr. Ramsey arrived. The manager frowned. "That's no reason to cry, Miss Williams. You should be very proud of your son. Joining the army, is he?"

Doris nodded.

"The best Service, congratulations! Be proud; we need many more like him."

He glanced briefly in Michael's direction and Michael felt his face get hot.

"Don't you go making the lad feel guilty, Mr. Ramsey," said Ethel. "He's only a boy."

Mr. Ramsey turned his attention to unlocking the doors. He entered the shop just as Mr. Swinton and Miss Dewey arrived. Michael went straight to his counter. He folded away the dust cloths from the menswear cabinets, gave the glass tops a wipe with the duster kept in a drawer by the register, and set out the tie and handkerchief displays. He was checking the cash chute when Mr. Porter and Sheelagh arrived. Instead of going straight to his office, as he normally did, Porter stood in the center of the store, between ladies' headscarves and children's underwear, and waved the staff together.

"It is a sad day for this country," he said, then paused and looked around at the gathered staff. "It is a tragedy to be at war again. I know we will all be thinking of our boys, our brave troops, who must go to fight in the trenches against that bounder, Hitler. But rest assured that this time we will finish the Hun off properly."

He caught sight of Mrs. Williams, red-eyed and snuffling, and aimed his next comments at her.

"We must stay strong. We must support our troops in any way we can; in *every* way that we can."

He took a longer pause and stared solemnly around the group. His voice took on a more businesslike tone.

"However, life must go on. I'm sure you heard on the wireless that we must all have these new blackout curtains. I'm expecting a big run on black fabric, so I hope we're prepared. Ladies, it may be necessary for you to remain late this evening to facilitate our customers. It will be our contribution to the war effort, eh? Swinton, make sure we have enough of that material in the storeroom and check with the authorities as to exactly what fabric is appropriate. Put a rush order in for more if you have to."

He smiled, in the same artificial way Aunty Wyn smiled at her customers.

"All right, that will be all. Carry on. Let's not waste time."

He continued to his office, and the staff dispersed to their different counters.

The day passed slowly. Though Porter had been right about the rush on black fabric, no one was interested in purchasing gentlemen's handkerchiefs, or ties, so Michael was glad when it was time to go home. There were no more air raid sirens and he was home by six thirty. He ate, drank his tea, and helped Aunty Wyn to clean up and put away the dishes. She had spent the day making their blackout curtains and asked him to fit hooks, close to the ceiling, in each room to hang them on. Michael did as he was asked, conscious of the time as he did so. He was determined to go and see Beth this evening and see what news they had of Paul.

"I'm going over to the Howard's now."

"You'll have to put up the blackout first. I'm too old to be climbing up and doing that."

"All right, give them to me then."

"It's not dark yet. I'm not wasting electricity and shutting out God's light until I have to. You can go after it gets dark."

"But it won't be dark before nine."

"Well, you can go then. You don't have to be out all evening, do you?"

"But you always want me back before ten thirty."

"And plenty late enough that is," she replied sharply. "I can't imagine what you boys find to talk about all the time anyway."

Michael felt his face flush. He wondered what Wyn would say if he told her about Beth. He didn't dare. He looked at his aunt and noticed again the fine lines all around her mouth, like a string purse with the string pulled tight.

"Will I have to do this every night?"

He tried to keep the resentment out of his voice.

"Of course you will. It's the law to have them up."

"But will I have to stay here until it's done?"

"I don't know what's got into you, lad. Do you think I can climb up that stepladder and put them up on my own?"

"Fine!" The Howards had a rule that Beth could be out until ten thirty on weekends, but weeknights she was not allowed out in the evenings at all, and must be in bed by nine thirty. Maybe once he'd put the bloody blackout up he could still get to talk to her for a few minutes, if he ran.

"I'll be in my room."

"No you won't. You can stay down here. I have some sewing to do on the machine before the light fades."

He waited until he heard the treadle's steady rhythm overhead before he turned on the wireless, lowering the volume to a barely audible level. He half-listened to the music while he fretted and fumed and watched the light fade, painfully slowly. At least the winter was coming; it would get dark earlier then. She couldn't stop him seeing Beth for long.

1940

Destruction and Construction

Huddled under the kitchen table, gas masks close by, Wyn and Michael listened to the aircraft overhead. They both wore their tin hats, and Michael chewed on a cheese and beetroot sandwich. Wyn said it was pointless trying to cook an evening meal. She said she would only have the potatoes coming to the boil and the siren would go off. They had sandwiches most evenings, though Michael hated the bread.

"It's gray," he complained the first time he saw the new "standard" loaf. "And it's got bits in," he added poking at a dark speck he thought might be an insect.

"Don't examine it, just eat it. They can't waste precious energy bleaching the flour, that's what they said on the radio. You just be thankful it isn't rationed yet, boy. You'd know what hunger was then!"

They heard the antiaircraft guns thudding skyward from Feltrim Hill. Wyn and Michael flinched as bombs dull-pounded in the distance. Suddenly there was a tremendous explosion, very close, and the darkened kitchen was momentarily illuminated by an orange flash. Michael jumped, and his head hit the underside of the table. An upstairs window smashed, cutlery rattled in drawers, and plates slipped from the dresser shelves and crashed onto the tiled floor. Wyn instinctively clutched at Michael's arm, her fingers pressing through his sweater and into his skin. People began shouting and screaming in the road outside. Michael and Wyn remained huddled in their inadequate shelter, straining to decipher the sounds from the street. She gradually relinquished her grip on his arm. Michael watched his aunt. Her lips were moving rapidly, and he thought she must be praying.

"Will I go and see what's happened?"

"No, the all clear hasn't sounded yet. Stay where you are."

They were quiet for a few minutes, before Michael spoke again.

"Paul's home on leave."

"I didn't know he'd been away."

Michael realized his mistake.

"Only for some training. Anyway, he asked if I would help them build their Anderson shelter next weekend."

"I suppose that's another excuse for you to spend your time over there?"

He ignored the jibe.

"It's getting brighter in the evenings now; you'll have me in until later, doing the blackouts."

They could hear fire wardens shouting instructions, then a fire truck arriving.

Michael had accepted her ruling about the blackout curtains, but in the subsequent winter evenings he could put them up as soon as he came home from work, which meant he was then free to go out when he liked, providing there wasn't an air raid and there were a lot of them.

Sometimes it took him hours to get home from work too, if the sirens sounded and he had to duck into a shelter. The wardens wouldn't let anyone stay on the street. Everyone said the Germans were trying to hit the aeroplane factory, that's why they kept coming back. But they hadn't got it yet.

"Why can't they get under the table, like we do? Or under the stairs? Why do they need an Anderson shelter?"

His aunt's voice jarred his thoughts.

"They're a big family, they couldn't fit. There's four of them, five when Paul's home. Maggie lives with James's family now, her husband."

"How long is it going to take?"

Wyn was always irritable these days, whenever he mentioned going out. He'd tried to persuade her to go to the local shelter when the sirens went off, but she said she didn't want to mix with every Tom, Dick, and Harry. The table was good enough for her.

"For them to make the shelter? I don't know, a couple of weekends anyway."

"Well, if you're at work, you will come home here first, won't you? I'll not have you doing manual labor in that suit."

Once the war began Mr. Higgins wrote and told Mr. Porter he wouldn't be coming back. He signed up with the navy and died three months later when his ship was hit in the English Channel. It meant that Michael's job in the shop was probably permanent, though Porter never suggested a raise.

"I always come home first, Aunty Wyn. You know I do."

He thought she enjoyed trying to make him a prisoner in the house. He only felt sorry for her occasionally. Like in the depth of winter when it got dark long before he got home, and he knew she had to sit in the gloomy kitchen, fire unlit, waiting for him. He wished again that she would go to the shelters.

"I could always take you down to the shelter when I'm going out. You wouldn't be on your own then."

He saw her mouth tighten and her jaw set in the willful expression he knew so well.

"I will be fine here, on my own, thank you."

They continued to sit, in silence, in the cramped and uncomfortable space. Soon they could hear no more aircraft and no more explosions. Then the all clear sounded. They removed their helmets and Michael climbed out from under the table; his legs were stiff and his back ached. He helped Wyn to struggle out too. She crawled out on her hands and knees and Michael helped her to her feet. It was a while before she could straighten up. He bent and picked up the gas masks. They always left the two cushions and the helmets under the table. It was easier.

While Wyn tidied up the broken plates he went into the front parlor and peeped into the street from behind the curtains. It was the Johnson's house opposite that had been hit. The firefighters were still there, though there wasn't a lot of fire, just a crater where the house had been and piles of smoking rubble. In the soft blue light of the full moon and the few flickering flames he could see some of the neighbors watching the firefighters. He scanned the faces, but couldn't see any of the Johnsons. He looked up at the moon. It used to be called a full moon. They called it a bomber's moon now.

"Come on, boys; put your backs into it. Hitler isn't going to wait for us to finish, you know."

Mr. Howard stood over the muddy hole, smiling, a cup of tea in his hand. The three young men stopped digging and looked up.

"You can always borrow my shovel if you're in that much of a hurry, Dad," said Paul climbing out of the hole. "Do *we* get a cup of tea, by any chance?"

It was their second weekend working on the shelter. Paul had managed to wangle another pass, and they all wanted to finish it before he went back. Mrs. Howard emerged from the kitchen carrying a tray of cups and a large plate of sandwiches.

"Sorry, boys, your father wouldn't wait for his."

George threw down his pick and stretched up a hand for his younger brother to help him out of the muddy hole.

"Come on, Michael," he said, as Michael wiped the sweat from his forehead. "You look like you need a break too. There'll be none left if Paul gets to the food first."

Paul laughed and helped them both out. All three sat on the mound of earth.

Mrs. Howard offered the tray of tea and sandwiches to the boys and called over her shoulder, "Come on girls, there's some for you too!"

Evelyn and Beth came from the small vegetable plot at the side of the garden where they were weeding.

"What a bunch of busy beavers," said Tom Howard smiling at the group. "And thank you for giving a hand, Michael; it's very much appreciated."

"You're welcome, Mr. Howard."

Beth gave Michael a fleeting, secret smile. Evelyn took a cup and a sandwich and sat on the kitchen step next to her sister.

"I suppose I have to get used to this kind of work. I'm going to be doing a lot of it," she said.

"Did you hear, Michael?" said Mrs. Howard, ensuring he took a sandwich before her eldest son helped himself to a second. "Evelyn is going into the land army."

"Yep, digging for victory, that's me," said Ev and sipped on her steaming cup of tea.

"I just can't imagine you up to your neck in cow manure and pig swill," said George, swallowing his second sandwich in a single mouthful.

"At least I don't have the manners of a pig," retorted his sister. "Anyway, I'll be working on a fruit and veg farm, not with animals."

George laughed. "You poor innocent, how do you think it's fertilized? Tighten your belts everyone, especially if you're expecting Farmer Ev to feed you."

"All right, you two, stop the bickering, time to get back to work. And the rest of you, tea break's over." Tom Howard examined the hole. "You know, I think it's probably deep enough." He looked at the construction manual again. "It says the shelter has to be part in, part out, of the ground." He looked toward the side of the house. A six-foot-long tunnel of corrugated iron stood beside the wall. "Let's try it."

The four men lifted the shelter and maneuvered it into the hole. It stuck out of the ground about three feet.

"Perfect," said George. "That's what you get for having two engineers on the job." He smiled at his father. "Now all we have to do is put the back on, fill in around the edges, and cover the top with all that earth."

There was a collective groan from the boys, but they set to and within a couple of hours the shelter was complete. It only remained to dig out a couple of steps down and hang the door. They could put some plank flooring in afterward.

Evelyn came over to inspect their work.

"Are we all supposed to fit in there?"

"Not you, Farmer Giles, you'll be sleeping with the chickens."

Paul stepped down into the shelter.

"It's certainly going to be cozy in here."

"It will be better to sleep out here than be in and out of our beds all night."

"Is Michael going to stay here too?" asked Evelyn fluttering her eyelashes at Beth. The younger girl stuck out her tongue at her sister.

"A good day's work," said Mr. Howard, ignoring the byplay. "Let's get in and get cleaned up."

They all followed him into the house, though Michael hung back waiting for Beth. He winked and smiled at her and she smiled back. He loved this family. He wished they were his.

The Raid

Michael was glad it was Wednesday, his half day, and he could leave the shop early. They were never busy these days, and he got bored listening to the women talking about how they managed their rationing books and made up new recipes with "half nothing." Sometimes, when Mr. Porter was out at the bank, he went into the storeroom to talk to Mr. Swinton. Michael was worried about him; the old man always looked tired these days. He'd volunteered to be a fire warden and spent several evenings a week on fire watch. Michael didn't think he was really able for it.

The sirens sounded soon after Michael left the shop. He ran to the top of Old Market and into Mary Street, where he knew there was a large, underground shelter. He heard them even before he got there, the noise getting deafening as they came closer. As he reached the shelter he looked up to see the dark swarm of German aircraft approaching the city, flying low. He could even see the black crosses painted under their wings.

A policeman shouted at him, "Get inside, lad. Stop hanging about gawping at them," and Michael hurried down the steep concrete steps and into the gloomy space, already crowded. Everyone was quiet for a while as they listened to the deep throb of the many, slow-moving aircraft. Some even stared upward, as if they could actually *see* the enemy flying overhead. As the sound moved further away an old man spoke.

"There's an awful lot of the buggers up there this time."

A few people close to Michael agreed.

"It sounds like they're heading for Filton Airfield."

Michael nodded. "That's what it looked like as I came down."

They were quiet again except for a small baby, who whimpered softly in its mother's arms.

"My dad says they follow the river up, that's how they know where to go. They've got maps," said a young woman.

Then the bombs began to fall. Explosion after explosion detonated, like rolling thunder in the distance.

"Pity the poor bastards that are getting that," said the old man and a woman snapped, "Mind your language, there's children here."

The old man apologized.

"My bet is they have the factory this time. That's why the daylight raid; to make sure," said a younger man who held a little boy on his lap.

Michael thought of Mr. Howard and George. He hoped they were in a shelter too.

They soon heard the aircraft returning, followed by antiaircraft fire. Five minutes later the all clear sounded, and the mass of people slowly filed up the steps into the daylight. Michael's heart pounded in nervous anticipation as he hurried toward home. He hoped the man in the shelter was wrong.

"They got the factory! They've wrecked it!" a woman on a bike shouted to another woman standing at the roadside.

"Are there many injured?" called someone behind him.

"They think there's lots of casualties."

Michael began to run.

He arrived at the Howard house just as a man on a bike wheeled around the corner and came to an abrupt stop at the gate. Dismounting hastily, the man threw his bike against the hedge and almost pushed Michael out of the way in his rush up the path. Michael followed him, trying to catch his breath, as the man hammered on the front door.

Mrs. Howard opened the door. She looked pale, but not really surprised. The man snatched off his cap.

"Hello, Mr. Foley." She spoke quietly.

The man stood, twirling his cap in his hands. "I'm very sorry, Mrs. Howard."

She looked like her knees were crumpling. The man stepped forward and caught her as she fell. He looked back at Michael. "Give me a hand, son."

The two clumsily helped the woman into the front room and lowered her onto the couch. They stood in silence, and the man fanned her with his cap. She opened her eyes and stared up at them.

"Get her a glass of water, will you, lad?"

When Michael returned, Mrs. Howard was sitting up, her head in her hands. The man had seated himself in the armchair opposite, in Mr. Howard's armchair. Michael handed her the glass.

"What happened?" she said, raising her head and looking pleadingly at her visitor.

"It was the start of the lunch hour. We were all coming out of the factory to have our sandwiches in the fresh air. Tom and George were ahead of me. We heard the sirens, but the aircraft seemed to appear at the same time. Came out of nowhere, they did, flying low, so we wouldn't see them 'til the last minute. They just kept coming. I saw Tom and George run to the shelter on the far side of the runway. They were faster than me. I turned back into the hangar." He stopped and shook his head. "They didn't stand a chance. It was a direct hit. There must have been ten or eleven of the lads in the shelter. Only one young lad survived and he's badly hurt. I think they've taken him to Frenchay Hospital. I asked the foreman if I could come here. I'm very sorry, Mrs. Howard. Is there anything I can do for you?"

"Where are they?"

The man looked uncomfortable.

"I'm not rightly sure, Mrs. Howard. There were so many. They hit the shelter, but they hit part of the assembly shed and the finishing hangar too. There's an awful lot of dead and injured."

"I want to see them."

"Can I get one of the neighbors in for you?"

Her voice got louder and more insistent.

"Where have they taken them? I want to see them."

The man looked at Michael for support. "I'm sure they'll be along to tell you shortly. It's too early to know where they will take them yet. I think it would be best if you stayed here, just for the minute."

Mrs. Howard glanced at Michael, seeming to see him for the first time. "Oh! Michael!"

She stretched out her hand and Michael stepped forward. He sat on the sofa beside her and put his arm around her shoulder. She didn't cry. She was very still.

"I'll get one of the neighbors," said Foley and Michael nodded.

As the man closed the front door behind him Mrs. Howard looked up at Michael, her eyes wide.

"Oh, Michael, Beth! She will be home soon."

He'd already thought of that. His head was a rush of thoughts. Who was going to tell her? How could you tell her that her father and brother were dead? Both dead! Dead! Just like that! Where was Paul? He knew his friend was now in flight training, but where? He hadn't been allowed to say before he left. They would have to contact Evelyn and Maggie too. He would have to tell Aunty Wyn where he was, as well, or she would be worried.

The man arrived back with Mrs. Young, a woman Michael had met a few times in the Howard house.

"Hello, Michael lad. Hello, Margaret love. I'm so sorry."

Mrs. Howard looked up at her friend. "Both of them, Helen. Both of them!"

"I know, love." The woman knelt and put her arms out. Mrs. Howard leaned forward into them and began to cry. Michael carefully extracted his arm and stood up.

"I've to run and tell Aunty Wyn where I am, Mrs. Howard. I'll be back before Beth gets home, I promise."

Mrs. Young looked up at him and nodded.

"I have to get back too," said Foley. "I just wanted to be the one to tell you." He tried to smile at the grieving woman. "Tom was a good man, Missus, and a good friend. And young George was a chip off the old block." He stood at the sitting room door. "I'll call in again, Mrs. Howard. I'm sure the police will be along shortly, when they know. I'm very sorry."

He left the house with Michael. As they walked down the path the man took a deep breath. He gave his eyes a swift wipe with his sleeve and tugged his cap out of his pocket, then looked sideways at Michael. "Are you all right, lad?"

Michael nodded.

"It's a bad business. I don't think they'll ever find them. Blown to bits they were. It's a mess out there."

He patted Michael on the shoulder and climbed on his bike. Michael closed the gate behind him and ran the half mile to his home, tears blurring his vision.

He pushed open the back door and called for his aunt. He ran through the kitchen and into the hall, his breath coming in chest-aching sobs. He called her again, and she emerged from the sewing room, his bedroom, at the top of the stairs.

"Beth's dad and brother have been killed."

He watched as she made her way down the stairs. He tried to stifle his sobs.

"I have to go back. I don't know when I'll be home. I don't know what I'll have to do."

She arrived at the bottom step and looked at him.

"Who's Beth, Michael? Get a hold of yourself, boy. Who's Beth? Where are you going?" He gripped a rail of the banister, the sharp, squared edges cutting into his palm and tried to catch his breath and stop crying.

"She's Paul's sister," he sobbed. "Mr. Howard and George! They've both been killed in the aircraft factory. I have to go back."

"Well, don't you think you'd better get out of your good suit before you do?"

"Bugger the bloody suit," he shouted and barely noticed the shocked look on his aunt's face as he turned and left.

When Michael arrived back, there were more women in the house. Two were in the kitchen making tea and three more were in the sitting room. Mrs. Howard was still on the couch where he'd left her. Mrs. Young sat beside her, holding her hand.

"Has Beth come home yet?"

Mrs. Howard looked up and Mrs. Young shook her head.

He didn't know what else to say. One of the women came from the kitchen carrying a tray of cups, saucers, milk, and even some sugar. The other woman followed carrying the teapot topped with a quilted cozy. He stepped out of the way.

"I'll wait for her outside, will I, Mrs. Howard?"

"Yes, please, Michael dear. Look after her, won't you? Don't let her be frightened."

He nodded and went to sit on the front step in the warm, September sunshine. He was sweating from all the running, but he felt cold. He gripped his hands together, to stop the shivering and watched the road for Beth's arrival. She was running when she came, and he jumped up and hurried to meet her.

"Have they been hurt, Michael? Someone said the factory has been hit. What's happened?"

He put his arms around her and held her very tight. He felt her crying.

She raised her tear-stained face. "Where's Mum?"

"She's in the sitting room."

"Who is it, Michael? Who's hurt? Is it Dad?"

He took the neatly folded handkerchief from his pocket and handed it to her. She was trembling.

"Both of them, Beth," he said, very quietly.

She looked up at him, startled. "Where's Mum? I want to see Mum."

They were standing just outside the gate. He opened it and ushered her through, keeping his arm tight around her. He led her up the path and into the house. The women stepped back when they saw her and Mrs. Howard stood. Beth rushed in and flung her arms around her mother.

"What's happened, Mum? Where are they? Are they badly hurt?"

Margaret Howard kissed her daughter's head over and over, stroking her hair at the same time. They were small, soft kisses, like how you would soothe a baby, Michael thought. Everyone in the room was quiet.

Eventually Beth stepped back a little from her mother and stared into her eyes.

"They're gone, aren't they?"

Her mother nodded.

Beth broke into wracking sobs; Margaret wrapped her arms tightly around her daughter. Michael came forward and put his arms around them both.

A policeman arrived an hour later and confirmed what they already knew. They had been taken to the city morgue, he said, and a friend or family member could go and identify them after six o'clock. He suggested it be a friend. Mr. Foley had returned with his wife and said he would do it. Michael told the constable about Paul and how they didn't know where he was. The policeman took the details and said he would look after that. One of the Howard's neighbors said he would go and fetch Evelyn from the farm and someone else said Maggie was on her way.

When the two young women arrived, there were more tears. Mrs. Young brought in Spam sandwiches and someone else brought potato scones, but no one was hungry. It was late in the evening before all the neighbors left. There was no word of Paul, but the policeman had told them it might take a couple of days to locate him and get him home. The siren sounded again around half eleven and Michael followed Mrs. Howard and her three daughters to the Anderson shelter in the back garden. They spent the night there, huddled in the muddy dampness. They cried and were silent and Mrs. Howard began to talk about the funeral arrangements.

Morning

Michael watched the first pale light filter in through the narrow entrance of the shelter and listened to the birds as their lonely calls slowly built to the dawn chorus. His back hurt from being pressed against the corrugated wall, but he tried to remain still. His legs ached too, from being cramped in the small space, but he tried not to think about it. Beth's head rested on his shoulder. It had taken a long time for her to go to sleep and he didn't want to wake her. As the light grew he saw the dark shapes of Mrs. Howard, Evelyn and Maggie huddled together opposite him, their coats tucked around them like blankets.

Aunty Wyn was probably mad as hell at him for swearing at her yesterday, and she wouldn't like it that he hadn't come home, either. Michael wondered what time it was. He would have to go into work some time. Mr. Porter didn't accept air raids as an excuse for being late, and Michael certainly didn't intend to try and explain about Beth.

He didn't think he'd slept at all, but he *had* done a great deal of thinking. There were two air raid warnings and two "all clears" during the night, but when they sounded Evelyn said there was no point going back into the house; they'd only have to come out again. They all agreed.

He looked across and saw that Mrs. Howard was watching him. She gave him a faint smile. A bird sang close by, a gentle, sweet song. Probably a blackbird, Michael thought, but it woke Beth. She stirred, raised her head, and peered up at him. She looked confused for a moment, but when she glanced across at her mother, she cried again. Mrs. Howard eased herself forward, trying not to disturb the other two girls, and held her daughter's hand. Evelyn and Maggie woke anyway. They all sat in numb silence, but when the blackbird sang again, Mrs. Howard sighed and began slowly to stand up.

"I suppose we should go in now. I think I'll make a cup of tea."

"I'll help," said Maggie, and followed her mother as she struggled out of their cluttered refuge.

Beth, still snuggled close to Michael, said nothing. Evelyn sat staring at the floor between them. "We'll manage, Beth. *Somehow*, we'll manage. We have to look after Mum."

Beth nodded.

Evelyn looked across at Michael, "Don't you have to get to work?"

"I suppose so. I don't know what time it is."

"It must be after seven anyway," she said trying to angle her watch to read the time in the dim light.

Beth sat upright and Michael finally stretched his legs.

Evelyn stood. "We'll be all right, Michael. You go on to work. We'll manage."

He stood too, head bent and his shoulders hunched to avoid the low roof. "Can't I do anything?"

Beth reached up and caught his hand.

"No, it's all right, Michael. We'll be fine. You go. Your aunt will be wondering where on earth you are."

"She knows. But I suppose I'd better go home and let her know I'm all right before I go into work. Are you sure you don't need me for anything?"

"I'm sure. Come back after work if you like."

"I will." He leaned down and kissed the top of her head.

Wyn was sitting at the kitchen table when he arrived home. She looked as if she'd been there a long time.

"Where have you been?"

He was tired. "I told you, I was over at the Howard's."

"All night?"

"Yes. We stayed in the shelter. There were two air raids."

"I am well aware of that."

He shrugged, "It didn't look like anything round here was hit, as I walked home."

"Not that it would seem to matter to you if it did," she snapped.

He sighed and sank into the chair opposite to her.

"I had to go; they needed me. I told you, Mr. Howard and George were both killed in that raid on the aircraft factory."

"I fail to see what use you could have been."

He looked into her cold, angry eyes.

"I was just there, if they needed me."

"Well, that's nice for them."

Michael didn't know what to say. They sat in a silence that made him feel increasingly uncomfortable.

"Look, I'm sorry, Aunty Wyn. I know you're angry with me, and I'm sorry I didn't come home, but I couldn't. And you were all right anyway, nothing happened to you."

There was more silence, and he could hear the methodical, slow, drip of water into the sink. Aunty Wyn kept saying the tap didn't need fixing, but it did.

"And do you intend to tell me who this Beth person is?"

His head dropped forward and he sighed. So this was it, this was what she was really angry about. He knew she'd find out about Beth one day, but he just felt too tired to deal with it this morning.

"I explained yesterday; she's Paul's sister." He stood and pushed his chair into the table. "I have to have a wash and get into work. I'm probably late as it is."

"You look a mess. Your suit is covered in mud."

"The shelter was muddy."

"If I remember rightly, I told you to get out of your suit before you went over there."

Despite his tiredness he could feel his anger rising again. He turned away. "I'm going to change my shirt," he said as he walked out to the hall. "I'll brush the mud off while I'm at it." And he added, "I'll talk to you tonight."

He trudged up the stairs, changed his shirt, ran a comb through his tangled hair, and tried to brush the dried mud from his trousers. As he hurried back downstairs he used his handkerchief to rub at his teeth. When he arrived at the front door, he turned and saw that she was still sitting at the table, and was watching him. "See you tonight," he called, and opened the front door.

He didn't slam it behind him. But he wanted to.

Michael thought about his decision all the way into town. It was nine fifteen when he arrived at the shop. As he walked resolutely past the counters and display stands he saw Mr. Porter glance out of his office window and check his watch. Michael went straight to the short flight of stairs leading to Porter's office. There were only a few customers in the shop, and he was aware of the staff watching him as he knocked on the door.

Porter's "Come," was immediate.

Michael entered. He stood just inside the door waiting for the man to look up.

"Close the door, boy."

He closed the door and remained where he was.

"I assume you have a good reason for being late? I don't recall any sirens this morning." Porter tidied the small sheaf of papers on his desk and scribbled his signature on the top page. "Nobody else was late."

He looked up at Michael for the first time since he'd entered the office.

"I also hope there is a very good explanation why you have come to work looking like a common beggar?" Behind his wire-framed glasses, his bulbous blue eyes were as unforgiving as his sister's.

"I want to hand in my resignation, sir."

The man's face turned a darker shade of red.

"You what?"

"I want to hand in my resignation, sir. I'm going to sign up."

"What the hell do you mean you're going to sign up? You're too damn young to sign up."

"I'm eighteen. I'm going to join the RAF and when I'm qualified I'm going to become a pilot, if I can."

"And how do you know they'll take you? Have you been to the recruiting office?"

"No, sir. I'm going there when I leave here."

"Does my sister know about this?"

"No, sir. I'm going to tell her later, after I've done it."

Porter gave a snort of derision.

"Ha! She's not going to let you go off and get yourself killed."

"I don't think she can stop me."

Porter stared at him.

"Do you have any idea what you are getting into, young man?"

"Yes, sir, I do. The war's not going to end soon. I'd be called up anyway. I'd rather choose what service I go into, before I get my conscription papers."

"And what about your prospects here? Are you going to throw all that away?"

"Like I said, sir, I'm probably going to get called up anyway in the end. If you're prepared to take me back when the war's over, I will be very grateful. If you don't, I'll just have to get another job."

"Well, if that's all the gratitude you have, you'd best be off. I hope they take you in the service, lad, because there'll be no job for you here if you come crawling back."

He waved his hand in dismissal and returned to his paperwork.

Michael left the office. Sheelagh stood near the bottom of the steps.

"Are you all right?"

He looked at her wearily. "Yes, I'm fine. I'm going to sign up. Say goodbye to Mr. Swinton for me, will you? I'd better not go in there; that miserable bastard," he inclined his head toward the office, "would probably fire him just for talking to me."

She put out her hand and touched his arm.

"Will you be all right?"

He nodded.

"Does Aunty Wyn know?"

"No, I have to tell her when I get home." He gave a rueful smile.

She smiled back.

"Good luck. Keep in touch, will you, somehow? Write to me or something?"

"I will. Take care."

He retraced his steps to the exit. He knew the staff had watched the exchange in the office. It didn't take much to work out he was leaving. As he passed her counter Doris whispered, "Good luck, lad, mind yourself."

Mr. Ramsey stood by the door, waiting to greet customers.

"Off then, are you, Mr. Kelly?"

Michael stopped.

"Yes, sir."

"Signing up, are you?"

"Yes, sir."

"Good for you, boy, good for you. We'll be thinking of you. Best of luck, boy."

To Michael's surprise the manager put out his hand. Michael shook it and left the shop.

The rest of the morning felt very strange. At the RAF recruiting office Michael explained that he wanted to be a pilot. They asked him about school and what he was good at and what he knew about the RAF. All the stuff Paul had talked to him about came back to him. He told them he knew he had to be an aircraftsman first and that only when he made the rank of sergeant could he apply to be a pilot. The recruiting officer nodded. Michael thought the man didn't look much older than himself, but he had several ribbons on his jacket, and a stiff leg. He told Michael being a pilot was a goal worth working toward.

"You have to be fit and you have to be pretty sharp. We don't want idiots up there."

He rubbed his leg while he spoke and Michael guessed he was a pilot who had been injured, but he didn't like to ask.

"Just fill out the forms and we'll get you started. When would you be ready to go?"

Michael shrugged. "Right away, I suppose. Well, perhaps tomorrow."

The man smiled. "We have a new intake going to basic training in two weeks. Will that be soon enough for you? We have to get all your paperwork together."

Michael nodded, though he didn't know what he was going to do for two weeks.

"You'll just need your personal kit, wash things, razor, underwear, that sort of stuff, and enough civvies for three days. We'll have you kitted out in uniform by then."

It was barely midday when Michael completed the form filling. He left the office clutching some of the papers he was told to get signed by a doctor and, "A person of authority who knows you personally." He decided he would ask Father Denton; he certainly wasn't going to ask his old boss.

He stood on the pavement outside the recruitment center and wondered what to do next. He didn't want to go home. He decided to go to the Howard's. He'd tell Beth first.

The house seemed to be full of people. He found her in the kitchen helping Maggie and Evelyn get food ready.

"What are you doing here?" she asked, wiping her hands on her apron. Her eyes were red and swollen. "Why aren't you at work?"

"Can I talk to you, somewhere quiet?"

"Go on out the back, Beth. We can manage here," said Evelyn.

Michael followed her out to the vegetable plot.

"What's happened, Michael? Have you been fired?"

"No. I handed in my notice."

"You what! Why? What happened?"

"I've signed up."

Her eyes widened. "But you can't."

He was surprised. "Why not?"

She had no answer. "Where are you going? What are you going to do?"

"Same as Paul."

"Oh, Michael." Tears brimmed in her eyes.

"Please don't cry, Beth. I have to. They're going to start conscripting soon anyway. I might as well choose where I go. I want to do it," he added with more determination.

She turned away from him, but he caught her arm and turned her back. He stared hard into her soft brown eyes.

"I love you, Beth."

She looked up at him, her face solemn.

"I love you, too."

They hugged each other tightly, and he smoothed her hair, as her mother had done the day before.

"Hi, you two."

They sprang apart, and Michael turned to see Paul standing on the kitchen step. Beth ran forward and put her arms around her brother as Michael watched. Paul gave Michael a small nod over his sister's shoulder.

"They told you then?" asked Michael.

Paul nodded again.

"I'm sorry, Paul."

Beth let her brother go. "Has Mum seen you?"

"Yes, she's in with Aunty Phyllis and Uncle Joe."

"How long are you home for? How did you get here so quickly? Who told you?"

"Just a couple of days. Captain Crandall told me and said I could leave immediately. I made the sleeper train from Torquay." He reached for Beth's hand. "Are you OK?"

"I'm fine." She stretched her other hand out to Michael. "Michael has signed up."

"He has?" Paul turned to his friend, "You have? I thought you didn't like the idea."

"I don't, but I'm not a coward," Michael responded defensively.

"I know you're not, Mike. Who did you sign with?"

Michael explained again what he'd done and told them both about his brief conversation with Mr. Porter.

"That's no harm. You weren't meant to sell buttons and bows."

Michael smiled at his friend's old joke.

"Now, all I've got to do is tell Aunty Wyn."

"I don't envy you, mate. When are you going to do that?"

"When I leave here, I suppose."

Paul turned his attention back to his sister.

"Are there any plans for the funerals yet?"

"Next week. Uncle Joe's helping Mum sort it out now, and the funeral director is coming round this afternoon."

The three sat on the step and talked. Maggie brought out three plates of food, and when they were finished Michael said he'd better go. He was getting more and more nervous about telling Aunty Wyn.

Paul took the plates back into the kitchen and Beth walked Michael around the side of the house and out to the gate.

"I meant it, Beth. I do love you."

"I know."

"I'll come back when I can. It may not be this evening. It all depends how she takes it."

"All right. We have a house full anyway."

"Tell Paul I'll see him before he goes back."

She nodded and he left to walk, reluctantly, home.

Wyn was not as angry as Michael expected. In fact she took it very quietly. When Michael told her he'd enlisted, she asked him if he'd spoken to her brother yet. He told the story of his day again, leaving out how angry Porter had been. Wyn didn't make any comment. When he'd finished telling her about signing up and how he would be getting his papers and leaving in two weeks, she simply pressed her lips tightly together and said she'd better get the supper.

After supper she sat in her rocking chair and stared into the empty fireplace. He spread the newspaper out on the table and started polishing the shoes. When he glanced over at her, his aunt seemed very small and very old.

"Will you be all right, when I'm gone?"

"I'm sure I'll manage."

"I got four shillings for signing up. I can give you that instead of my wages. I'll send my pay every week."

She said nothing.

"I'll be able to go to the funerals before I go. They think they will be next Wednesday."

"And will you be accompanying this Beth person?"

He threw down the brush. "She's Paul's sister. It's her father and brother that have died." His voice rose defiantly, "Yes, I will be there with her."

Wyn was silent for a while.

"Well, I don't suppose you'll be seeing much of her when you go off to war."

Goodbyes

The next day, before Paul went back to camp, Michael bombarded him with questions about being an aircraftsman, flight training, and mostly about being a pilot.

"What's it like when you actually leave the ground? How do you keep it going straight? What's the view like? Is it very quiet?"

"It's really fantastic, Mike. When you're up there, it's like looking down at a huge map. You can see everything, churches, houses, parks, cars."

"Is that how they got the factory? I heard someone say they used a map to find it."

"Yes, they teach us to follow roads, or rivers, or railways lines when we can, to make sure we're on the right track. It's easy, just like in geography class."

"How long does it take to learn? The flying I mean?"

"I hope to have my wings in the next two weeks, which means I'll be a qualified pilot. I just have to do my night training. Then we go overseas to train on the big ones. We'll be going to Canada or Africa for that. I can't wait."

"I'm going to try for it, Paul. I never thought I would, but the more I think about it, the more I want to fly. I suppose I've been listening to you for too long."

"Great! You'll make it, Mike. I know you will. Perhaps we'll be in the same squadron."

They were sitting on the back step again. Paul picked up a small stone and threw it at the Anderson shelter.

"Thanks for being here for Mum and Beth and the girls. I'm sorry I won't be able to get back for the funerals. They said they can't give me more leave, not in the middle of flight training."

"That's all right. They're glad you got home at all. I'll be here."

"I know. I really do appreciate it, Mike. I know all the relatives will be here, but you're closer to us than most of them."

"Do you think they'll be able to cope? Afterwards, I mean. I'll be leaving, myself, on Saturday week."

"Yes, I think so. Mum's pretty tough and all the neighbors will be here. Of course the money's going to be tight, but Beth will be getting a job soon, and Mum says she's going back to work too. With my money as well, they should manage."

The two young men sat in companionable silence, each with his own thoughts, until the kitchen door opened behind them. They turned and saw Evelyn smiling down at them.

"Dodging work again are you boys? Mum wants you, Paul; the priest's here."

Paul went into the house, and Evelyn took his place on the step.

"I hear you've signed up?"

Michael nodded.

"What about our Beth? You're going to go off and leave her then, are you?" Michael knew she was teasing, but he didn't feel like laughing.

"Paul says I'll get a few days leave after my basic training, and that takes six weeks. It won't be too long before I get back. After that I don't know. Will she be all right, do you think, Ev?"

Evelyn gave his arm a quick squeeze. "Of course she will. Us Howards are tough."

Michael smiled. "Yes, so Paul just told me."

"We'll mind her, don't you worry, Mike. You just look after yourself. We've had enough death in this family." She leaned over and gave him an unexpected kiss on the cheek. "You're a good person, Michael Kelly. I hope you join the family for real one day."

He was startled, by the kiss and the comment. He stared at her in astonishment. She laughed, stood, and went back into the kitchen.

Over the next two weeks Michael spent as much time as he could with Beth, and away from his home. His aunt continued her aloof silence, and he felt uncomfortable staying in the house. Whenever he *was* there, he used the time to do odd jobs. Fixing large hooks at the sides of the window frames meant his aunt could hook back the blackout curtains during the daytime and wouldn't have to use the stepladder, as he did, every night. He wondered why he hadn't thought of it before. Sorting through his few belongings, he found the collection of jigsaw puzzles. He hesitated for only a moment before tossing them, with a satisfying clatter, into a large rubbish sack. He kept the atlas.

Michael spent a full morning fixing and oiling the latch and hinges on the back gate and several hours another day cleaning out the area under the stairs. It was a dumping place for so many items Aunty Wyn never got around to sorting. With her grudging permission he threw out two old and battered trunks filled with yellowing newspapers and fashion-magazine cuttings she used to create dress patterns. He discarded broken shelving and large bags full of fabric scraps and ribbon trim. When the space was empty and cleaned, he put in a small, upholstered chair that he took from the front parlor. The space was now a secure and comfortable niche for his aunt to shelter in, during raids. She would no longer have to crawl under the table and sit on the floor.

She didn't thank him.

It was a double funeral, both coffins placed in front of the altar, side by side. The church was full and two priests conducted the service. Michael sat in the second row, behind the Howard family and next to Beth's Aunty Phyllis. Her uncle Joe, Mrs. Howard's brother, sat in the front row, next to his sister. Beth didn't turn around during the whole service, but Michael heard her quiet sobs and saw her sisters tuck their arms around her as they clung together in mutual grief and support. When the coffins were carried out of the church, Beth waited to be last out of the front row, so that she could walk beside Michael.

He felt a large lump in his throat, and his eyes leaked tears, though he tried hard not to cry. He was amazed at how calm Mrs. Howard was for the Mass and at the burial. He didn't know how she was able to talk quite normally to everyone who came back to the house afterward. Michael was in charge of offering the men beer instead of tea, if they wanted it, and Mrs. Howard gave him a small bottle of Advocaat and said he was only to offer it to the older ladies. In the kitchen, when he poured the first glass of the thick, yellow liquid, he took a sip. It was creamy and sweet like cold custard, he thought. The label said it was made from eggs and sugar and brandy, but he didn't taste much brandy in it. All the older ladies accepted his offer of the sweet drink, though the next day he found one glass of the congealed liquid abandoned behind the couch in the sitting room. It didn't pour out even when he tipped it upside down.

On the Friday before his departure he wrapped the clothes he would not be taking, including the suit, in brown paper. He tied the neat parcel with twine and pushed it far under his bed, out of the way. When Michael asked his aunt for money to buy a small suitcase for the things he *would* be taking with him, she gave him an old brown cardboard suitcase she fetched from her bedroom. One of the catches was broken, but she said the other one worked fine. He put his few personal belongings into it and tied the battered case with twine too, in case the remaining catch gave way.

That evening he went over to say goodbye to the Howards. The house was quiet now. Maggie had gone back to her husband's family and Evelyn had returned to the farm and her land-army job. When he arrived, Mrs. Howard and Beth were sitting in the kitchen, listening to "Band Wagon" on the wireless. Mrs. Howard even laughed at some of the jokes. Michael sat with them for as long as he could, and when he said he really should leave, Mrs. Howard gave him a hug and wished him well and said she looked forward to seeing how smart he looked in his uniform. Beth kissed him at the front door and gave him a small silver medal of Saint Christopher, the patron saint of travelers. He kept it in his hand all the way home.

He said goodbye to Aunty Wyn the following morning. He wasn't sure whether to hug her or not, but she stood stiffly at the door, her hand on the latch, so he gave her a fleeting kiss on the cheek and left.

"I'll write," he said as he closed the gate. He glanced back when he got to the end of the road, but she had already closed the door.

Michael walked into town and stood outside the bus station with the other recruits. A different officer, a sergeant someone said, did a roll call. When a mud-spattered truck, painted in camouflage browns and greens, arrived and rattled to a halt they all climbed into the back and sat on the bench seats on either side. Their baggage was piled between the two bench rows on the floor. Michael thought some of the lads must have packed everything they owned, judging by the size of their suitcases.

First News

Michael struggled to keep his balance on the lorry bench. He thought there must be about twenty-five of them crammed onto the uncomfortable seats, and all of them rocked and swayed as the lorry sped through the outskirts of Bristol. When it turned a particularly sharp bend, he was thrown forward and would have lost his balance entirely but for the young man beside him who grabbed at his arm and pulled him back. His neighbor then introduced himself.

"Francis Aloysius Murphy, recently from Dublin, and intent upon taking the king's shilling no matter what me grandfather says."

Michael smiled at his companion's accent.

"I'm Michael Kelly." He held out his hand.

"That's a grand Irish name." Murphy took his hand and shook it energetically, "But yer accent's a bit off. So it must be the Bristol Kelly's ye are?"

His companion laughed at his own joke and Michael didn't explain his name.

Francis Murphy amused the group for the rest of the journey. He told his fellow travelers to, "Call me Frank, I only use the full title for formal introductions," then proceed to tell them about the uncle he was named after. He also told them how his great uncle, Francis Padraig Murphy, had tragically died when he lit his pipe too close to his poteen still. He explained that poteen was the "Irish elixir of the Gods, brewed by men of taste, with a disinclination to pay liquor taxes." They all laughed when he told how, "The poor man's wake and burial was put off for an entire week," because the explosion had destroyed all the illicit liquor they had. "It took us the week," Frank explained, "to make more of the better quality, liquid lightning."

Once he got started, Francis Murphy didn't stop. He described how another uncle disliked work so much that he worked out a scheme for avoiding it.

"Didn't he travel the country, seeking out local matchmakers and enquiring about any likely widows living locally? A terrible man for the women was Uncle Jack." Frank shook his head in mock despair. "But he pretty much made a living out of it, inveigling his way into a poor woman's heart and her home, staying 'til he wore out his welcome, then heading off to the next parish." Frank gave Michael a nudge and a wink. "He said he never threw a stone over an orphanage wall, for fear of hitting one of his own, don't you know!" He looked around his captive audience and smiled. "I'm told he died in bed. Hardly surprising with his reputation, and I'll warrant it wasn't his own!"

There was an easy camaraderie among the group by the time they reached the barracks. The vehicle came to a halt outside a building with "Drill Hall" written on a sign over the door. Michael followed the others as they climbed down from the truck, collected their bags and suitcases, and went inside. A waiting sergeant ordered them to, "Form two lines, you ugly bunch. Straight lines, you morons! And face Captain Warren there." He indicated a young man, not much older than themselves and stood to one side as Captain Warren administered the oath of allegiance. When they repeated the piece that said, "To our Sovereign King and his heirs and successors," Frank, who was standing behind Michael, whispered, "Me grandfather would turn in his grave if he heard me," but he continued to recite the rest of the oath, loud and clear, along with the others.

They then took turns to give their details to a clerk, sign several more papers, and on completion of the formalities they re-formed their two lines. A corporal, armed with a clipboard and pen, told them they were allocated Hut 7. The sergeant bellowed, "Right turn, quick march," and, after a brief confusion of feet shuffling and sideways glances to ensure they were all on the same foot, the group marched out of the Drill Hall, in reasonable formation, still carrying their bags.

Hut 7 was indistinguishable from all the other long and narrow wooden huts that edged the vast drill square where several groups of young men marched, jogged, marked time, and exercised in ragged unison.

Inside, the hut smelled of stale cigarette smoke, old socks, and disinfectant. A doorless room on the left of the entrance held a line of washbowls, set in a long, wooden counter. On the right, in a partitioned recess, Michael saw three toilet stalls and a urinal. Two lines of cots ran the length of the hut, with lockers and narrow wardrobes between each one. A stove, with a pile of wood beside it, stood at the far end, with a cluster of chairs around it.

Michael, tired and hungry, was grateful when everyone completed their unpacking and the corporal directed them to the mess hall for supper.

The next two days passed in a seemingly endless series of lines as they were issued everything from meals to uniforms and kit bags to dog tags. They learned to answer to their dog tag number and to obey instructions promptly, ending each short response with, "Sir," and a sharp salute. They were questioned by medics and clerks about every topic from childhood diseases to next of kin.

Michael's work experience in Porter's Emporium proved useful. Many of his companions had no idea of their hat, shirt, or shoe sizes, and the first dress inspection reminded him of a film he'd seen, starring Buster Keaton, where all the policemen wore ill-fitting uniforms. The drill sergeant, the same one who had met them the first evening, was an aggressive man with a bad case of acne and a habit of squinting his eyes when he gave orders. He yelled at the worst dressed to get themselves back to stores, learn how to use a tape measure, and, "Get reissued with proper-fitting uniforms, you sorry excuse for fighting men." Meanwhile, the others were instructed on the cleanliness requirements for their huts, each man allocated a particular chore.

On the second day another sergeant, whom they quickly nicknamed Hitler, caught Frank sneaking a cigarette when he was supposed to be cleaning the toilets. Hitler ordered him to run around the perimeter of the drill yard ten times. When Frank completed his punishment and returned to the billet, wheezing and coughing, he muttered to Michael, "The bastard nearly killed me. Has no one told him you get more out of a fella by kindness than by shouting?" Then he added, "I should have listened to me poor grandfather." This became his ongoing cry as he continued to try and subvert the discipline of the barracks.

By the third day the new recruits were adequately uniformed, could stand to attention, and give a passable salute, though marching in unison was still a challenge. Their civilian clothing was parceled up and taken to be mailed back to families and train passes were issued. Driven by truck to the local station, they boarded a train for Bridlington which, they were told, would be their basic training camp.

At their destination, they again boarded a convoy of trucks and were driven into town. The trucks pulled to a halt on the seafront. Michael stared in awe at the sea. He'd never visited the seaside before, though the salt smell stirred faint memories of a boat journey, long ago, and he felt a, surprising, momentary clench of fear in his stomach.

A corporal watched as they disembarked and unloaded their kit bags. He explained that, as there were not enough military billets for all the recruits, "You jammy buggers get these digs." He indicated the brightly-painted guesthouses, each with a distinctive sign hanging on the front gate proclaiming its name.

Michael and Frank were assigned a double room on the second floor of a lodging house called "Sea Vista" and Frank suggested that maybe they were keeping "the fighting Irish" together. The clerk said roll call would be on the seafront at 7:30 sharp the next morning, added that the mess hall was actually a commandeered restaurant, "round the corner on Blythe Street," then dismissed them to find their accommodation.

Michael and Frank slept well. The beds were so comfortable after the military-issue cots they'd had for the last three nights and two to a room was better than twenty-five to a barracks hut. They woke early the next morning, washed, dressed, and hurried to the unusual mess hall for a breakfast of cereal, tea, and toast. It seemed strange to be eating such plain fare in such fancy surroundings.

They walked back to the seafront and watched in amusement as sixty or seventy young men, in various stages of dress, wandered bleary-eyed out of the different colored guesthouses to assemble on the unorthodox barracks square. Frank leaned back on the promenade railing, sucking on one of his usual, home-rolled cigarettes and gave Michael a running commentary.

"Would you look at yer man coming out of 'Sandy Haven?' I swear he's going to fall over any minute if he doesn't haul up his trousers. It doesn't look like anyone showed *him* how to use a tape measure!"

A few minutes later he pointed again, "Would you look at himself, by 'Beau Bay?' It looks like his boots are on the wrong feet. Wait 'til the sarge sees that!"

The drill sergeant waited, frowning, as the motley group assembled. At 7:30 exactly he yelled at them to line up, alphabetically, in three lines, and call out their numbers so that a clerk could check them off. It took some time for the new recruits to sort themselves out and Michael noticed the sergeant, a short man with a large stomach, rapping his baton impatiently on his palm while they did so.

Once registered and their lines straightened, they drilled up and down the promenade for the rest of the day, only stopping for a brief break at noon. A mobile canteen, set up at the end of the prom, served each airman a Spam sandwich and a tin mug full of tea. Frank examined his tea briefly before handing it back up to one of the WVS ladies.

"Could I have one without milk, darlin'? It stands a better chance of being warm."

"We've been told to put the milk in first, so that you don't use so much."

"But I don't want to use any *at all*, love."

"It comes with milk," she snapped and looked beyond him to the next airman. "Next."

"Then I suppose a spoon of sugar is out of the question?"

"There's a war on, young man. You can waste your own sugar ration in your tea if you wish. Next."

Frank gave her his most charming smile before walking away to sit on a bench with Michael.

"I thought we were supposed to be heroes!" He inclined his head back to the canteen truck. "And I thought *they*," he indicated over his shoulder to the mobile canteen, "were supposed to be angels of mercy."

"That's the nurses."

"Ould battleaxe," the Irishman muttered, with a good-natured grin, before sipping on the opaque, pallid brew.

After that, they drilled every morning, a monotony that had several of the recruits wondering if they were ever going to move on to actual duties. In the afternoons they were taught basic mechanics in the "mess hall," and in the evenings they were expected to study the issued aircraft manuals. Michael felt homesick for Beth, though not for Wyn. Even the war seemed distant. With no major targets in, or near, the sleepy town they had few air raids, and many of the recruits, including Michael, found it eerily quiet at night.

"Bugger all for them to bomb up here," said one elderly local who watched the drills most days and got talking to the lads when they stopped for lunch. "Watching you young lads is about all the military action we see."

Frank and Michael soon became close friends. Lying on their beds in the evenings they exchanged stories. As time went on Michael told Frank what little he knew about his Irish family.

"Do you know County Galway?" he asked one night as they lay in the dark and he watched the orange-red glow of one of Frank's ever-present cigarettes.

"Sure, that's the other side of the world. That's the Wild West, boy. I'd never been outside of Dublin at all, until I had the mad notion to try and kill that bastard Hitler single-handed and make myself a hero. More fool me. I should have listened to my grandfather. No sense, me!"

Michael finally took some time from his studies to write his first letters. Frank had slipped into town for the evening, "looking for a bit of entertainment, don't you know, lad. Them sergeants is altogether too serious. You have to have a bit of fun, sometime."

He asked Michael to join him, but Michael said he wanted to write letters instead. His first was to Beth.

Sea Vista,
The Promenade,
Bridlington,
Yorkshire.

Dear Beth,

Sorry I haven't written before, but it has been pretty busy. We were moved here after the first three days. Bridlington is a nice town, though we don't see much of it, except the seafront. Sergeant Hughes says we will be here for six weeks. He's the one who drills us every day. All we seem to be doing is PE and learning to march. Six weeks of that seems stupid, but we do look a lot more like we belong in the uniform now, we can at least stay in step and turn the same way at the same time. There are about sixty of us here and we are staying in guesthouses, which seems a bit strange but they don't have enough military billets, they say, so they've commandeered these. No one is going on holidays to the seaside anyway these days, the beaches are mined and there are big signs to keep off. Our billet is on the seafront, which is nice, and the locals are very friendly.

He went on to tell her about the studying he was doing and about the different aircraft and concluded with,

I have made friends with a lad from Dublin, Frank Murphy. I think you'd like him, he's very funny.

I think about you all the time and I miss you. How are you? I hope you will write soon,

Take care of yourself,
Love,
Michael

He also wrote a brief note to Wyn saying he was fine and hoping she was fine too. He decided he didn't have much interesting news, so he wouldn't write to Sheelagh yet. He received a reply from Beth in less than a week. Mail was given out at roll call, but the recruits didn't have the opportunity to read their letters until they broke for lunch. All morning as he quick marched, right turned, about turned, and stood at ease Michael was aware of the envelope in his breast pocket. It felt like a thick letter. All morning he wondered what she wrote, missing his step twice for not concentrating on the sergeant's orders. The second time the sarge made him do a drill sequence in front of the others. He didn't mind; it was nearly time for the lunch break.

When Michael finally opened the envelope, he saw that, as well as a letter from her, Beth had enclosed his letter too. He glanced at that first and was surprised to see a great deal of it blacked out. He unfolded her letter and read.

> *Dear Michael,*
>
> *I was afraid you had forgotten me. It was difficult to understand your letter because there was a stamp on it that said it had been read by the censors and they had blacked out all sorts of bits. You can see what I mean when you look at it.*
>
> *Anyway, we are fine. It still seems very strange when Dad and George don't come home in the evenings, but I know lots of other people are in the same boat and have lost members of their family, and some don't even have graves to visit. We just have to get on with it. Mum is great and is looking for a job; she has also volunteered with the WVS and is going to help serve tea and biscuits at Southmead Hospital, in the outpatient departments. She says it will keep her busy and that she should be doing more for the war effort anyway.*
>
> *Evelyn is back with the land army and brings home veg. and some fruit when she can. Our vegetable plot is doing well and digging for victory makes me feel like I'm being a bit useful.*
>
> *Do write again soon, but I think you will have to be careful what you say or it will just be a lot of black lines again. I hope you will be stationed near home when all your training is finished,*
>
> *All my love,*
> *Beth*

The recruits had been told to be careful what they wrote and not to give any information away, but Michael didn't think that had meant about marching on a seafront. He realized he would have to be much more careful, especially if a stranger might read the personal stuff he wrote to Beth. He showed the censored letter to Frank.

"Begod, if that's what they're doing to yours; imagine what they'll do to mine."

"Why?"

"We Irish have a bit of a history of not getting on too well with the Brits, Mikey. Did you not know?" he laughed. "And good old Erin has chosen to stay out of this fight. We're officially neutral. They're probably keeping an extra close eye on me, to make sure I'm not spying."

Frank's comment surprised Michael, and he had new respect for his friend. It must have been hard enough for Frank to sign up if his Irish family didn't want him to. But if the British didn't trust him when he got here, that must be terrible, especially when he didn't *have* to join the services *at all*!

Michael read Beth's letter twice more before the corporal blew his whistle for them to reassemble. He tucked it into his wallet and wished basic training was finished and he could see her again.

First Leave

Michael could just make out the platform clock in the dark. Eleven o'clock. He hadn't realized the journey would take so long, or that the train would stop at every station on the way. Now he wasn't sure what to do. Beth and Aunty Wyn both knew he was coming for the weekend, but he'd told Beth he hoped to call in to see her for a while before going home. A weekend was such a short time, and he'd been looking forward so much to seeing her again. He kicked at an imagined stone. He'd just have to wait until tomorrow. Even Aunty Wyn would probably have given up by now and be in bed. He might be locked out.

Michael walked out of the station and down the ramp to the main road, kit bag on his shoulder, still wondering what to do. A van slowed to a stop beside him.

"Where are you going, lad? Can I give you a lift? I'm heading toward Filton."

He had to go home. He didn't have much choice.

"Yes, please. Anywhere up the Gloucester Road will be fine."

He climbed in and the man offered him a cigarette. Michael declined.

"Have you come far?"

Michael looked at him for a moment before answering.

"No! Not too far."

"Well, I'm sure your family will be glad to see you."

As they drove through the deserted center of the city the driver explained that he was an undertaker. "Doing a couple of pickups. There's no shortage of work these days, though that doesn't please me like it should."

Michael gave a quick glance over his shoulder.

"It's all right, lad, relax. I don't have any customers in the back yet."

He chuckled and continued driving slowly as he peered into the darkness ahead. With a new moon and no streetlights it was difficult to see.

"Still can't get used to driving in the pitch dark. Just as well there aren't too many cars about."

A shadowy figure waved at them from the side of the road. As they came closer they saw the white gloves and helmet of a warden. The undertaker pulled his van to a halt and wound down the window. The warden leaned in.

"Douse that bloody butt. I can fine you for that, you know."

"Sorry, sorry." The undertaker carefully tamped his cigarette out in the ashtray and tucked the stub behind his ear.

The warden impatiently waved them on and the driver muttered, "Petty little dictator," under his breath as they drove away.

Michael got out of the van at the top of Muller Road, thanked the driver, and walked the rest of the way home to Glenfrome Road. Turning the key in the lock, he was relieved to find the front door wasn't bolted. He carefully eased open the door and entered the hallway. He'd forgotten the smell, a dry, "old people's" mixture of mothballs and dust. He'd always disliked the smell of mothballs. Aunty Wyn was so afraid of moths damaging the fabrics in her sewing room that she liberally scattered the pungent-smelling items everywhere. She left them at the back of shelves, in cupboards, under his bed, and he even remembered finding one in the pocket of his trousers once. He closed the door as quietly as he could and saw a dim yellow glow coming from the kitchen. He called softly, "Aunty Wyn, it's me, Michael. Aunty Wyn, can you hear me?"

There was no reply. It was probably just the flickering light from the fire that he could see, though it wasn't very like her to leave a fire burning if she was going to bed. He put down his kit bag, removed his boots and padded silently along the hall and into the kitchen, just in case.

She sat slumped in her rocking chair, with the Bible on her lap. A candle flickered in a sconce on the shelf beside her. She was snoring softly. Michael stood in the doorway watching her; he'd never seen her asleep before. Her mouth was slightly open, and her glasses had slipped to the end of her nose. She still wore the same, old-fashioned, long black clothes she'd always worn. He smiled, trying to imagine her in any of the knee-length outfits that were all the fashion now. No, she never would. She was an old lady, her face creased in countless fine lines, like a scrunched-up piece of parchment and her thin, white hair pulled back in a meager bun.

"Aunty Wyn," he said softly, not wanting to startle her.

The sleeping woman stirred and opened her eyes. He gently spoke her name again. She straightened her glasses and peered toward the door.

"Michael?"

He stepped forward. "Yes, it's me. Sorry, I didn't want to frighten you." He felt awkward as he gave her a half smile. "Hello, how are you?"

"I'm fine, fine," she nodded and peremptorily gestured him forward. He came and stood in front of her. She scanned him up and down.

"You look very smart in your uniform, Michael." Wyn lifted the Bible from her lap and offered it to him. "Put it in the drawer, would you, boy?"

He did as she asked, then she waved him to a kitchen chair, "Well, sit down, lad. I got your note. I've been waiting for you since two o'clock."

He pulled a chair out from the table and sat. "I didn't know it was going to take me this long to get here."

"Wartime," she said with a shrug. "Everything takes longer than expected, even queuing for a loaf of bread. So, how have you been?"

"Fine."

"And you're here for the weekend?"

He nodded. "I have to report to my new posting then."

"Where will that be?"

"I don't know yet. We'll be told when we get back."

"Have you eaten?"

"Yes thanks, I got a sandwich at Crewe station."

"I've made up your bed. Are you tired?"

He nodded, "I am a bit. How have things been here, all right? Not too many air raids?"

"No, once they hit the aircraft factory I think they moved on. We still get a few."

He didn't think he'd ever had a conversation this long with her before. Maybe she missed him. Or maybe she'd just been lonely.

"Have you been using under the stairs for a shelter?"

She nodded and gave a whisper of a smile, "I think I even slept through one or two of the raids. That chair is more comfortable than crouching under the table."

Michael nodded and yawned. "Would you mind if I went straight up to bed, Aunty Wyn? I'm pretty tired. Thanks for waiting for me. It's nice to be home."

He meant it. She might be a bit strict, but this was home, the only one he could remember. Who else would have taken him? What would an orphanage have been like?

His aunt stood and picked up the candle sconce. "No, of course, we can talk in the morning. You go to bed now. I'll go too. Is the front door locked?"

"I'll do it as I go. Can you see all right, with just the candle?"

"I'm fine. I'm used to the dark now."

He stepped to one side and she walked toward the door. As she passed him she stopped, sniffed, then turned sharply and stared at him.

"So! You've picked up that filthy habit have you? You've only been gone a few weeks. It didn't take you long, did it, Michael Kelly?"

He didn't understand what she meant for a moment; then he remembered the undertaker's cigarette.

"I got a lift home from the station. He was smoking."

Her disbelief was obvious, "You reek of tobacco smoke. Don't ever bring that disgusting practice, or smell, into this house."

He watched her as she continued along the hallway without another word. As she reached the bottom of the stairs he said, "Goodnight."

She didn't reply. He watched her climb the stairs and sighed. Why did he think things would change, just because he'd been away for a few weeks? She'd never change. Still, he'd see Beth tomorrow. He knew *she'd* be glad to see him.

Promises

Beth wouldn't be finished in class until four o'clock, and Michael didn't know how to fill the time until then. Wyn had a few chores for him, but he'd finished them by midmorning. He decided to visit the Howard graves before he walked into town. It was just over two months since the factory bombing.

Two vases of fresh flowers were set neatly at the head of each earth mound. He recognized the flowers from the Howard garden. Mrs. Howard always had bunches of them in the house at this time of year, even though Michael thought they smelled funny, like pepper. As he stood at the foot of George's grave, head bowed, Michael thought about the two men buried there. He thought about the time they built the Anderson shelter and all the mealtimes he'd shared in their house and how he'd had to ask Mr. Howard's permission to date Beth. He remembered what the man, Foley, had said about them being blown to bits and wondered just how much of them was buried here. He sighed, said a silent prayer, and blessed himself before leaving the cemetery and walking leisurely into town.

It was a fresh, late-autumn day, dry and cold. Along Belton Avenue the fallen leaves lay on the path and road in a thick carpet of yellow and orange. Men no longer swept paths and roadways clear of nature's discards. Michael couldn't remember the last time he'd seen the city workmen and their red-painted city handcarts. He supposed the men had more important wartime jobs now.

He wasn't sure where to go or what to do to fill the time, but found himself following his old, familiar walk to work, along Clarence Road and down into Old Market. Passing under a clock outside a jeweler's shop, he saw it was nearly twelve thirty. Continuing his walk up Castle Street toward the shop, he remembered that Sheelagh usually took her lunch break around this time and often went to Lyons Tea House, on the corner. He decided to go there and wait.

As Sheelagh entered and saw him she stopped abruptly. Michael, too, was surprised. He had never before realized how pretty Sheelagh was. She wore a slim-fitting, barely knee-length suit that showed off her trim figure. Her auburn hair, close-cropped and soft-curled, framed her pale, slightly freckled face, and the soft blue of the suit accentuated her violet-blue eyes. He thought she was quite tall for a girl too.

"Michael! Well, look at you! Wow, you look handsome in the uniform; it suits you. May I join you, or are you waiting for someone else?"

He smiled as he stood and gave her a mock salute. "No, I was waiting for you."

She tucked herself into the seat opposite him, and they ordered two teas from the young waitress.

"So, how are you doing? How is the RAF treating you?"

He shrugged. "It's early days yet. I've only learned to square bash really. We start doing the real training when we get our posting."

"Where will you be?"

"I don't know; they won't tell us until we go back. How's everyone in the shop?"

She gasped and put her hand to her mouth, "Of course, you don't know. I was waiting until I had an address for you. I'm sorry, Michael, Mr. Swinton died. He was on fire watch, and some kind of incendiary bomb hit a house. They say he tried to help the people get out, but there was an explosion. They think it was the gas. He died instantly, they said. It happened the week after you left."

Michael had a fleeting image of himself and the old man perched on their packing cases in the back alley behind the shop, drinking tea and eating homemade cake. He remembered how comfortably they worked together in the gloomy cavern of the storeroom and he pictured his mentor as he pushed the outsized hampers out into the shop and wheeled them from counter to counter to deliver the merchandise. He was a nice old man, always friendly, always pleasant. It wasn't fair.

"I'm sorry, Michael. I should have told you straight away."

He shook his head. "That's all right." He looked at his sister, "It's what happens in a war, isn't it? How's his wife?"

"I think she's gone to live with a daughter in Penryth, in Cornwall. It's safer there."

He nodded. "She used to send in cakes and biscuits." He sipped his tea. "Who's in the stores now?"

"They have another old man working in there. Hastings is his name. Dad offered the job to Colm, but he said he wasn't going to work in any storeroom."

"Colm? Our brother, Colm?" Michael asked in astonishment.

"Oh, dear, a lot really *has* happened since you left, hasn't it? Yes, he turned up here a couple of weeks ago. Seems the university closed some of its departments and his was one. He's over twenty, so the next thing is he would have been called up for active service, but he failed his medical. Apparently he's deaf, though I find that hard to believe."

"Deaf?"

She nodded. "Even before he got his call-up papers, I gather he got a private medical. His father paid for it. The doctor said he was unfit for service due to hearing loss."

"Really?"

"Like I said, he doesn't seem deaf to me."

"So, what's he doing down here, in Bristol?"

"His mother was worried about him. You know, with the Blitz happening in London. So she wrote to Mum and Dad and asked if he could come and stay here for a while. He stayed with us for a week, but he's renting a flat in Clifton now."

"Is he working?"

"The Sinclairs asked Dad to give him a job but, like I said, he wasn't interested. I think he's got one now. I've no idea what it is. Anyway, what about you? How long are you home for? What are you going to do while you're here? Was Aunty Wyn glad to see you?"

He hadn't seen his sister since he quit his job and walked out of the shop, but he found it easy to talk to her now. He told her about the Howards and what happened the day the Germans bombed the aircraft factory. He spoke about his friend Paul, who was now overseas, but he didn't know where. And he told Sheelagh about Beth.

"We've been going out for nearly two years now. I think her sister, Evelyn, was in your class at school."

"Evelyn Howard? *Mad* Ev? That's her sister?"

"Mad Ev?"

"Oh, we just called her that. She was always doing crazy things and getting into trouble with the nuns."

He smiled. "Yes, that sounds like Ev, though she's calmed down a bit these days. Beth's not a bit like her. She's very quiet, shy really."

"Is she pretty?"

The question caught him by surprise, and he felt a little awkward trying to answer it. Eventually he smiled and nodded. "Prettier than any girl I know."

Sheelagh returned his smile. "What does she do?"

"She finished school in the summer. She's doing a Pitman's shorthand and typing course now, so that she can be a secretary or something."

"Maybe I'll get to meet her some time?"

"Maybe." He frowned. "Aunty Wyn doesn't like the idea of me having a girlfriend, so it would probably be better if you didn't mention it to her, or your parents, if you don't mind?"

"I won't. I hardly see Aunty Wyn anyway. Daddy still goes over on his own most Sundays to collect his rent. I only see her on the odd occasion. You know, high days and holidays." She grimaced.

"Is he still mad at me for leaving?"

"Who? Daddy? I don't think so. His bark is worse than his bite, Michael. You just don't know him very well. I think he was just concerned about Aunty Wyn living on her own when you said you were leaving. To tell the truth, I think he was actually afraid she would have to come and live with us. Even *he's* afraid of her."

"Well, she seems to be doing fine."

"She's always seemed like a bit of a dragon. In fact," she said, making a wry face, "I've always thought all she needed was a broomstick and a black cat."

They both laughed. Sheelagh looked at her watch. "I have to get back, Michael; Miss Dewey will be waiting to go for her lunch. Thanks for coming to see me. Will I see you again before you go back?"

"I don't know, but if not, I'll write to you."

She stood. "Will you be back for Christmas? It would be strange without you."

"I really don't know."

Michael paid for the teas, and they walked out of the shop together. Sheelagh paused and turned to her brother.

"Where are you going now, Michael?"

"I'll walk up and meet Beth from college."

"All right. Take care. It was nice to see you." She suddenly put her arms around his neck and gave him a swift kiss, then laughed as she rubbed the dark red lipstick from his cheek. "I know we weren't very close growing up, but we *are* brother and sister. I'd hate to lose you."

"I know," he said, smiling down at her, taken aback by the kiss. "The war makes you think about that kind of stuff, doesn't it?"

She nodded and glanced at her watch. "I must go, I'm late. *Please* write soon. 'Bye, take care." She turned and hurried down the road, turning once to wave. He stood where she'd left him, until he saw her enter the shop.

Once Sheelagh was gone Michael's thoughts immediately turned to Beth. He hurried up Park Street to meet her at the college, even though he knew he would be far too early. He arrived and, as it was only two o'clock, he wandered into the park opposite the college entrance. He sat on a bench where he could see the entrance and thoughts about the war crowded his head. It changed everything and everyone. He thought about the unfair deaths, like Mr. Swinton's, and the Howard's, and the Jackson family in the house opposite theirs. None of them were even in the services; they were just trying to live their ordinary lives. The war brought people closer though, he thought; just look at his meeting and conversation with Sheelagh! He couldn't imagine that happening if he was still working in the shop. And, despite her criticisms, he thought Aunty Wyn was more concerned about him, now that he'd signed up.

The college doors opened, and a swarm of young women hurried down the steps, chattering and laughing. He scanned the crowd for Beth, but she saw him first, shouting his name and dodging her way through the clusters of women. She ran across the road, and he hurried out through the park gates to meet her. They collided in a mutual bear hug on the path, and he lifted her off the ground laughing.

"Michael, put me down. They're all looking."

He laughed, "I don't care." But he set her down, cupped her face in his hands, and kissed her, very gently. "Hello," he said.

They walked back to the Howard house, hand in hand. Beth kept looking at him sideways and smiling.

"What?"

"You look so nice in your uniform. I'd forgotten how good-looking you are," she walked on tiptoe for a moment, trying to match his height, "and how tall."

He stopped, turned toward her, and brushed a wisp of hair from her face. "I never forget how beautiful you are," he said and kissed her again.

The weekend passed quickly. He spent some of the time with Wyn, but more with Beth, although he didn't tell Wyn where he was going. It was easier to say he was meeting friends.

"You seem to have become very popular since you joined up," was her only comment. Beth said she understood why Michael didn't bring her home to introduce her to his aunt. She'd heard so many stories about the old woman from Paul and some from Michael as well. She said she thought Aunty Wyn sounded like a very intimidating woman.

On his last evening Michael and Beth sat in their usual place, on the back step. It was a cold, clear night, and the stars glittered like tiny pinpricks in the black velvet of the sky.

"I'll write to you every day," he promised, holding her two hands in his.

"I'll write back every day."

"Even if I don't get back for ages, just remember I still love you."

She nodded. "I love you too." They kissed.

"It's time for me to go, Beth."

"I know."

"I'll go in and say goodbye to your Mum."

Mrs. Howard hugged him and told him to take care. Beth walked with him to the end of the road. She cried when he held her close, and it took a long time before he could walk away. He, too, felt salt tears burning his eyes and falling unbidden. He continued home reluctantly.

But, she said she loved him. She *said* she *loved* him!

By the time he reached Glenfrome Road his tears had dried. Arriving at his front gate, he paused, looked up at the stars and grinned.

She said she loved him!

Moving On

As he climbed from the back of the lorry Michael saw Frank waiting for him at the entrance to the guesthouse.

"We're off to the sunny south, Mikey. We leave in the morning."

"Hi, it's nice to see you, too," said Michael. He put down his kit bag and shook his friend's hand. It *was* nice to see Frank, but he was missing Beth already, and he had no idea when he would see her again.

"Yes, yes. It's good to see you." Frank hiked Michael's bag onto his shoulder and hurried to cross the road. "Did you have a good leave?" he called. "How's the girlfriend?" Frank opened the guesthouse front door and entered. Michael followed. "We're off to Cornwall." Frank continued, "You and I are going together, along with Harry Fields and John Stapleton." He led Michael upstairs to their room. "Some of the lads have got different postings, so we're going out on the town tonight, for a bit of a farewell." He threw Michael's kit bag on the bed. "It's time we were off, there's no point in you unpacking. I told the lads we'd meet them on the prom at seven. Come on, Mikey, we're going to have a right old hooley before we leave here."

Michael protested; he'd been traveling all day. He was tired; they were going to be traveling again tomorrow. He didn't really feel like going out.

"Of course you do, Mikey. Isn't it a farewell to our friends? How could you not go?"

Michael reluctantly agreed. Up to now he'd been careful to avoid joining Frank on any of his drinking sorties. The Irishman's reputation had spread, early on, as a prime instigator in any drinking mischief that occurred in town. Michael didn't drink. Aunty Wyn's lectures on the subject convinced him it was, as she often told him, "A slippery slope.

211

The demon drink was a sure and fast way to hell." He'd always worried about his friend's weakness. But tonight Frank seemed determined that Michael should join him. He supposed the least he could do was look out for his friend and make sure he got home safely. He didn't actually have to drink any alcohol.

Michael's resolution dissolved as the evening progressed. By the time they left the last pub his head felt very fuzzy. As they staggered back to the guesthouse, it was he who leaned heavily on his friend for support. His legs felt decidedly rubbery, and his coordination didn't seem to be too good, though he wasn't sure Frank's was much better. They sang snatches of popular songs, interspersed with some of the bawdier ones they'd been singing earlier in the pub. "Lily of Laguna" faded into silence as they forgot the words, to be followed a few minutes later by "The Harlot of Jerusalem." Their enthusiasm for the rousing chorus threatened to topple their balance.

At one point Frank stopped and clutched his friend's arm. "Did I tell you about my friend Maurice, Mikey?"

Michael shook his head, stumbled, and nearly fell.

"I got a letter from him this morning. He's a good friend, Mikey. Joined the army the day the war was declared." He released Michael's arm and stared disconsolately at the ground. "He's been injured, poor bugger, while he was getting out of Dunkirk." Frank leaned against a garden wall to steady himself. "He was hit by machine-gun fire as he tried to get into a boat. He said they dragged him on board, but the docs don't think he'll ever walk again. He said there were hundreds of bodies floating in the water. Can you imagine that, Mikey?" He shook his head. "And the enemy was firing at them all the time." He took a deep breath. "Poor bugger! War's a bad business, Mikey, a bad business."

He pushed himself away from the wall and continued walking. Michael watched him go. He remembered the jigsaw puzzle that the Porters had given him one Christmas, of the Battle of Trafalgar. He suddenly remembered all the bodies floating in the water around the ships and men waving their arms and looking like they were screaming for help or drowning. His stomach clenched and he thought he might be sick. There were so many ways you could die in a war.

He took a deep breath and nodded. "Bad business, very bad," he muttered and hurried to catch up with his friend.

When they arrived at the guesthouse, Michael tripped and stumbled as he tried to navigate the stairs. He giggled and Frank tried to shush him. He began to laugh, and there were a few shouts of, "Keep it down out there," and, "Shut up, you noisy buggers," from different rooms.

Arriving outside their room, Frank tried to hold Michael upright with one hand while he fumbled in his pocket with the other, to find their room key. He finally found it, opened the door, and unceremoniously dumped Michael onto his bed before falling back onto his own.

Michael remembered nothing else until he woke the next morning fully dressed, snuggled beside his kit bag, his mouth dry, his tongue furred, and his pulse pounding audibly in his head.

As he struggled to remember the previous night he heard noise from the street below and realized it was Corporal Withers. He scrambled off his bed and shook his roommate, who had obviously slept in his uniform too.

"Get up, Frank. We're late for roll call."

Frank rolled over in his bed and clamped his pillow over his head. "Jaysus, can a man not sleep in a bit of peace and quiet in his own bed. Leave me alone, will ya?"

Michael continued to shake him until his friend pushed the pillow away, opened one, bloodshot eye and grudgingly sat up. Frank slowly swung his feet to the floor, still muttering, pulled up his socks, and groped his way into his boots. The two then stumbled down the stairs and out onto the Promenade. Michael saw a few other drinking comrades from the previous night also running from their various billets. Some even looked worse than he felt. The drill sergeant watched them scramble into place and shook his head in mock despair. When the full company was assembled, he walked slowly between the arrow-straight lines of men.

"I should have you all on KP, you shoddy bunch of layabouts," he bellowed, "except there's no bloody kitchen to send you to." He came to a halt in front of Michael. "Sweet suffering Lucifer, what do you look like? Did you sleep in your bloody uniform, airman?"

Michael stared straight ahead. "No, sir. I mean, yes, sir." He risked a quick look at the sergeant. The man's face was bright red, the veins standing out on his neck, "No, sir."

"Make up your mind, you wittering imbecile."

"No, sir. I mean, yes, sir."

"Oh, for the love of heaven, shut up airman, before I put you on report for a month."

"Yes, sir."

Michael's head was still pounding, but now he felt sweat breaking out on his face and in the small of his back. His knees felt weak, and he wished the parade was over and he could go and throw up over the nearby sea wall. The sergeant shook his head, "It smells like Bailey's Brewery out here." He continued to the end of the line and turned into the second row. Michael heard him roar, "Get a shave, you scruffy gorilla; I don't want to see that growth on yer face," as he passed behind him.

Despite his disparaging comments, the sergeant didn't put any of them on report. His inspection complete, he wished them well in their new postings and warned them to be ready to take the transportation to the railway at ten hundred hours. "And for pity's sake tidy yourselves up. You all look downright 'orrible. And *you* are what the country is relying on?"

They were dismissed. Some of the recruits went to thank him, but others, like Michael, were more interested in getting a cup of tea from the mobile canteen and something to cure their sore heads.

The trip to Cornwall was uneventful. Michael spent most of it sleeping. Despite his promise, it was two days before he wrote to Beth with his latest news.

> *My Dear Beth,*
> *Sorry to tell you that I will not be home for*
> *Christmas. We have been told we're only here for a short*
> *time then Frank, me, and ten others will be transferred*
> *to flight training! Can you believe that? It looks like I'm*
> *going to make it! I hope Frank will keep out of trouble*
> *in the meantime. I think his drinking and messing*

around is his way of dealing with the war.

 I miss you so much, Beth, and look forward to getting your letters. Sorry it took so long for me to write, they are keeping us pretty busy here. I've no idea when I'll see you again but hopefully we'll have some leave when our flight training is over.

 Say hello to all your family. Any news of where Paul is?

 Take care of yourself. I keep your Saint Christopher medal with me all the time, so you know I'll be safe. Have a good Christmas. I'll be thinking of you.

Love,
Michael

1941

Flying

Michael learned fast. He loved the flying. Paul had been right. He loved the way the throb of the engines vibrated in his belly as the aircraft sped down the runway and the way the earth suddenly fell away beneath him as he took off. The houses, streets, and trees became smaller and smaller as the aircraft climbed, so that the landscape looked like model railway scenes he'd seen in shopwindows at Christmas time. He was filled with exhilaration as the aircraft rose toward the endless blue of the sky or the artificial ceiling of wispy, cotton candy clouds. *Per Ardua ad Astra* was the RAF motto, "Through Adversity to the Stars." Michael liked the motto. He studied hard to become a good pilot and in only a few weeks qualified for his first solo flight.

Afterwards, when he taxied the small aircraft back onto the ramp and parked, his instructor, Flight Sergeant Robley, stood waiting for him.

"Congratulations, lad. How was that?"

"It felt terrific, sir. I'm surprised. I didn't even feel that nervous in the end; at least not once I took off without problems."

At debriefing, he wrote in his logbook:

March 6th 1941. 0.9.00 - 0.9. 47 hours. Solo command. Tiger Moth.

He was a pilot!

Toward the end of March, as Michael made his routine check of the flight-operations board, he saw that he, along with the rest of his group, was rostered for a week's home leave. Sergeant Robley stood beside the board.

"It might be your last leave for a while, lad, make the most of it."

Michael knew they were due to be posted overseas some time soon. They'd already been told that advanced flight training was too difficult in Britain, with the Luftwaffe a constant threat. So this must be it. He wondered where they would be going. Paul went to Canada.

Several of his companions questioned the sergeant but he would only tell them to enjoy their leave and come back well-rested. Michael hurried to his billet to pack. He couldn't wait to see Beth.

He arrived at Glenfrome Road soon after midday, let himself into the house, and called, "Aunty Wyn, it's me. I'm home."

He saw her working at the kitchen table, but she didn't respond to his call. Michael dropped his kit bag and banged the front door closed. She looked up, startled. In the kitchen, women's clothes, scissors, a tape measure, pins and patterns littered the table and chairs.

"Hello. Sorry if I frightened you. I did shout."

She frowned. "What are you doing here? I wasn't expecting you."

"I know, I'm sorry. I couldn't let you know in advance; they only told us yesterday."

"I have some ladies coming in, any minute. They need me to do these alterations for them. I can't send them away."

It was as if he hadn't been away at all.

"That's all right. I'll go out," he assured her; relieved he wouldn't have to make excuses. "I'll come back later, when they've gone."

"That would be good." She gave him the smallest wisp of a smile, "Then I'll make you some supper. I have to finish this before they come."

Michael watched her gather some of the debris from the table and put it into her sewing box. She looked old. The skin on her hands seemed paper thin; her thin face was a tracery of fine lines. How old was she? She must be getting hard of hearing too if she didn't hear him open the front door or call her name.

"It's been very quiet in the house without you, boy," she said, giving him a quick pat on the arm. She closed the lid of the sewing box. "We can sit and talk tonight." She walked out into the hall. "Put that upstairs before someone trips on it," she said indicating his kit bag, then she went into the front parlor and closed the door.

Michael did as she asked, called goodbye on his way out, and hurried over to the Howard's.

He knocked on the door several times, but there was no answer. Disappointed, but with nothing else to do, he sat on the front porch

220

steps to wait. In one of her letters Beth said she'd completed her typing course and was looking for a job. Perhaps she'd found one, although she hadn't mentioned it.

Almost two hours passed before he saw her turn the corner of the road and walk toward the house. He remained sitting, enjoying being able to watch her when she didn't know he was there. Her hair was hidden under a brightly colored scarf, knotted at her forehead, and she wore an old coat he remembered Mrs. Howard used to wear, years ago. The coat was unbuttoned and Michael was surprised to see that, under it, she wore what looked like a man's shirt, with her hands thrust deep into the pockets of baggy, khaki overalls. As she came closer he saw smudges and streaks of dirt, or grease, on her face.

Beth didn't see him until she was almost at the gate and Michael stood. She stopped still, in disbelief, before letting out a squeal of delight and running into his arms. He held her tight, kissing her forehead, her nose, her eyes, and her lips. He stood back to look at her and she laughed.

"Oh, Michael, look at your face; you're covered in grease. Oh, I'm so sorry."

Digging around in her coat pocket she found a handkerchief and tried to clean off the black smudges while he stood and smiled at her. Even with all the oil streaks and the strange clothes, he thought she was still the prettiest girl he'd ever seen. He took her hand from his face and kissed it.

"What on earth are you doing dressed like that, Beth Howard? You look like you've been crawling under cars."

She blushed. "I'm sorry, Michael. I didn't want to tell you until I saw you." She dug into her pockets again and brought out a key. "Come on into the house and I'll explain."

She opened the door, and he followed her through the hall and into the kitchen where she tossed her coat across a chair, then turned to look at him.

"You look wonderful, why didn't you tell me you were coming?" She fussed with her hair, tucking stray wisps under the scarf, then trying to wipe her face with the greasy handkerchief.

"I think you're wasting your time," he laughed, happy just to look at her.

221

She shrugged and gave up. "All right, let me make a cup of tea and we can sit and chat. I'll go and clean up properly in a minute."

He sat at the kitchen table, watched as she made the tea, and listened as she explained her appearance.

"When I finished my Pitman's course I started looking for a job. Then I got a letter from the Ministry of Works saying that they noted I wasn't working. They told me I had to report for work at Thristle Engineering Works." She put the teapot on the table and smiled. "So I did." "They have me making gun sights. It's not too bad. I don't mind it really," she gestured at her appearance, "but, as you can see, it *is* a bit mucky when I have to clean the machine."

"You're working on machinery?"

She nodded. "I can even service it. That's what I was doing today. I suppose I could have asked to work in the land army, like Ev, but then I would be away most of the time. Ev lives at the farm. She only comes back at weekends, if she can borrow a bike. This way I can come home every day, after my shift, and be with Mum. She would be on her own otherwise, with everyone gone."

As she spoke she cut slices of bread and took a jar of homemade pickled onions from the pantry. "Look, our own onions, we grew them ourselves," she said proudly. She made sandwiches and joined him at the table.

"Now, enough about me! What have you been up to, Michael? I haven't seen you for over four months. You write about your friend Frank more than you write about yourself. Tell me."

"I've made it, Beth. I'm a pilot."

She jumped up and ran around the table to hug him. "Oh, Michael! Why didn't you tell me?" She stood back and looked at his uniform jacket. "I didn't even notice your wings. I'm sorry. I was just so pleased to see you."

He stood and gave her a sharp salute.

"Flying Officer Second Class, Michael Kelly, at your service."

He loved the look on her face as she beamed up at him. He'd looked forward to this moment all the way home, he felt so proud. He explained how he still had a lot of training to do before they let him fly on missions, but at least he'd got this far.

They spent the rest of the afternoon catching up on all the news they'd been unable to write in their letters. When Mrs. Howard came home she seemed to be as happy to see him as Beth *and* as impressed with his new rank. It was after eight o'clock before he remembered Aunty Wyn and said he'd better go home.

"But I'm here for a week, Beth, and I'll see you every day, I promise."

She laughed, "You'd better, Michael Kelly, or I'll run off with a soldier!"

They kissed goodbye and he hurried home.

The week went too quickly. Even Wyn seemed pleased to have him home. She didn't question where he went each day, so Michael decided not mention Beth. Keen to avoid any arguments he continued to tell her he was meeting his friends.

On the night before his leave ended he told Beth about going overseas. Even though she knew it would happen soon, she struggled to hold back her tears.

"When I get back, I want to introduce you to Aunty Wyn. I should have done it this time, but it's been so nice and peaceful I didn't want to risk it. I admit I'm a coward where she's concerned. But I'll do it next time, I promise. Can you wait for me, Beth?"

"Of course I can, my love. Just be sure you take care of yourself and come home safe."

"I will."

She brushed away her tears and snuggled closer to him and linked her arm through his.

"The war can't last forever, Michael. Mr. Churchill says it will be over soon."

"Well, don't believe all he says, sweetheart. Will you tell Paul I'm thinking of him when you write to him? Our letters don't seem to catch up with each other too often."

"I will. He always asks for you. I wish you two got leave at the same time."

"Perhaps next time."

They parted reluctantly and Michael hurried home to pack his kit bag ready for his early departure in the morning.

Journeys

Michael found the heat oppressive and the pounding of the ship's engines pulsed through his entire body. The smell of stale sweat and old food made him feel ill. He lay in his hammock, staring up at the gray-painted, metal plating over his head and wondering how much longer he could last before he joined his shipmates in the "head." He'd learned that was the naval name for the latrines. Though the ship was rolling, Frank kept telling him that as long as he stayed in his hammock he was actually staying still. Michael said it was a good theory and if he kept his eyes closed it almost worked, but he couldn't shut out the smells.

They'd been confined to quarters for most of the four-week voyage, except for brief exercise periods on deck. Two thousand of them, soldiers and airmen, lived cheek by jowl. Frank and Michael shared their particular living quarters with twenty other airmen. The cramped space was deep in the belly of the vessel, close to the engine room. Their hammocks were slung everywhere, even over the mess tables. The mess was their eating, sleeping, and living quarters all in one, and it smelled like it. Michael remembered reading about slave ships when he was in school. He knew slaves were part of what made Bristol wealthy in the old days, but he'd never really thought about what it must have been like on those ships. He had even more sympathy for the slaves now.

When he first heard they were going to Africa, he had been excited, but four weeks on the boat had done a great deal to quell Michael's enthusiasm. He had his nineteenth birthday on the journey, though he didn't mention it. As the boat traveled south, following the distant, dark smudge of the African coastline, then rounded the Cape of Good Hope and steamed slowly northward up the east coast, he constantly tried to pinpoint their final destination. He spent hours studying his dog-eared atlas. For days now they had all been saying that *surely* they would land soon. At times he almost wished he was back in Porter's Emporium, wearing a neat suit, clean socks, and a fresh shirt.

He decided he couldn't take the noise and the smells any longer and swung out of his hammock. He picked his way between the tables and men, toward the "head" ducking his head to avoid other hammocks. As he did so a young airman clattered down the metal ladder shouting, "We're going in. I saw the port. We're going to dock. We've arrived, lads."

The men cheered and shouted questions at the airman. Michael forgot feeling ill. He smiled across at Frank, who was playing cards. He'd played cards for most of the journey, not seeming to notice the smells or the stomach-churning motion of the boat.

Africa! Who would have believed they would ever be in Africa?

Kit bags were hastily packed, dirty clothes thrown in with the clean, the wet with the dry, as they waited for the orders to disembark. Once the boat docked it seemed like hours passed before the order for his mess to muster on deck was called over the speaker system. They lined up to climb the steep metal-rung ladder and then stood on deck breathing in the moist heat and their first, pungent smells of Africa.

When they disembarked and reassembled on the quayside, Michael still felt as if the ground heaved and rolled beneath him. A few of the men even got sick.

Frank nudged his friend, "So? Where are we, Mikey? Do you know?"

"I think its Durban."

The sergeant chivvied latecomers into line; then inspected his group.

"All right, lads, look lively. Get yourselves and your bags on board those trucks over there, quick as you like. We don't have time to hang around here sightseeing."

"Where are we going?" called one lad from the back.

"Train station, lad, you're off to Bulawayo."

There was a collective groan from the men.

"How far is that, sarge?"

"Never you mind, lad, just get in the truck."

"Some airmen, us," muttered Frank. "Wouldn't you think they could have flown us instead of making us float down here in bloody Noah's Ark for weeks on end? And now they're sending us on a train journey?"

Michael pulled the atlas out of his kit bag again and studied the map of Africa to find Bulawayo.

"We're going north," he told his friend, "Bulawayo's in Rhodesia."

He and Frank threw their kit bags onto the back of the open truck and climbed aboard. Others joined them. When the truck was full, they took off over the rutted, garbage-strewn streets to the station. Michael and the others stared at the beggars, many of them crippled, who squatted at the roadside and raised their hands in silent supplication. Laughing urchins, their brown faces snot-smeared and powdered with street dust ran after the truck, begging, waving, and shouting, their tattered clothing fluttering around them. The young airmen twisted and turned to see as much as they could of the unfamiliar town and its people. They did see an occasional white man, in linen suit and Panama hat, going about his business along the cluttered, raised sidewalks. Some of the men waved and smiled, but the few white women they saw ignored their passing.

The train left three hours late. The wooden-slatted seats were narrow, hard, and uncomfortable, but Michael was exhausted. Rocked gently by the tickety-ta rhythm of the train, he fell into a deep, dreamless sleep.

He woke to the purple-pink light of an early dawn. He stood and stretched his legs. Stepping over his still-sleeping companions, he slid open the carriage door and moved out into the corridor. He joined others who were already gathered there, leaning out of the windows, seeking a breath of cool air. The servicemen watched in silence as the sun rose. The colors of the sky rapidly turned from purple, to red, then a deep burnt gold before the landscape flooded with the hard, bright light of an African sun. The men squinted their eyes against the glare and scanned the unfamiliar countryside.

"Bloody hell, look at *them*," said the young man beside Michael, pointing at a herd of giraffe stampeding away from the train in a yellow-ochre dust cloud. "I've only ever seen one of those before, in our local zoo."

"This is the biggest bloody zoo you're ever likely to see, mate," said another. He pointed toward the horizon, "Look, there's an elephant."

"Bloody hell," the first man repeated, in awe.

Michael narrowed his eyes further, "That's not an elephant, it's a rock." His companions laughed, then the rock moved and loped off waving its trunk and they laughed louder.

The young men took it in turns to point out the different animals and, as his eyes became more accustomed to scanning the tufted, strawlike grass and scrub, Michael spotted a pride of lions. They crouched low over a dead animal, jostling to get at the carcass, snarling at each other with bared teeth and bloody jaws.

"I wish my Ma could see this," said the airman beside him. "We're a long way from the damned war out here, that's for sure."

Michael nodded. He wished he could write to Beth about it all. He'd have great stories when he got back.

They disembarked at a busy rural station and were driven in yet another bone-rattling truck through the small local town. It looked a bit like the Western towns Michael had seen in cowboy films. Several miles later they arrived at a makeshift collection of Nissen huts, clustered at one end of a dusty runway. A limp wind sock hung over a squat control tower, and several airmen in khaki shorts and shirts sat outside the huts on packing crates, camp seats, and supply boxes. They played cards, smoked, or just watched the newcomers climb stiffly down from their vehicle. Frank looked around.

"I suppose this is the airfield, but it looks like someone forgot to bring the aircraft."

"No point having them sitting on the ground, mate. They're on flight ops," said one of the khaki-clad men. "Welcome to Camp Nowhere." He extended his hand, and Michael and Frank introduced themselves. He said his name was Brian Hopkins, from Newcastle. A sergeant shouted for roll call, and Hopkins gave them a casual salute before returning to his friends.

It took a while to get used to their new quarters. They were hot, Spartan, and bug infested. But the flying was exciting, the companionship good, and the people in the town welcoming. They invited the off-duty young men for meals in their homes and threw socials for them at the weekends, though always ensuring that their daughters were well chaperoned. The months sped by. The airmen learned far more about navigation than they had at home base. Compass readings and knowledge of the stars became new and essential navigational tools above the vast, rich farmlands of Rhodesia, where there were few city landmarks to guide them.

Michael enjoyed it all. He learned about a variety of weather conditions and survival techniques. He learned how to judge wind speed and direction from various clues, even from the thin wisps of smoke drifting from fires in the kraals. He learned more about flying and the Liberator, his assigned aircraft, every day and was almost disappointed when their six-month training was completed.

The boat journey home was as unpleasant as the one out. Nearing northern waters, the cold, December weather signaled the exchange of their tropical khakis for the old, standard, blue-wool uniform. It felt uncomfortably heavy and itchy after the tropical kit.

The tanned but weary airmen disembarked at Southampton and were disappointed to learn that they then had to spend a day in barracks, debriefing.

"Typical," said Frank. "Four weeks to debrief us on the boat, when we've bugger all to do, but they wait until we get back here and all we can think about is seeing our families."

"I didn't think you were going home."

"Well, no, I'm not, not exactly. We only have five days, Mikey; sure I would hardly be there when I'd have to come back. No! There's a certain lady in Berkshire whose acquaintanceship I intend to renew." He gave Michael a wink. "It seems I might have some of my uncle's charms, Mikey, if you know what I mean. She's a widow lady, and she says she only loves to hear my beautiful Irish accent!"

Michael shook his head. "And to think I considered introducing you to Beth's sister."

"Is that the Evelyn one?"

"Yes. One of the few women I thought might be able to manage you, but I'm not sure Beth would be too pleased."

"Once I've sown my wild oats, Mikey, I'll be the model husband. It's just that I'm not quite ready, not yet awhile."

They signed in at the debriefing, found seats near the back of the room, and listened as various officers addressed them.

"Think before you drink!" said an older wing commander, scanning the crowd of young men. "I know it's nice to celebrate being home, but you never know who's listening. Watch what you say, don't give information away that might be useful to the enemy!" He elaborated on his theme for some time and then sat while another officer gave them a lecture on "Upholding the Honor of the Service."

"So many men, wearing these uniforms, have died defending this country. Respect their memories, respect yourselves, and always remember our motto, '*Per Ardua ad Astra* ... Through Adversity to the Stars.' Only your best is good enough."

The final speaker congratulated them on completing their training and warned them about the vast differences between flight training and active duty. He urged them to constantly respect and learn from their superiors, help their juniors, and become valued members of their squadrons and crews.

The speakers all hammered at their messages, and the airmen fidgeted in their seats and hoped they would be in time to find transport home that evening. They were eventually discharged, and Michael's group was instructed to report to the home camp at Brize Norton for allocation to squadrons and active duty in five days.

Beth said Michael's dark tan really suited him. On his second night home they walked into town to see the film *Rebecca*. As they went she kept glancing at him and smiling, saying she couldn't believe how handsome he was. He shrugged his lack of interest, but walked a little taller. On the way home, she told him she thought he was far more handsome than Laurence Olivier, the star of the film, and she'd always thought *he* was *very* handsome.

At the top of West Street, Michael sidestepped and gently tugged her through the gate and into the churchyard of Holy Trinity Church. She thought he was joking; the film had been scary, and she'd spent a great deal of the evening clinging to his arm. She thought he was trying to scare her again. "It's all right, I just want to talk to you for a minute," he said and guided her to sit on the low wall bordering the graveyard. Once there he fumbled in his jacket pocket, took a deep breath, and knelt on one knee.

"My dear, sweet, Beth, I think I have loved you since the very first time I ever saw you." He opened a small black box and held the contents up to her, "Will you marry me?"

Despite the darkness, she could see a single, tiny diamond sparkling brightly in the moonlight. It glinted from the center of a thin, gold band.

"Oh, Michael, it's beautiful." She took the ring from the box, slipped it onto her finger, and stretched out her hand to admire it. Michael remained on one knee.

"How did you know my size? It fits perfectly."

"Beth, I think I'm kneeling on a stone. Given that you've put the ring on, does that mean you will?"

She laughed and gave him a gentle push, "Get up, you clown, of course I will."

He stood, put his arms around her, and pulled her close.

"Get on with it, man," said a soldier walking past with a young woman on his arm. Beth looked around, startled, then turned back and gave Michael a long, lingering kiss.

"That's more like it," said the soldier as he and his companion continued up the road. "Good luck to you both."

Beth and Michael laughed and kissed again. They kissed for a long, long time. When they stopped, she stretched her hand out to admire her ring.

"It really is beautiful, Michael. Where did you get it? It must have cost a fortune."

"We had a free day in Durban, before we boarded the ship home. They mine diamonds in South Africa."

He didn't tell her he'd saved his money for months *and* borrowed some of Frank's card winnings. He didn't tell Aunty Wyn that he'd got an increase in his pay either. Anyway, it was all worth it. She said yes.

As they turned into the Howard's road Beth stopped walking.

"What about your aunt, Michael?" she glanced toward her home. "And what about Mum? I can't really leave her right now; it's not a year since Dad and George died. Your aunt hasn't even met me!"

"I know," he smiled down at her and tried to gently smooth away her frown with his finger. "We'll work it out somehow. Let's talk about it tomorrow. Let's just be happy tonight."

She gave a slight shake of her head.

"Perhaps I should keep it in the box for now, until we talk to them." She eased the ring from her finger, and Michael reluctantly fished in his pocket, pulled out the box, and handed it to her.

"All right." He was disappointed, but he knew she was probably right. "As long as that doesn't mean you've changed your mind already. Does it?"

She smiled up at him. "No, I don't think I'll ever do that, my love. I think I loved you before you even realized I existed."

She took a final, wistful look at the ring before placing it in the black, velvet-lined box and tucking it into her pocket.

They walked the rest of the way in silence. Michael's thoughts turned, yet again, to deciding how he would break the news of his engagement to Aunty Wyn. He hadn't even *thought* about how it would affect Mrs. Howard until Beth mentioned it. She didn't *seem* as if she needed to be minded that much. She seemed to be coping very well. .... Perhaps they could all live together?

He was relieved that his aunt was in bed when he got home, but he knew he couldn't put it off for long.

Confrontation

Wyn washed a cup and handed it to Michael.

"Aunty Wyn, do you have any ladies coming in tomorrow night for fittings?"

"No, it only seems to be alterations these days. Everybody's scrimping and saving. Why?"

"I want to bring someone 'round to meet you."

"Do you indeed! And who might that be? One of the new friends you seem to be out with all the time?"

Michael dried another dish and put it on the dresser. He'd been thinking about how to talk to her all morning.

"Well, yes, she *is* a friend."

Wyn stopped with a bowl in her hand. "She?"

"Yes. I've told you about her before."

He'd thought he could handle this. What the hell was wrong with him? Michael looked at the old woman standing in front of him and wondered just how old she was. He'd never remembered her mentioning her birthday. But she *was* an old woman, he thought, a lonely and bitter old woman. He realized he'd never seen her with any friends, not real friends, not unless you counted her regular customers. It must have been pretty lonely for her all these years with only him for company. Was that why she didn't have any friends? Because she had to look after him?

Wyn peered up at him from over the wire rims of her glasses. Water from the dish in her hand dripped onto the tiled floor, but she didn't seem to notice. She frowned.

"Well, boy. Is that all you're going to say? That you've told me about her before?"

He felt his face getting hot and his heart beating faster. Dammit, he'd rather be doing his first solo night flight again, than standing facing his aunt in this small kitchen.

"Yes. It's Beth Howard, Paul's sister."

"Ah, the young lady you stayed out all night with."

He decided to ignore the barb.

"Yes, that's the one."

"And why would I want to meet her?"

He took a deep breath and looked his aunt firmly in the eye.

"Because I'm going to marry her."

"You what?" Her voice was quiet, her eyes flint-hard.

"I'm going to marry her, Aunty Wyn. I love her."

She turned her attention to the dish in her hand, shook the remaining drips off into the sink, and put it down on the draining board. He watched as she dried her hands on her apron. They were like birds' claws, thin, bony and bent.

"You're going to marry her?"

"Yes."

He watched as she walked unhurriedly to her chair and sat.

"And what about me? What am I supposed to do?"

He put down the cloth and went to sit opposite her.

"I've been thinking about that ..."

Before he could complete his sentence she cut across him.

"Well I'm glad to hear that. I thought you had made your decision already."

"Well I have, but ..."

"Ah ...'but.' Yes, of course, 'but' ..."

"Look, Aunty Wyn, ..."

"Don't '*look*, Aunty Wyn' me!" she spoke quietly. "You seem to have forgotten that *I'm* the one who took you in, fed you, and clothed you. *I* took you when no one else wanted you. *I* was the one who looked after you when you were sick, taught you your manners and the Bible, and saw to it that you knew right from wrong...or so I thought. And *this* is the thanks I get? '*Look*, Aunty Wyn?' I didn't have to take you in, remember. But I did. And *this* is how you intend to show your gratitude? Going off to marry this hussy."

"She's not a hussy. And I'm grateful for everything you've done for me. I always have been. If you gave her half a chance I know you'd like her."

"I don't have to like her. You're not going to marry her."

He wanted to shout at her. "I'm in the war now. I'm going to be flying on missions. I could be killed at any time. Just look at the number of casualties!" *She* listened to the news; *she* knew how many casualties the RAF had. Why couldn't she understand? Just because she'd never married didn't mean she should try and stop him. He couldn't live with her forever. Who knew how long this war was going to go on? Or if he would survive it.

Michael was now as angry as his aunt.

"Yes, I am, Aunty Wyn." He tried to not let his rage sound in his voice.

"You seem to have forgotten something, young man. My brother and I are still your guardians, whether you like it or not, and you are still underage until you are twenty-one. You need our permission before you can marry anyone. And *I,* for *one,* certainly do *not* give my permission."

Refused permission! Like he was a small child!

"But there's a war on. I could be dead before I'm twenty-one."

"Then better to leave her as single and untarnished goods, than a widow."

He couldn't believe she said that. Tarnished goods! How dare she!

"Beth is the woman I have chosen to marry. And she has accepted. You can't stop me forever. Once I'm twenty-one you can't stop me."

She stared calmly up at him.

"Don't raise your voice to me, Michael. That's more than a year away. I'm sure you will be well over this infatuation by then, when you've grown up a bit and have had time to consider."

He tried to match her calm tone.

"It is *not* an infatuation and I will *not* get over it. I'm grown up *now* and there is nothing to consider."

He stormed from the kitchen, snatched his jacket from the hall stand, and pulled open the front door. Turning, he called back to the still-sitting woman, "If we have to wait until then, we will. But we'll get married eventually, with or without, your bloody permission."

He slammed the door and left.

Later that evening, sitting on the couch in the Howard's front room, Michael told Beth about the confrontation. She held his hands tightly in hers.

"Of course we can wait. It isn't that long, my love. We were probably going to do that anyway."

He nodded. "I'm sorry, Beth, perhaps when she calms down a bit. There's no point in trying to talk to her now, not when she's like this."

"Can we tell Mum anyway? I know I said I wanted to wait, but I could hardly keep it secret last night. I slept with the ring under my pillow. I know she'll be pleased, and we can tell her it will be at least a year before we get married. We'll have plenty of time to sort things out."

He agreed and they went into the kitchen, where Margaret Howard was preparing supper. She cried when they told her. She hugged Beth first, then Michael, then both of them.

"Your father would have been so pleased, Beth, and your brother George. I'm so happy for you both. The girls will be thrilled... so will Paul. And wait 'til we tell Evelyn! She's been hoping this would happen for a long time." She smiled at Michael and hugged him again. "We all have, Michael dear." She turned to her daughter. "Are you going to show me the ring, or am I going to have to search you for it?"

Beth laughed and ran upstairs. Mrs. Howard blew her nose and wiped away stray tears.

"Thank you, Michael. I know you've made her so happy and I know you'll be good to her."

Beth clattered back down the stairs, two steps at a time. Once in the kitchen she opened the box and showed her mother the ring.

"It's beautiful, Michael. It's a very pretty setting; perfect for our Beth." The woman looked from one to the other, "So, when are you going to name the day?"

Beth and Michael exchanged glances.

"Not for ages yet, Mum. We have to wait until Michael's twenty-one. His aunt isn't very pleased."

"Oh, dear, I'm sorry to hear that, Michael. But I'm sure she'll get used to the idea. She's probably just afraid she'll be losing you."

Michael, still angry at Wyn's decision, was not prepared to make excuses for his aunt. He shrugged.

She continued, "Well, that doesn't stop us *thinking* about it, does it? It will give us something to look forward to." She smiled at her daughter. "I wish I'd kept my wedding dress, Beth. Getting one these days is not going to be easy."

"Oh Mum, I haven't even started to think about that yet. We have time."

Michael wished, yet again, that Aunty Wyn was as nice as Mrs. Howard.

The atmosphere at home was strained for the rest of his leave. Michael spent as much time as he could with Beth, meeting her at work, on her lunch break, and walking her home in the evenings. On Sheelagh's half day off work he met his sister and told her about the engagement. She said that now she definitely had to meet her sister-in-law-to-be and that she would like to treat them both to a meal one evening at the Trocadero.

"Would you mind if I brought Colm? I think he should meet the new member of the family too, don't you?"

Michael was indifferent, but it was Sheelagh's treat, and if she wanted to bring their brother, then Michael wouldn't object. He supposed Colm was family anyway, though he didn't feel much like it.

The evening was fun. Beth and Sheelagh got on very well, and even Colm seemed less of a boor than Michael remembered. He told a lot of funny stories which had Beth and Sheelagh laughing. The only time it got serious was when he started talking about how he went to Ireland for their father's funeral. Michael didn't know Colm had been back at all. It seemed he was the only one who hadn't visited his family, *and* the only one not to see his father again even if it *was* only at his funeral. He was jealous. When Colm made a sneering, joking remark about how quaint, even stupid, the Irish people he'd met were, Michael glanced across at Sheelagh. Her face was red and her blue eyes almost sparked as she snapped at her brother, interrupting him.

"I don't think that's funny at all, Colm. I saw him before he died, when he was in hospital. It was very sad. They might be poor, but they are lovely people and they are our family. Don't talk about them like that."

Michael thought she was going to cry. He was angry at his brother too, and he could see Beth felt awkward. Colm quickly apologized, saying he thought that maybe he'd had too much to drink. Michael agreed, though he didn't say so and he didn't think it excused his brother either. But it was Sheelagh's treat and he didn't want to make things worse, so he said nothing. Sheelagh went to the ladies' room and by the time she came back the conversation had turned to rationing, always a favorite subject. Colm offered to get Sheelagh and Beth stockings, which were almost impossible to buy any more and even some chocolate.

"I can't imagine how you can do that," said Sheelagh. "Even working in the shop I can't get stockings."

"Ask no questions, sister dear, ask no questions. You just let me know what you want, and I will see if I can get them for you."

She looked at him with distaste. "If you are talking black market, Colm, you can keep them, thank you. I don't want to know about it."

He shrugged. "Suit yourself."

He didn't seem a bit abashed and flashed a disdainful look at Michael.

At the end of the evening Colm and Sheelagh promised to keep in touch with Beth while Michael was away. They all hugged and said goodnight. On the way home Beth told Michael she liked his sister and hoped they would be good friends. She said nothing about Colm.

Placement

Michael studied the notice board and found his name.

"Flight Sergeant Michael Kelly. 120 Squadron, Coastal Command, Nutt's Corner, County Antrim."

"Can you believe it, Mikey? Nutt's Corner! Isn't that the perfect place for us?"

"Are we in the same squadron, Frank?"

"Of course we are, mate. They couldn't separate us now. Sure, aren't we joined at the hip?"

Michael laughed. "So, Flight Sergeant Murphy, given that you know everything, when are we going?"

"Isn't it right there in front of you, lad." Frank pointed to another list, under the first one. "We go this evening."

"And where is County Antrim, exactly?"

"It's in Northern Ireland, boyo, on the shores of Lough Neagh. Have you not checked it up on your precious atlas? Or have you finally worn it out?"

"Ireland?"

After all this time! Michael had given up any idea of getting to Ireland, or trying to meet his Irish family, while the war was on. Now he was going to be based there!

As they walked away from the notice board and back to their billet one question buzzed in his head.

"Is Antrim far from Galway, Frank?"

"Not that far. But there is the little problem of the border, Mikey. There's a bit of a difference between *Ireland*, Eire as we like to call it, and *Northern* Ireland. You know, we were not too anxious to support the Brits in a war. Not after hundreds of years of occupation by the buggers."

"But they don't support Hitler, do they?"

"No, that's why hundreds of the likes of me have signed up. But we have to come to England to do it. The South is officially neutral, my friend. It's only Northern Ireland that's involved in the war."

Michael couldn't believe it. He would be so close, and yet it *still* wasn't going to happen! He *still* wouldn't be able to see them.

"We can't cross the border?"

"Not legally. If we did, we could end up in an internment camp for the rest of the war. Not that that would be such a problem for me, I suppose. My grandfather would be just as well pleased and me Ma would be relieved I was out of it." He smiled. "Sure, they would probably bring me a file in a cake or something." His smile faded. "Of course, it might be more serious for you, being a Brit and all. Well, you are, as far as the authorities are concerned anyway."

He stopped walking and turned to face Michael.

"Sorry, Mikey, I shouldn't make jokes about this. I know what you're thinking. Don't look so down, Mikey me boy." He patted his friend on the shoulder. "I've heard that the border's as leaky as a sieve. We might be able to find a way. Let me look into it when we get there, see what we can do. I have a cousin. Well, he's actually a second cousin, once removed, but he lives close to the border and he might just be able to give us some help." He smiled. "We'll just have to see when we get there. But no, I don't think County Galway is that far from Antrim. Sure the whole island's not the size of Rhodesia."

Michael could think of nothing else for the rest of the day. He wanted to write to Beth and tell her, but knew the letter would be censored. Eventually he sent her a brief, carefully worded note that he hoped she would decipher.

> *Dear Beth,*
>
> *Just a quick note to tell you how happy I will be to see my brother and sister, soon. At least I hope to. Must dash now.*
>
> *Love,*
> *Michael*

He didn't realize how confusing the note would be. Beth told him later that it was ages before she realized she had the wrong brother and sister. She thought Michael meant Sheelagh and Colm and that he was telling her he was going to be posted near Bristol. She was so excited about it. It never occurred to her that he meant Mary and Pierce.

They landed at their new base close to midnight. Michael was met by an orderly who told him he would be joining a duty crew at 07:00 hours the next morning. He was replacing a copilot given extended leave due to illness. After saying goodnight to Frank and getting directions to his quarters, Michael unpacked and climbed into bed. His first active duty! He would be flying his first mission in less than eight hours! He was nervous, no point pretending he wasn't. His stomach felt tight, his breathing shallow, and his forehead was a bit clammy. Would he remember everything? Would he be scared if they encountered the enemy? It was all very well enjoying flying, but this was a bit different. He turned over the pillow, finding a cool surface, tugged the rough blankets up to his chin, and closed his eyes in the forlorn hope that he might get some sleep.

Michael rose early, gave himself several nicks with the razor in his haste to shave, and hurried to find the briefing room and meet the rest of his crew. He introduced himself to his skipper, Flight Lieutenant Alan Purdy. He's not much older than me, he thought. Like the recruiting officer in Bristol.

The briefing was detailed. They studied Atlantic charts, aerial photographs of allied and enemy ships, submarines and enemy aircraft. They scanned weather reports and incident logs, while the skipper explained to Michael that their mission was primarily to seek out and destroy enemy submarines in the North Atlantic.

The briefing over, the crew walked across the ramp to their aircraft. The wireless operator, an older man called Tug Wilson, asked Michael if he'd remembered the pigeons. Michael decided this was some kind of initiation joke they pulled on new pilots.

"No, I thought I'd bring my rubber duck instead, it makes less noise."

The crew laughed and Michael thought he'd passed the test, but when they got to the aircraft there was a wicker basket on the ground under the wing. He looked at the wireless operator, his eyebrows raised. Tug nodded.

"Real pigeons?" asked Michael in disbelief.

Tug nodded again. "You see! You flyboys think you know everything, but they didn't teach you this in flight training, did they?" He picked up the basket and followed Michael on board. "Bloody wireless lets us down sometimes. That's when these babies come in useful. They're homing pigeons. Useful if we go in the drink too, because for sure the damn wireless won't work then. These feathered friends could save our lives." He pushed the basket under his seat. "Of course, that's only if I remember to fix a message to their legs." He laughed and patted Michael on the back. "You just better hope I don't get too forgetful in an emergency."

"Didn't you know that's why there's a law banning pigeon shooting?" said the navigator, as he struggled to get past Michael and into his seat.

"I hadn't thought about it, with aircraft," Michael responded. "I thought it might be how spies did it."

"Oh yes, a good spy always has a pigeon in his pocket," laughed Tug, as he settled himself into his cubby. Michael watched the gunners disperse to their positions. Despite all his training, the muscles across his shoulders felt taut, and the toast and tea he snatched in the canteen had turned into a solid and surprisingly heavy, lump in his stomach. He wiped his damp hands on his trousers and hoped no one noticed.

Michael squeezed past the navigator, over the pedestal, and into his seat. He said a brief, silent prayer.

1942

Taking Risks

Michael quickly became a seasoned member of the crew. At Christmas he managed to get leave for a couple of days, but when he chose to spend Christmas day with Beth and her family instead of with the Porters, it was yet another cause for ill feeling between himself and his aunt.

"I would have thought it was the least you could do. My brother *has* been your benefactor you know."

"With all due respect, Aunty Wyn, I don't feel that I have benefited that much."

"What kind of ungrateful remark is that supposed to be?"

"I'm not talking about you, Aunty Wyn. Of course I'm grateful to you. But he just used me as cheap labor."

"He wanted you to learn the business from the bottom up. He would have left you the business. He promised me. And then you just threw it in his face. If you would just get down off your high horse and try and be nice to him, patch things up a bit, I'm sure he would take you back when the war is over."

"I'm not sure I want him to take me back."

"Of course you do, don't talk such nonsense. Not want to inherit a thriving business like Porter's Emporium? We would be wealthy."

Her comment startled Michael. *We* would be wealthy? He was sure she was older than her brother. Did she think she was going to live forever?

She was barely civil for the rest of his brief visit.

Returning to Northern Ireland, Michael saw in the New Year flying over the dark and forbidding North Atlantic. In the cold of a dismal New Year's dawn they spotted a U-boat just as it was submerging. The skipper timed his drop perfectly, and the submarine exploded upward in a fountain of sea foam, metal shards, and flames. The aircraft circled the wreckage to confirm the strike. They saw bodies floating, face downwards in the oil-slicked water, but no survivors. He heard the navigator behind him mutter, "Happy bloody New Year."

It was Michael's first strike. As they continued their flight he thought of Beth's father and her brother; he remembered the Jackson's who had lived across the street and old Mr. Swinton who died trying to save people from a fire. He didn't feel guilty about the killing. He did feel uncomfortable. No one spoke much for the rest of the day.

With time he got used to the bombing, and when, on other missions, they did spot survivors, they radioed base to let ships in the area know. Some were rescued, but most died in the freezing waters long before help arrived.

By the end of February, Michael had flown numerous missions, and he and his crew scored several strikes on enemy submarines. He'd hardly had a chance to talk to Frank and compare notes on their sorties, but they did arrange to put in a request for the same furlough dates and Frank made enquiries about his cousin. In late March the two young airmen's requests for three-day passes were granted and their plan took shape.

The Journey

Michael and Frank, dressed in borrowed civilian clothing, sat in the back of a farmer's cart that reeked of animal manure. It was drawn by a horse that moved so slowly Michael thought it was sleepwalking. The carter didn't seem much more alert and Michael's anxiety grew. He looked across at his friend.

"Are you sure this is going to be all right, Frank?"

They hadn't seen a house for miles. The dirt track wound its way into the distance ahead of them. There were no signposts, or signs of life, visible through the mist, except for the occasional bleat of a sheep.

"Will you stop worrying, boyo? I told you I'd get you across the border and I will. I'm sure we could probably have done it on the main road. They don't stop everyone, but your accent stands out a bit, don't you know. Now relax, will you? We'll be in Dundalk before you know it, and we can get the train to Dublin from there. Enjoy the land of your forefathers, Mikey. Isn't it beautiful?"

Michael tugged the collar of his jacket up higher, to try and prevent the steady drizzle of rain from running down the back of his neck. The jacket smelled musty, and in his opinion there was precious little scenery to enjoy in the cold, rain-sodden early morning. He was cold, wet, and uneasy.

Frank had somehow arranged for this unexpected transport to get them across the border, from Newry to Dundalk, via the back roads. With no civilian clothes in camp the carter, a distant relation of Frank's second cousin, once removed, also provided clothes for them both. Though he said he didn't realize what a "tall bucko" Michael was.

The damp air carried the bitterly cold wind of a late winter, and Michael was more than a little uncomfortable about how the local Irish constabulary would react if they found a British airman in their midst. He knew they were required to take him into custody and detain him for the duration of the war. Frank said that they would, in fact, probably turn a blind eye. Michael said that that was easy for him to say. *He* was all right. *He* had an Irish passport.

Perhaps, Michael thought, he'd been too hasty when Frank suggested the trip. Perhaps he'd been too anxious to meet the brother and sister Sheelagh told him about.

What the hell was he doing here?

The old carter turned and gave them a toothless smile. "Not long now, lads. Another half hour and we'll be there."

An hour and a half later, long after Michael became convinced they had been traveling in circles, the carter let them off on the outskirts of Dundalk. They found their way into the town, and Frank asked for directions to the station. By late afternoon they were sitting in the third class carriage of an all-stops train to Dublin.

The journey passed slowly, and it was nine o'clock in the evening before they pulled into Amiens Street Station. Frank's three brothers were waiting for them. The two friends climbed, stiff-limbed, down from the carriage, and Frank was immediately overwhelmed by his brothers' welcome. They all spoke at once as they took it in turns to hug him.

"Jayz, Frankie, did you travel in a cattle truck?"

"You smell a bit ripe, man."

"We were here for the last two trains; we thought you weren't coming after all."

Michael wondered how Frank had managed to tell them of his arrival, without alerting the censors. His friend introduced Michael and Frank's youngest brother, Donal, suggested they adjourn to a local bar to "dry out and have a sup," before they went home. Michael thought that it was late and that he wasn't actually wet. He also got the impression that the three brothers had already had a sup or two, but Frank said it was a grand idea, so they set off for O'Toole's pub.

It was almost eleven o'clock before they caught the last tram to the Murphy family home in Fairview. Mrs. Murphy didn't seem a bit concerned at their late arrival. She made a big fuss of her son and his friend.

"My darlin' boy! Frankie, would you look at the state of you!" She turned to Michael, "And is this the friend you've been telling us about?" She took Michael's hand and shook it. "Welcome lad, welcome. We're delighted to meet you at last, aren't we, lads? Michael, isn't it?"

Once she had made sure they were well and that her sons had provided them with "a small drop of the craythur to keep out the chills," Mrs. Murphy gave them fresh clothing and told them to go and change. She said that she'd give their traveling clothing "a bit of a clean" and let them air out on the washing line overnight.

"There's a grand breeze blowing out there. That will get rid of most of the smell. You don't want to meet your family smelling like a farmyard, do you, Michael lad?"

When they returned to the kitchen, Frank's mother told them to sit at the table and served them generous helpings of cabbage and bacon. She placed a large tureen of potatoes and a dish of butter in front of them and sat to watch them eat.

The brothers continued to compete for Frank's attention as they ate. Even Frank's mother interrupted now and again, adding a piece to a story, or correcting an error. With the whole family laughing and joking, shouting and interrupting, Michael found it difficult to follow what they were saying. Even Frank's accent seemed to be stronger since he arrived home. It suddenly occurred to Michael to wonder if he were going to have the same difficulty understanding Mary and Pierce. That would be a disaster! After all this time! And after wanting to meet and talk with them for so long.

No. Sheelagh hadn't said anything about not understanding them. He was just tired *and* a little muddle-headed by the drink. He finished his meal, leaned back in his chair, and looked around the table. It was great to be here, the food was good, the home cozy, and the family so friendly. He was beginning to enjoy the adventure.

The Meeting

Early the following morning Frank accompanied Michael to the railway station and bought his ticket, so that there would be no awkward questions about Michael's accent. He also made enquiries and learned there was a bus service that went twice daily from Ballyfin to Doonbeg. He handed Michael the train ticket and walked with him to the platform. There they shook hands and Michael climbed into an empty carriage. Frank slammed the door closed behind him.

"Don't forget! You've to be back here tomorrow afternoon. We can't be late back," he shouted as the guard blew his whistle and waved his flag. "The train for Dundalk leaves at five. Be here!" he yelled as the train pulled out.

"I will," called Michael, then gave his friend a thumbs-up sign before closing the window against the smoke and smuts of the engine and settling down for the journey.

On arrival in the busy Ballyfin station Michael asked an elderly woman, carrying a basket of eggs, for directions to the bus. He kept his voice low, almost a whisper, to avoid giving away his accent.

"I can't hear you, lad," she said impatiently, cupping her ear. "Speak up."

He spoke a little louder, glancing over his shoulder to make sure he hadn't attracted unwanted attention. He was suddenly acutely aware that, against all his military training, he was out of uniform and in a foreign country where, if Frank was to be believed, British military in particular were not very welcome! He hunched his shoulders, trying to make himself less noticeable. The woman didn't seem to notice his accent, or his furtive behavior, and pointed across the road to the bus stop.

"You're in luck, lad. It hasn't left yet. Always late, it is, since they started repairing the bridge up at Clonhessy's Pass. "

He thanked her, hurried across the road, and boarded the bus. Once he'd purchased his ticket from the driver he took a seat at the back, out of the way. As the bus rattled out of the town Michael felt as if his heart had skipped a beat and he gave an involuntary gasp. He had no address for Mary. He couldn't remember her married name either. He felt beads of sweat form over his top lip and his heart beat a little faster. How could he be so bloody stupid? To come all this way and not know where he was going!

He knew the village was Doonbeg, the name stuck in his head from the first time Sheelagh mentioned it. But she'd never mentioned a precise address and it never occurred to him to ask her for one. Why would he, he argued to himself as he stared out at patchwork fields and whitewashed cottages? He hadn't really expected to come here for a long time, not until after the war. His breath fogged a small circle on the window. He rubbed it clear with the back of his hand. What *was* the damned address! Could he really be so stupid as to get this close, put himself in this much danger, and still not find them?

After almost an hour's travel and several stops, they passed a road sign for Doonbeg. A few minutes later the bus slowed into the village. The driver energetically applied the brakes, Michael stood and, the rackety vehicle came to an abrupt stop outside a post office. Michael walked to the front of the bus, nodded his thanks to the driver and stepped down onto the pavement. He stayed there and watched, as the bus drove away.

He glanced up and down the street, wondering what he should do next. Nothing looked familiar. He wracked his memory for any clues Sheelagh might have given. He thought he remembered her saying Mary had a little "sell-everything" kind of a shop. The village wasn't that big, surely it would be somewhere nearby. The shops would probably all be here; it looked like this was the main street.

There were several small shops tight beside each other along the narrow road. One had boxes and sacks of vegetables displayed outside; another had boots and shoes hanging on poles fastened to large hooks over the entrance. There was a neat, double-fronted, clothing store with assorted bolts of cloth piled in one window and a solitary, sun-faded mannequin dressed in a tweed skirt, twinset, and pearls, in the other. The mannequin was surrounded by a clutter of children's clothes, sturdy underwear, and a variety of woolen garments, hats, shawls, gloves and sweaters, many of which looked homemade. Further down the street, Michael saw a gray stone house with a slightly recessed doorway. He walked toward it, passing a butcher shop as he did so. Dead rabbits hung in the window, and he was surprised at the variety of other meat on display. There was bacon, sausages, different cuts of meat and large chunks of lard. Rationing at home meant there was very little available in most shops, but especially in butchers'.

He continued on down the street, peering into the different shopwindows, looking for a clue. There was no name, or sign, over the entrance to the little store, but some instinct drew him toward it. It just, might, be the one. As he got closer he could see a confusion of goods through the dusty window. There were lucky bags and combs, packets of biscuits, ribbons and all sorts of canned goods. Yes! This could be it. An old woman stepped out onto the pavement clutching a jug of foamy milk. He stood to one side to let her pass and stepped into the tiny shop.

"Yes, sir, can I help you?"

His mouth went dry. He stood looking at the young woman behind the counter. She didn't look a bit like Sheelagh. Though she was only a little shorter, she was much rounder than his sister, and not at all elegant, or fashionable. Her hair was pulled back in an untidy bun, and she wore a loose, long-sleeved blouse with a wool shawl draped over her shoulders. The shop smelled of cheese and milk and dust. The young woman watched him.

"Can I get you something, sir?"

She smiled. She had perfect, even, white teeth and a friendly smile. Her pale brown eyes and hair were a bit like his Beth's.

"Mary."

Her smile faded. She stared up at him; a frown creased her forehead.

"Yes."

"Mary Kelly?"

"I was. I'm Mary Daly now."

"I couldn't remember that."

As he spoke, her hands moved to catch the points of her shawl, and she tugged them across her chest as if it would protect her from bad news. Her hands closed into tight fists.

"I'm Michael."

Her crossed arms pressed in, even tighter, to her body. She shook her head slightly.

"Michael? ... My Michael? ... *Our* Michael?"

He nodded.

She didn't move, but her eyes quickly filled with tears which fell, unheeded.

"Michael!" she repeated. She was still for an instant longer before she unclenched her fists, reached out, raised the counter flap, stepped through, and grasped at her brother's upper arms. Her two hands gripped them so tight it almost hurt him. She stared up into his face, tears washing her cheeks, yet a bright and beautiful smile on her face.

"I want to hug you, but I want to look at you as well. Oh, Michael!"

She finally released her grip only to throw her arms around him, hold him close, and lay her head on his chest, still crying.

Michael held her tight. He kissed the top of her head. He hadn't ever imagined it would be like this. He couldn't believe his sister was so pleased to see him. Only Beth had ever held him like this.

Her crying soon lessened and Mary stepped back. She dabbed at her face with her shawl and looked up at him, shamefaced.

"Oh, Michael, I'm sorry. What must you be thinking of me? Sure I could frighten you right back out the door with my carry-on." She thrust a hand into the pocket of her skirt and tugged out a handkerchief. She patted at her tears; but then her hands fell to her side, and she just stood and stared at him, still smiling.

"I can't believe it. You! Here at last." She studied him from head to foot. He was painfully aware of the ill-fitting clothes Frank's contact had provided. He must look such a sight. He should have remembered to comb his hair too. It was probably a mess.

"You look so handsome," she said, smiling up at him. "And you've grown so tall. And your beautiful, brown eyes! I should have known you from the eyes, Michael. Your beautiful, sad, brown eyes." She shook her head, "What am I thinking of. Sure my wits have left me entirely. Come in, Michael, come in."

She put a hand on his back and ushered him toward the small door at the rear of the shop. Before she followed him she deftly flipped the sign on the shop door to CLOSED.

"Go in, go in. Joe is up the yard pottering in the vegetable plot. Go on in, Michael, I'll call him."

Memories

Michael opened the door and bent his head slightly to enter the back room. He immediately had the strange feeling that he was stepping back in time, though nothing seemed familiar. It was a warm, welcoming feeling.

A young girl, her curly auburn hair tied back with a blue ribbon, sat on the stone-flagged floor playing with a doll. She looked up as Michael entered, and he saw she had the same startling blue eyes as Sheelagh. She looked like a tiny version of his sister. He smiled down at her.

"Hello."

Mary followed him in. "Look, Norah love. It's Michael. Your Uncle Michael! Come and say 'hello.'"

The little girl stood, still clutching her doll, and came toward him. "Say 'hello,' alanna. Have you lost your tongue?" her mother urged.

The child tucked herself shyly behind her mother's skirt and peeped out at him. Michael bent and held out his hand, palm up.

"Hello, Norah. I've heard about you. How are you?"

He smiled and continued to hold out his hand. She came, slowly, out from her hiding place and cautiously touched his fingers, then turned and ran to a half door at the rear of the room. She pushed up the latch and ran out into the yard. Michael stood and Mary shrugged.

"When she gets to know you, she won't leave you alone. Will you come and meet Joe?"

"Of course I will."

It all seemed so natural. He felt quite comfortable in this unfamiliar place, with this woman he didn't know. At least, didn't remember. He glanced briefly around the room before following Mary. The bleak, winter light poured through the half door, open at the top, and

255

through a single, deeply recessed window. On the window ledge sat a blue-flowered mug, filled with pale lemon primroses. Even *they* seemed vaguely familiar.

A red, well-worn armchair sat to one side of a range which filled almost one wall. Strawlike stuffing pushed out through a cluster of small holes on the side of the chair closest to the fire. Beside the chair was an open-weave basket piled high with what looked, to Michael, like clumps of dried earth. A larger, round-backed, wooden chair sat on the other side of the fireplace. A strangely familiar, earthy smell filled the room.

Despite the open door, the room was warm, heated by the range fire. Over the range, close to the low ceiling, stretched a long and cluttered mantelpiece. Several, faded, sepia-toned photographs caught Michael's attention. They were crowded on either side of an old, brass clock, behind which was stuffed a collection of letters and paperwork. Two brass candlesticks flanked the photographs, and beyond them were two plaster statues, one of the Infant of Prague and the other of Mary with the infant Jesus.

"Joe, Joe, come quick, come and see."

Through the half door Michael saw Mary calling to a man digging at the top of the yard. The man looked up, thrust the fork deep into the earth, and started down the sloped garden to the house, scattering chickens as he went. On his way he scooped the little girl up in his arms, kissed her nose, and came the rest of the way, smiling. Michael stepped into the yard and watched. The man was slim, but muscular, his coloring similar to Mary's. He wore heavy brown leather boots, and his kneed, brown corduroy pants were held up by both belt and suspenders. His collarless shirt was mud and sweat-stained. He looked like he hadn't shaved for a day or two.

"Look, Joe," Mary caught Michael's arm, showing him off. "It's Michael."

The man looked from his wife to Michael. "Michael! Your brother Michael? Jesus, man, where did you come from?" He put down his daughter and thrust out his hand. "Sure, we thought you dead and gone this long time."

"We did not, Joe Daly. Didn't Sheelagh tell us he was fine?"

Joe was shaking Michael's hand enthusiastically. "Ah, you know what I mean, woman," he laughed, "Don't be arguing with me in front of yer long lost brother. Come in, man, come in."

He opened the half door and stood back for Michael and the child to enter. He followed with Mary, giving her a hug and a quick kiss as they went.

"I'm sure you have Mary in a right old state. Are you going to make us a cup of tea, love, and we'll make the man welcome. Sit down, Michael, sit down. Make yourself at home." He gestured toward the large wooden chair and said in a lower voice, "I'd offer you something stronger than tea, but herself won't allow it in the house. Let me wash the dirt from my hands and I'll be with you."

Michael shook his head. "Tea will be fine."

He studied the photographs on the mantelpiece, peering closer at one particular picture of five young children. Mary joined him.

"Is that us?"

She nodded, "Aunty Bridgie had it taken, not long before you all went to England." She pointed to a small boy in the center of the picture. "That's you." He saw that the children's faces were solemn, and the little boy, that was him, looked as if he was about to cry. "That's Sheelagh," Mary continued, "and me, on either side of you, and then Colm and Pierce." She whirled to face him. "Oh, my Lord! Pierce! We have to tell Pierce. Joe, we have to let Pierce know!"

Joe dried his hands on the towel and laughed at her. "I know. I've already thought of that." He glanced at the clock. "He took a load to Ballyfin this morning. He should be passing here soon, on his way home. I'll go out and see if I can wave him down. If I've missed him, I'll walk over to Glendarrig and bring him back with me."

"Thank you, Joe. Do you need something to eat first?"

"Just give me a cup of tea in my hand, Mary love. Heaven forbid I should miss him."

Mary hurried to make the tea. "Can you give me a minute 'til I get this done, Michael, then we can talk in peace?"

"Of course," he said, and took the opportunity to examine the rest of the photographs.

Michael recognized Colm and Sheelagh in their Communion finery, and then his glance stopped at one of a small, serious-looking young boy with curly hair. The child's jacket and short pants both looked too large for him. Comparing it to the group picture, Michael assumed it was himself. At the far end of the mantelpiece he saw a larger picture of a young couple in old-fashioned clothes. The woman sat, hands clasped in her lap, staring out somber-faced. She wore a dark, full-length dress and unbuttoned coat. Her face was partly shadowed by a large-brimmed hat, heavily trimmed with flowers. A tall, well-built man stood beside her, wearing a three-piece suit with high-buttoned waistcoat and a looped watch chain. His hair was slicked down from a side parting and his top lip completely hidden by a bushy mustache. His high, starched collar looked tight and uncomfortable, and he had a small flower in the buttonhole.

"That's Mammy and the Da, on their wedding day," said Mary. "It doesn't do her justice though. She was beautiful."

She took the steaming kettle from the hearth and busied herself making tea. Michael continued to stare at the photograph of the parents he couldn't remember and would never know.

"Here's your tea, Michael. And there's yours, Joe, now off you go and watch for Pierce."

She brought her own cup and sat in the red chair. Michael sat opposite.

"Now! Tell me everything, Michael. How long will you be here for? Tell me about your home in England. What was it like going to school over there? Did you miss us? Tell me about the lady who took you in and what you're doing now. I know Sheelagh told me some of it, but I want to know everything, from the very beginning!"

Pierce

Mary listened, engrossed, as Michael told her about his life, his home, and his aunt. When she mentioned the letters she had written to him over the years, Michael said he only learned about them recently. That Sheelagh had told him about them. Even then, he said, when he confronted his aunt and Jim Porter, they avoided answering his questions about them. Michael saw how hurt and angry this made Mary. He was careful not to tell her how Porter, and his aunt, often referred to Irish people as riffraff and ne'er-do-wells.

He patiently answered all of her questions, even though he thought his story was boring. He couldn't really understand his sister's curiosity. He was far more interested in learning about her and about Doonbeg and Glendarrig where she said he was born. He had so many questions he wanted to ask, *if* he ever got the opportunity to ask them!

Norah crept onto her mother's lap. With her thumb thrust into her mouth and her blue-eyed gaze never leaving his face, she listened to her uncle almost as intently as her mother did.

Michael explained to Mary why he left Porter's shop and joined the RAF.

"You see!" said Mary, "Sheelagh didn't tell me all of that. She just said you left the shop and signed up. She didn't explain why." Her expression changed. "I'm so sorry those people died. Your friends." She shook her head, "It must be terrible over there, with the bombs and everything." Her expression changed again as she smiled, "And you're a pilot! A *real* pilot, fancy that! That must be so exciting, Michael. Aren't you nervous up there, so far from the ground?" Without waiting for a reply she added, "And what about Colm, Michael? The last we heard about him he was at that university and Sheelagh said that meant he didn't have to do military service."

Michael laughed at her rapid change of subjects and decided to tackle her last question first. He told her how Colm's situation had changed and how his university department closed because of the war. He explained how his brother *might* have been called up then but that a doctor said he had a hearing problem. Michael didn't say that Sheelagh didn't believe it.

"Colm is in Bristol now. His mother didn't want him staying in London, because of the Blitz."

"I'm sorry he's deaf. I hope it's not too bad. Aunty Bridgie, God rest her soul, got fierce deaf. I had to shout everything. But I'm glad that he's living in Bristol, near you and Sheelagh. It's been so difficult, imagining you all separated. I'm glad you are closer together now."

Michael wasn't sure he felt any closer to his brother, even if he *did* live in Bristol, but he didn't say anything.

When he told her of his time in Africa, she gently nudged Norah.

"Did you hear that, Norah love, your Uncle Michael has seen real, live lions and elephants?"

The child nodded, but her thumb remained firmly in place.

"How long can you stay with us, Michael? You *will* be staying, won't you?"

"I can stay the night, if that's all right with you?"

"Oh, Michael! Only one night? Of course that's all right, but I hoped you could stay for longer than that."

Just as Mary was asking him if he was courting, they heard the bell on the shop door tinkle and then Joe's voice, followed by another man's response. Michael jumped up and turned toward the door. Joe opened it, stepped into the small room and smiled at Michael, then stood to one side. A second man entered and stopped just inside the door. In that single, frozen moment Michael took in every detail of the brother he had forgotten.

Dressed in a similar fashion to Joe, Pierce wore stout workman's boots, heavy-duty corduroy trousers, held up by belt and braces, and a collarless shirt with the sleeves rolled up. He was slim-built, like Joe, with the ruddy complexion of a man who worked outdoors all his life. His hair was an unruly thatch of curls, the same, rich auburn as Sheelagh's, but Michael noticed that his brother's eyes were more green than blue, and they were as gentle as Sheelagh's were fiery.

No one spoke; even the room seemed to hold its breath. Pierce strode forward and threw his arms around his youngest brother. He hugged him tight and Michael hugged him back. With no need for words, the two brothers, separated for seventeen years, said almost everything they needed to say in that one, long, silent embrace. Everyone in the room remained quiet. As the brothers released their grip Michael became aware that another person stood in the doorway. She stood there, patiently watching them, a soft smile on her face and a single tear escaping down her cheek.

Pierce stepped back from Michael and followed his gaze. He held his hand out to the woman. "I'm sorry, Mavourneen." She took Pierce's hand and he brought her forward to Michael. "Michael, this is my fiancée. Maeve, Maeve Egan. Maeve, this is my brother, Michael."

She stepped forward, hastily brushed the tear from her face, and extended her hand.

"I'm pleased to meet you," said Michael, shaking her hand warmly. He turned back to his brother, "And you too, Pierce. It's been so long."

Mary noisily blew her nose into her handkerchief and chided her husband. "Joe, where are your manners? Will you fetch chairs for everyone?" She lifted Norah down from her lap. "Come on, alanna. We have tea to brew and a meal to fix. Sit down, Maeve. Were you working this morning?" She turned to Michael, "Maeve is a nurse in the hospital, above in Ballyfin." She turned back to the young woman, "You must be tired, Maeve. Sit down there," she indicated her own chair, "and I'll get you a nice cup of tea. Will you have one, Pierce? Sure you will. I'll see if I have any nice biscuits in the shop for you to have. Just 'til I get us something proper to eat." She beamed at her husband and her two brothers. "I wasn't expecting all this excitement and all these visitors today. But it's a grand, *grand* day."

Joe laughed at his wife's fluster. "Are you ready to take a breath now, Mary love? So that someone else can get a word in?" She blushed, and waved her hand at him in mock dismissal as she hurried past him into the shop. He pulled a chair from the table and set it near the others by the fire. "Sit down there, Pierce, and get to know your brother a bit while I distract your demented sister."

Pierce continued to stare at Michael. "I can't believe it. After all these years of wondering and waiting and then, here you are, just like that. Like it's any other day!" He shook his head. "How are you, Michael? How have you been?" He sat. "Dear God, I've missed you."

His head dropped and he was very still. Maeve leaned across to rest her hand on his arm. Michael too felt overcome. He waited, in silence. Pierce took a deep breath, recovered himself and started to ply his brother with all the questions Michael had just finished answering for Mary.

The meal was over and Norah put to bed before Michael got *his* turn to question *them.* He had almost as many questions, and his brother and sister were eager to answer, sharing their stories and welcoming him back into their lives. Maeve and Joe sat back in the dim twilight of the room, bystanders in this long-awaited reunion, as the two brothers and their sister laughed and cried, remembered and healed.

When the clock on the mantle chimed ten, Pierce said they would have to go. He must drive Maeve back to Ballyfin. "But I'll be over early in the morning. We have to spend more time together before you leave. I'll drive you to the station, Michael, for the late-morning train to Dublin. Won't that be enough time for you to meet up with your friend?"

Michael nodded. "I'm sure that will be fine."

He didn't know how he was going to say goodbye when the time came.

After Maeve and Pierce left, Mary showed Michael upstairs. She opened the door into a tiny bedroom. A single, narrow bed appeared crowded into one corner by an upright piano. A sturdy nightstand stood at the foot of the bed with a white, china commode on its bottom shelf. Mary bustled and fussed as she prepared his bed. She folded down the sheets, smoothed the faded quilt, and plumped up the feather pillows. She fetched a blue china jug and bowl from the other bedroom and placed them on the nightstand, then neatly arranged a towel beside them. She stepped back to look at her handiwork then excused herself again, saying she needed to get some soap from the shop. Michael took the opportunity to unpack the few things he'd brought with him and looked around for somewhere to put them. The nightstand, bed, and piano were the only pieces of furniture in the room. He put his belongings on top of the piano. It was filmed with a pale layer of dust, and its two brass candle sconces were dull and unpolished. He lifted the lid and silently fingered the keys, then turned to the window. Raising a corner of the crocheted, lace curtain, he peered briefly into the deserted main street before turning his attention back to the room. The wallpaper was a light brown, with tiny pink flowers. It had peeled away from the wall in one corner. A dark, oppressive picture of the Sacred Heart hung over the head of the bed.

Mary returned with the soap. As she removed the tissue paper wrapping and put the soap in the small china dish beside the bowl Michael smelled a faint whisper of lilacs, like the ones in Beth's garden.

Mary finally said goodnight. When she was gone, Michael undressed and climbed into bed. He lay awake for a long time after the house went silent. He felt so close to these people. Only now did he have time to think clearly about the day, his visit, and everything he'd heard. His family had made the past so vivid for him. He almost thought he *remembered* living in this house with all of them. Mary had told him how four of them slept in the single bed he now filled and how Aunty Bridgie had tried so hard to keep them all together as a family. Could he really remember the day Sheelagh, Colm, and himself were driven away on their father's cart? Did he miss Pierce, that day, when his eldest brother, was not there to say goodbye? Pierce remembered and still seemed upset by it.

And they had never forgotten me, he thought, even though I didn't know they existed until a few years ago. He felt angry he had to leave so soon. Why now, when he had just found them?

"As soon as this bloody war is over," he said quietly. "I *promise* I will be back."

Eventually, he slept.

Early Morning

Michael lay, snug in his bed, listening to the early-morning sounds of the house. He heard Mary and Joe whispering quietly in their bedroom next door. He heard his brother-in-law creep past his own bedroom door, step quietly down the stairs, and out through the shop. The bell tinkled softly as he did so. Michael even knew where his brother-in-law was going. The previous evening, Joe told him he had to deliver a load of turnips to Rathfen and hoped to be back in time to say goodbye. "Though I don't suppose you'll miss me with all the chattering Mary will be doing."

Michael heard Norah talking sleepily to her mother and Mary hushing her, saying she would wake her Uncle Michael.

How strange that sounded; it was hard to imagine himself as an uncle. What were uncles supposed to do? Michael listened as Mary ushered the little girl quietly downstairs. He wanted to join them, but he also wanted time to think again of all the stories he'd heard from his brother and sister the previous night. He wanted to be sure he would remember all the details.

He heard Mary's footsteps on the stairs again. She tapped gently on the door.

"Come in."

She carried the large black kettle from the range.

"I've some hot water for you, Michael. I'll put it in the jug." She tipped the steaming water into the blue and white china jug with the chipped handle. "Did you sleep well? That old bed has seen better days I'm afraid. If I'd known you were coming, I'd have got Joe to buy a new one from McNamara's in Ballyfin. They have all kinds of beds in there, now that they've opened their furniture department. I've been meaning to do it for a while now."

Michael hoisted himself up in the bed and sat watching as she poured the water.

"I slept fine, thank you, Mary. It's a really cozy bed. It's hard to believe I slept here before. It seems like a whole different world."

She put the empty kettle down on the floor and sat on the end of the bed.

"We're not very grand here, I'm afraid. We don't have servants and such, like you do over in England."

"Believe me, Mary, everyone doesn't have servants. We certainly don't. It's just me and Aunty Wyn."

"Sheelagh called her a dragon. Is she really nasty, Michael? Aunty Bridgie would have been brokenhearted if she'd thought you were unhappy." He saw her clench her hands together in her lap. "So would I."

"She's a tough lady all right, but I don't think she means harm. I don't think she's had an easy life herself. Her brother is a pretty tough character too. That's the man I worked for, in the shop."

Mary nodded. The previous evening she questioned him for a long time about Jim and Edith Porter and why Michael didn't stay with them.

He had shrugged as he answered. "I don't remember living with them at all. *I* thought I'd always been with Aunty Wyn. I suppose I was too young. And it never occurred to me to ask why she took me in. Lord knows why. I think part of me was always afraid to ask, in case I didn't like the answer." He shrugged again, feeling a little embarrassed. "It can't have been easy for her, being a spinster and all. I suppose I took me in because she wanted company and some security for her old age."

Michael did not really want to talk about the Porters again this morning, or if he had been happy or not. He glanced down at the quilt, "Did you sew this? Aunty Wyn sews, but she makes dresses and things, not stuff like this."

Mary nodded. "Aunty Bridgie and me made it, after you all left. She said it would help us to remember you all. See," she pointed to a pale lemon square of material, worn thin with age and washing. "That's a piece of Mammy's blouse and that red one there is a bit of an old ribbon I used to wear before Aunty Bridgie cut my hair. We put pieces from all of us around Mammy's." She pointed to another square.

"That's a bit from Pierce's shirttail and that," she pointed again, "was an old shirt you wore, though it was really a hand-me-down from Pierce and Colm."

He studied the quilt, shaking his head in disbelief. "So much of all of us, just in these small pieces of material."

They were both quiet. Norah called up the stairs. "I've finished my toast and milk, Mammy. Can I come up and see Uncle Michael now?"

Mary jumped up. "No, you can't, alanna." She hurried to the door. "We'll let the poor man get up and dress first. I'm coming now." She turned to Michael. "I'll go and make you some breakfast, Michael. Take your time. Come down when you're ready. I've to open the shop; the milk will be delivered directly. You could set your clock by Mattie O'Brien's deliveries."

"Thanks for the hot water."

She nodded and left. Michael snuggled back under the quilt. He would have to bring Beth to meet these people. They were a *real* family, just like hers. She would love them, he knew she would.

Michael washed, dressed, and came downstairs, tempted by the smell of bacon frying. Norah played with her doll on the stone-flagged floor, and Mary stood over the range turning bacon and sausages in the pan. Having greeted the child, Michael sat by the fire and watched his sister. Pierce arrived as Mary removed the bacon and sausages from the pan. She pressed two thick slices of bread into the sizzling fat.

"Perfect timing, Pierce Kelly. I suppose you'll have some of this."

"That would be grand, Mary. I've delivered two loads already this morning, with only a cup of tea to sustain me." He glanced at the clock, "And it's still only eight o'clock. Good morning, Michael, did you sleep well?"

Mary cracked four large eggs in beside the frying bread.

"Put some knives and forks on the table there, Pierce and Michael. This will be ready directly."

The brothers did as she asked and Mary brought two laden plates to the table.

"Wow! I'd forgotten what a real breakfast looked like," said Michael, then pointed and added, "What are they?"

Pierce laughed, "Do you not remember black-and-white pudding, Michael? Shame on you!"

"Pudding?"

Mary frowned at Pierce. "It's not that kind of pudding, Michael. Taste it, I'm sure you'll like it."

Norah watched as he ate.

Michael wasn't sure about the pudding; it tasted spicy and had a lot of small lumps in it. But he certainly wasn't going to offend his sister.

"It's all great, Mary," he said as he sipped a cup of steaming tea, hoping to rid his mouth of the unfamiliar taste. "Thank you. Even Mrs. Howard didn't cook a breakfast like this. And I haven't had a real egg in over a year. We usually get the powdered ones. They're pretty awful."

That started another whole discussion on the war, and Hitler, and how people were managing in Britain with the increasingly tough rationing.

"It's not too bad, I suppose," said Michael, accepting another sausage, pronging it on his fork, and holding it up. "We get these all right, but over there we dare not ask what's in them. Frank says he thinks they're mostly sawdust."

Pierce and Mary laughed and explained that they, too, had rationing, "Even though we're not in the war. They say it's because the shipping lanes are dangerous. Anything that comes from abroad is rationed."

"I have to say I miss the sugar," added Mary. "And the sweets. But at least we have plenty of this."

She offered Michael more bacon and sausage. He shook his head and thanked her again. He was conscious of the time passing, and he wanted to talk more with his brother before he had to leave.

Once Mary had cleared the table and washed the dishes she excused herself, saying she must work in the shop for a while.

"I'm sorry, Michael. I don't want to be away for a moment of your visit, but I *have* to get a few things done. Will you be all right here, with this lummox of a brother of ours?" She put her arm affectionately on Pierce's shoulder.

Pierce looked up and smiled at her. "Are you not afraid we'll talk about you when you're gone, Mary?" he said.

"I'm far more afraid I'll miss something Michael has to say," she replied. "It's such a short visit." She patted Pierce's shoulder. "But I have to be out there for the women collecting their milk. Come on, Norah love; let's see what we have to do in the shop."

She took the child's hand and they left.

The brothers spoke of Pierce's haulage business and how Pierce had taken Joe as his business partner. They spoke of their father and the woman he married after their mother's death. Michael asked Pierce questions he had been reluctant to ask Mary. She didn't seem comfortable speaking about their father and Michael had not wanted to upset her. Pierce tried to answer all his questions and added.

"She's right, you know. Mary, I mean. Sure you're hardly here and you'll be gone."

"I'll be back, don't worry." Michael grinned, "You'll be sick of me before you know it."

Pierce's smile faded. "No, Michael. Never! This is your home. It seems like Colm has taken completely to his new life over there, I can't imagine him coming back too often. But you seem like you belong here. I know we'll see you again."

Michael felt a little awkward, unsure how to respond, unused to a close family of his own like this. He remembered how often he had envied the Howards.

"I can't wait to bring Beth here. I know she'll love it."

"That's your fiancée?"

Michael nodded.

"When are you getting married?"

"Next year, I hope, as soon as I'm twenty-one. Mr. Porter and Aunty Wyn won't give their permission, so we have to wait."

"Twenty-one! Sure you're only a boy still, Michael Kelly. I'm just turned twenty-nine and I'm only now thinking about getting married."

"I thought you and Maeve were engaged."

"As indeed we are, but that's no reason to rush things, Michael. Sure, shouldn't we enjoy the engagement first?"

"I can't wait to marry Beth," said Michael. "It seems like we've been together for a long time already." He looked up at his brother. "Perhaps you could come over for the wedding, you and Maeve? And Mary and Joe, of course, and Norah."

Pierce shook his head. "Not as long as the war is on, Michael. I think we'd find it a bit hard to get over there at the moment, with all the travel restrictions."

Michael knew his brother was right, but the thought of the whole family being together was such a great idea.

"Perhaps it will be over by then," he said, without conviction. "Who knows?" He thought about his tattered atlas, where he still pencil-shaded the occupied, or enemy, countries. Italy, Japan, Hungary, and Greece were all darkened now, even France because it was being run by the Vichy government and the newspapers said they were Germany's puppets.

"At least the Americans are now in it with us," he said.

Pierce was nodding his agreement as Mary hurried in from the shop.

"Joe has just arrived. Will I get a bite to eat for you all, before Michael leaves?" She looked from one brother to the other.

Her husband followed her in, carrying Norah. "Will you relax for a bit, love? I've put up the CLOSED sign. Is that all right? So we can have an hour's peace before Michael here has to go."

"We've not long finished eating, Mary. I certainly don't need any more," said Pierce.

"So what has you both looking so serious?" she said.

Pierce stood from the table and stretched, his fingers almost touching the low ceiling. As he sat again he continued. "We were talking about the war, and getting married. Both very serious subjects, don't you know, Mary." He smiled at his sister.

"Does that mean you're finally going to make an honest woman of that poor Maeve, Pierce Kelly?" she responded. "Haven't you been courting her for years now? Isn't it about time?"

"Now, now, Mary," said her husband. "Didn't it take me years to talk you into it?"

She turned and scowled at her husband. "There was good reason for that delay, as well you know, Joe Daly!" she scolded. "Michael, don't mind these two. Would *you* like a little something to eat before you leave?"

Michael protested he was full and couldn't eat another thing.

"She's trying to make up for years of not being able to feed you up. Isn't that right, love?" said Joe.

Mary smiled, but a faint blush colored her cheeks.

The next hour was taken up with questions, answers, and fond remembrances—all the things they wanted to say before their brother left and it was too late.

Then it was time.

Michael collected his small bag from the bedroom, shook hands with Joe, and bent to say goodbye to Norah. The child threw her arms around his neck and gripped tightly. He scooped her up and, with Norah in his arms, led the small group through the shop and out to where the lorry was parked at the curbside.

"I'll drive him over, Joe," said Pierce. "I should be back before you go out again."

Joe nodded. Pierce rounded the lorry and climbed into the driver's side. Michael tossed his bag into the cab and gently set Norah down. He stood, looking at Mary. She had begun to cry again.

"Don't forget us, will you, Michael?" she said between quiet sobs.

He opened his arms and she went to him. They hugged for a long time.

"He's going to miss the train, Mary love," said Joe, as he gently pulled his wife away.

Michael nodded. "I promise I'll be back," he said. "And how could I forget you, Mary? I've only just found you. All of you! I'll be back as soon as I can, I promise. And I'll bring Beth with me."

Mary stepped back. "We'd like that. Wouldn't we, Joe? We would love to see you both, as soon as you can come." She dabbed at her eyes with the corner of her apron; then gently pushed Norah forward. "Say goodbye to your Uncle Michael, Norah."

The child thrust her arms up and Michael bent to her. He gave her a hug and a kiss, then straightened, shook hands again with Joe, kissed Mary, and climbed into the truck. Pierce already had the engine running, and once Michael was seated he edged the lorry slowly away from the curb.

Mary reached up and put her hand on the edge of the open window, "Please stay safe, Michael. I couldn't bear to lose you, now that we've found you."

She stepped back, and she, Joe, and Norah waved until the vehicle rounded the bend and Michael lost sight of them.

The guard was blowing his whistle as the two brothers arrived on the station platform. Pierce ran to the train and yanked open a carriage door. Michael threw in his bag and hastily jumped in after it. He turned, pulled the door closed, and opened the window as the train continued to gather speed out of the station.

"I *will* be back, Pierce, I promise," he shouted.

Pierce ran alongside the train. "You'd better, or Mary will never speak to you again!"

Michael laughed. Pierce reached the end of the platform and stopped running. He raised his hand and held it aloft in a final farewell. Michael waved in return and gave his brother a surreptitious salute.

A Race

Frank paced the platform while anxiously watching the time on the station clock. As soon as the Ballyfin train pulled in he scanned the small crowd of passengers for Michael. When Frank saw him alight from the third class carriage, at the back of the train, he waved his arms and whistled. Michael waved back.

He cupped his hands around his mouth and shouted, "Hurry, Michael. We've only got a few minutes." Michael hastened his pace. As he drew closer Frank added, "I thought you weren't going to make it. Your train is nearly an hour late. We're going to have to run." He snatched Michael's bag. "Follow me."

The two young men clattered down the stairs of the underpass, raced through the narrow tunnel, and ran up the steps on the other side, taking them two at a time. The guard slammed the last door closed and raised his flag just as they arrived at the platform. This time it was Michael who snatched open a carriage door. He jumped in, missed his footing and tumbled in a heap onto the grimy carriage floor. Frank followed, falling over his friend. Someone slammed the door closed behind them, and the two remained on the floor, breathless and laughing.

"By Jayz, that was close," said Frank, finally sitting up and brushing dust and dirt from the knees of his trousers. "I was already imagining the court-martial. This is the last train today. miss this and we'd have been on report and all hell would have broken loose. You put the heart across me, Michael Kelly, cutting it so fine."

Michael stood and brushed himself down. "Sorry, I thought I'd have plenty of time. I wasn't to know it was going to be so late."

He helped his friend up from the floor, and they settled themselves, facing each other, on the wooden seats. Both were quiet for a while, each occupied with his own thoughts. Frank broke the silence as the train rattled through the outskirts of Dublin.

"Well, Michael, me boyo, how was it? Did you find them? Did it go all right?"

Michael nodded. His eyes drifted over Frank's head to a faded sepia photograph of Bray fixed on the wood-paneled carriage wall. He noticed that the women in the photograph wore full-length dresses and carried lace umbrellas against the heat of a watery Irish sun. The gentlemen wore bowler hats and suits with waistcoats. How old *was* this train?

Frank remained quiet and, eventually, Michael lowered his gaze and looked at his friend.

"It was terrific, Frank," he said. "It really was. They are all so nice. They truly seemed to be happy to see me," he added, with a tinge of surprise in his voice.

"And why wouldn't they? Aren't you the prodigal son and all that?"

Michael smiled. "I'm hardly that! But I know what you mean."

They spent the rest of the journey exchanging stories about their brief visits. Michael was surprised that Frank could remember as much as he did. Most of his time seemed to have been spent in various Dublin bars drinking pints of "Arthur's best."

"I hadn't realized how much I missed Mr. Guinness's fine brew, Mikey. You know, I was almost resolved to go AWOL last night, but the banging head I had on me this morning persuaded me to go back to that watery stuff you people call beer."

When the train pulled into Dundalk it was already getting dark. Michael and Frank disembarked along with the rest of the passengers. Michael winced at the icy blast of wind that whistled through the station, promising snow. He tugged up the collar of his jacket and the two men left the station. They headed to the outskirts of town, where Frank had arranged to meet the carter.

There was no one there.

"If that bastard doesn't turn up, I will personally find him and ring his scrawny neck," said Frank as he paced back and forth at the side of the road.

"You're sure we were to meet him here?"

"Of course I am. Sure isn't this where he dropped us off? You heard me tell him, didn't you? Half an hour after the Dundalk train gets in, to meet us here, by the signpost. What's complicated about that? And it's well above a half hour already!"

They waited for a long time. Michael sat on a large rock watching his friend pace. Frank stamped his feet on the ground to keep them warm.

"What will we do if he doesn't turn up?"

"I'm not even going to think about it, Mikey. He'll be here directly. I know he will."

The angry Irishman continued to pace.

The chill wind numbed Michael's fingers, ears, and nose. He stared toward the town, hoping to catch sight of the missing carter, but couldn't see far in the dark. Thick clouds scudded over the moon, and the shadowed countryside was only visible occasionally. He strained to hear the sound of a horse and cart, but only the hoot of an owl and the wind rattling through the leafless hedge broke the silence; that and Frank's muttered curses. Michael didn't feel anxious at all. So what if they didn't get back? He could always return to Doonbeg, or Glendarrig. They would be glad to have him back. He could stay there, live there. The British couldn't come and find him and he was sure his family wouldn't give him up.

As the clouds cleared momentarily, he again stared down the thin ribbon of the road into town and thought he saw a shadow moving in the distance.

"Is that him?"

Frank pivoted and peered to where Michael indicated, but the clouds had closed in again.

"It better be, Michael. It bloody well better be. We must have been here over an hour."

Ten more minutes passed before they heard the distant creak of cartwheels, the slow clop of a horse's hooves, and the muffled sound of what could be a man singing. As the sound neared and the voice became clearer, Frank swore again. "He's drunk! The bastard's drunk."

Michael stood and waited patiently until the dark shadow became visible as horse, cart, and driver.

"How are ye, lads? Have ye been waiting long?"

"Bloody right! Where have you been, you bloody amadan? Don't you know we have to get back across the border as quick as we can?"

"Ah sure, don't fret yourself laddie. Amin't I here now? Climb up, boys, climb up, and we'll be on our way."

The two airmen threw their bags into the cart; Frank followed and pulled his friend up after him. The carter twisted in his seat.

"Are ye right, lads? I put a bit of straw back there for ye, for comfort like."

"Would you, for the love of God, get going? The sooner we are across the border the happier I'll be," snapped Frank.

Michael smiled at his friend; he'd never seen him this upset.

"Relax, Frank, we're on our way."

"I don't know what has you so bloody relaxed, my friend. There could be all kinds of military personnel out there." He gestured vaguely into the darkness. "And I, for one, don't want to end up in the cells."

"We had no problem getting here."

Frank made no response, and they traveled in silence for a while. The carter stopped singing and Michael thought he might even be asleep, but the horse kept moving in a slow, plodding trudge and seemed to know where he was going. Everything was peaceful for some time.

Michael heard the voices first. He kicked Frank, who sat up from where he'd been lying in the straw.

"What? What's wrong?"

Michael grabbed his friend's arm. "Be quiet, Frank."

"What?" whispered the Irishman quietly, looking around him.

"Can't you hear them?"

Frank was silent for a moment, then, "Shite," he muttered.

At the same time the carter began to sing again, sounding even more drunk than before.

"What are you doing, you stupid bastard, do you want to get us killed?" hissed Frank.

Michael's heart thundered in his chest. The warm, almost invincible feeling he had all day suddenly evaporated and a cold fear took its place. "Make him be quiet, Frank."

The carter sang even louder but, as he took a breath between verses, he whispered. "Get under the straw you eejits, and hide your bags too."

The two men scrambled to lie down, their bags by their sides, and tossed the straw over themselves as best they could. The carter stopped singing and spoke loudly to his horse. "Would you come on there, you flea-bitten ould nag? Do you want me arse in a sling for being home late, again?" Then he broke into another song.

"Halt! Who goes there?"

Michael heard the click of a gun bolt. Through the latticework of straw covering his face he saw the soft glow of a kerosene lamp.

"Whoa! Whoa there, girl." The cart slowed and he spoke again. "Ah Jayz, lads, are you going to get me in more trouble with the missus?" The cart stopped. "Wasn't she expectin' me back from the market a while back? What is it ye want, lads? What are ye doing out here in the middle of nowhere on a miserable cold night like this?" he belched noisily.

"What's your name, old man?"

"Brendan O'Duill, a loyal subject of his majesty and a law-abiding citizen going about his law-abiding business." The carter belched again, then hiccupped.

One of the soldiers laughed. "Let him go, Dave. He's just another drunken local."

"What do you have in the cart, old man?" said the first voice.

"Straw and pig shite, yer honor. Sure, didn't I tell you I'm back from the market? I took down two of my pigs. They can't rear pigs there, not like we do here. All skin and bone, their's are, only good for glue. They need our animals to breed from. But look for yourselves, lads, nothing like a bit of fresh pig shite for clearing yer head."

"Let him go, Dave, I'm not going to poke about in pig muck."

"Do you live close by, O'Duill?"

"I do, yer honor, just over the next ridge. Sure ye are welcome to join the wife and meself fer breakfast if you like. Once I've had a couple of hours sleep."

"Yes, right, thanks. Be on your way, old man, and be careful! You could get yourself shot wandering around out here drunk at this hour of the night."

The old man wished them goodnight, urged the horse forward, and began singing again. He sang for some time, while the two airmen remained silent and hidden in the cart. Eventually he pulled the animal to a halt and spoke softly.

"I think you can probably get up now, lads."

They pushed the straw away and sat up.

"That was close. Thanks, O'Duill."

"Miserable bastards!" muttered the old man. "What the hell are they doing out here? Nothing better to do with themselves, that's what. Don't they know there's a war on? They should be fighting them bloody Germans, not harassing the likes of us. Now, sit tight, lads, and let's get you to the house before we have any other encounters."

Once they were back in uniform, O'Duill drove them into Newry. From there the two men were soon thumbing a lift back to camp. They arrived at the gates with half an hour to spare. The sentry wrinkled his nose as they got close.

"Good God, lads, where did you two spend your leave?"

He hastily checked their papers, waved them through, and suggested they clean up before they went back on duty.

As they walked toward their barracks, Frank gave Michael a sideways glance, smiled, and winked.

Impatience

Michael and Beth sat in the Howard's kitchen. Four months had passed since his trip to Doonbeg. Though he had given hints, he hadn't directly mentioned it in his letters, afraid the censors might read them. Now, finally, he was home and able to tell her everything.

"I asked Mary and Pierce if they would come over for the wedding, with Joe of course, and Norah and Maeve. But they said it wasn't possible, what with the war and everything. It would have been perfect if they could."

It was summertime, and the back door was open to let in the warm, evening sunshine.

"Pierce is engaged to be married too, isn't he?" asked Beth.

"Yes, but I don't know when it will happen." Michael smiled. "He says he wants to enjoy the engagement first. Mary said he's just too lazy. She says she's going to have a word with Maeve and tell her to give him a push."

"They sound so nice, Michael. I'm so glad you went to visit them." She suddenly turned to him and frowned. "Though I would have killed you, Michael Kelly, if you had got caught. Have you no sense at all?"

He grinned and twisted his features into a funny face. She laughed.

"I can't wait to meet them."

They were quiet. A blackbird sang and Michael glanced out into the garden to where the Anderson shelter stood. Every time he saw the shelter it reminded him of the time he and the Howards had built it. Grass grew over the top now, softening its outline, disguising its function. He looked back at Beth. She was watching him.

"I know. I think of them every time I look at it too." She sighed, then smiled up at him. "Did you know Paul says he will give me away

278

at the wedding? And Evelyn is going to be my bridesmaid. Paul said he will get the leave somehow."

"Oh, great! So you're going to steal my best man! What am I supposed to do?"

She laughed. "I hadn't thought about that, sorry. You'll have to find someone else. What about your friend, Frank?"

He nodded. "Good idea, I'll ask him when I get back. I'll have to bring him home with me though, some time, so that you can meet him before the wedding. If we can."

"Are we going to set the date while you're here, Michael? Mum can't wait to send out invitations."

"I don't mind. When do you want to do it?"

"I think your birthday would be a perfect date."

"Really?"

"Why not?"

"May the second it is then! … But we don't have anywhere to live, Beth."

"I know. But, as long as the war is on you're only going to be home for short leaves, like now. You can stay here then. Mum said so. She says when the war's over, we can find our own place."

He liked the idea of coming home to the friendliness of the Howard house. It would be far more welcoming than the cold comfort of Glenfrome Road. Then he thought of Aunty Wyn and his mood changed. "I suppose it's time to tackle Aunty Wyn then? Will you come round and meet her? We can tell her we've set the date. You have to meet her some time, I suppose."

Beth nodded. "Would you like to invite her around here for tea? Mum said that might be a bit easier."

"I doubt she would come, but I'll ask her. For when?"

"You're only here for ten days. Let's get it over with. How about tomorrow?"

"I'll ask her," he said with a shrug.

"*Now* I'm nervous," said Beth, making a wry face.

Michael stretched across the table and took her hand. "Don't be. We're getting married, and if she doesn't like it, then that's just too bad. Come on, let's go for a walk. It's a lovely evening."

Wyn sat beside the empty fireplace, her Bible on her lap. Michael sat at his usual place beside the table.

"I'm busy. I have an alteration that needs doing before Wednesday," she said as she polished her glasses with the hem of her apron.

"You only need to come for an hour, just to meet Beth and her mother and sisters, and have some tea."

"I don't have the time."

"What about Thursday? You'll have finished the alteration by then, surely?"

"I have a fitting to do."

"All day?"

Wyn stared at him. Anger flared her nostrils, and her lips thinned to a fine line.

"I will not be bullied."

"You're not being bullied. You're being invited to tea, that's all."

"I don't want to go to tea."

"But you have to meet Beth."

"I don't *have* to do anything I don't want to do."

She opened the Bible, put her glasses firmly into place on the end of her nose, and began to read to herself, tracing the words with a thin, gnarled finger. The conversation was over.

Michael stood and looked down at her. "You are such a stubborn woman! I'm going out now, but I tell you this, Aunty Wyn. You *will* have to meet her. I'm going to marry Beth and you *will* meet her, whether you want to or not."

"… So, I will just have to bring you around to the house, then she can't duck out."

Michael had finished relating the conversation he'd had with his aunt, to Beth.

"I don't know what else we can do. I don't know what's got into her. She seems to be getting more and more difficult as she gets older."

Beth squeezed his hand. "That's probably it, she's old. She's probably lonely as well, especially with you away. She's not used to company. The war must be very frightening for her, as well."

Michael appreciated the excuses his fiancée was making for his aunt, but *he* was not as ready to excuse her.

"It's hard for everyone, why should *she* be an exception? You'd think she'd enjoy the company for a change. I'm sorry about this Beth. Do you mind coming over?"

"No, of course not, if that's how it has to be. I just hope she likes me."

Michael doubted it, in the mood his aunt was in, but he didn't say that.

"She says she's busy tomorrow and Thursday, so how about Friday evening? I can come over and collect you."

They agreed and Beth spent the rest of the week trying to decide what she should wear.

Wyn was carrying washing in from the yard when they arrived. She closed the back door and turned to see Michael and Beth standing at the hall door into the kitchen.

"Aunty Wyn, this is Beth Howard, my fiancée. Beth, this is my Aunty Wyn."

Beth stepped forward and extended her hand. Wyn ignored the gesture, brushed passed the young woman, and put the basket of washing on the table.

"Aunty Wyn, you can do that later."

She ignored Michael and began to fold the washing.

Beth spoke. "I have heard a lot about you, Miss Porter. I understand you are a wonderful dressmaker. A friend of my mother's, Mrs. Wilkins, said you made her daughter's wedding dress. She said it was beautiful."

Wyn gave the faintest nod of her head at the compliment and continued to fold pillowcases.

"I was wondering," Beth continued, "if you would consider making my wedding dress. If I can get some material, that is?"

Both Wyn and Michael stared at her in surprise. Michael raised his eyebrows and Beth blushed.

"I don't *make* clothes any more, young lady. My eyesight is too bad for that, and my fingers are too stiff. I only do alterations these days." She turned her attention back to her task. "And even *that* is becoming increasingly difficult," she added. She stopped folding again and gave Michael a withering look. "I had hoped my ward would look after me when I became too old to fend for myself, but obviously he has no such intention. I am to be put into the workhouse! *That's* how it's to be, I gather. So forgive me if I am not delighted that you have wheedled him away."

Beth's blush deepened.

"Oh, for God's sake, Aunty Wyn! There aren't any workhouses anymore! And even if there were, there's no way I'd let you go into one. I send you most of my pay now, and Beth and I will continue to make sure you are minded, even after we get married. Won't we, Beth?"

"Of course we will."

Wyn had now abandoned the washing and stood glaring at the young couple, her arms folded tightly at her waist.

"I'll thank you not to take the Lord's name in vain in my house, Michael Kelly." She turned to Beth, "And that might well be ... until your first child comes along! Then I'll be quickly forgotten. No one knows better than me the cost of rearing a child *and* the little thanks you get."

Michael threw his eyes to heaven in exasperation. "I give up. Come on, Beth. I'm sorry I brought you. I didn't think it would be as bad as this."

He put his arm lightly around Beth's waist and guided her toward the door. Beth took a few steps then twisted away from his arm and turned to face his aunt.

"I'm sorry you are not happy about our engagement, Miss Porter. I love Michael very much. You have reared him on your own, so I think you must take the credit for the gentle and kind person he is. I hope we will meet again soon, Miss Porter, and that you will give me a chance to show you how much I do, and will, care for Michael. And for you."

She turned and walked through the hall to the front door. Michael followed. He closed the front door behind them and whispered, "Wow! That was quite a speech, my shy little Beth. Thank you."

They returned to Beth's home. Mrs. Howard was surprised to see them back so soon.

"My aunt is being as difficult as ever," said Michael, dropping into a kitchen chair with a sigh. Mother and daughter exchanged glances and Beth nodded.

"She didn't make it easy, Mum. But I'm sure she'll come round eventually."

That Sunday Michael accompanied his aunt to Mass, as he usually did when he was home. When the service was over, they slowly filed out of the church along with the other parishioners but, instead of beginning the brisk walk home, Wyn stepped to one side and waved Michael on.

"You go ahead home. I want to have a quick word with my brother. I'll be home shortly. Put the kettle on when you get there."

It was the most she had said to him since Beth's visit. Michael nodded and left, guessing that his aunt wanted to complain about him, yet again, to Mr. Porter.

The kettle had boiled, and he was heating the teapot when Michael heard the distinctive sound of Porter's car outside. The old man must have given Wyn a lift home. That was a rare occurrence; he seldom drove her home and never since petrol rationing had begun. He collected his rent monthly now, his aunt had told Michael. He had also told Wyn that walking was good exercise anyway, though Michael had never seen Porter walking anywhere if he could drive.

Brother and sister both came into the house. Perhaps he was collecting the rent. The two men exchanged chill glances, but neither spoke. Wyn stood by the dresser and slowly removed her hat and gloves. Porter took a seat at the kitchen table, indicating that Michael should sit too.

"I have something I want to say to you, young man."

They had hardly spoken since Michael walked out of the shop almost two years before. What could the old man want with him now, Michael wondered.

"I understand you have been having an affair."

Wyn removed her coat and took it, her hat, and gloves out to the hallstand.

Michael stood abruptly, almost toppling his chair backward as he did so.

"I have *not* been having a bloody affair. I am engaged to a young lady of impeccable character, whom I have known for some time. In fact, she is the sister of my best friend. How *dare* you call it an affair! If you and Aunty Wyn hadn't refused permission, we would be married already. As it is, sir, we have decided that we will be married on my twenty-first birthday, when your permission is no longer required."

"Sit down, boy, sit down and watch your language. There's a lady present."

Michael sat. Wyn returned from the hall and quietly took her place in the rocking chair beside the fireplace. Porter cleared his throat and continued.

"Despite your hasty departure from my employment, I always considered you a good worker, boy. The late Mr. Swinton told me of your studious application to tasks in the storeroom, and Ramsey was most impressed with your aptitude on the shop floor."

Michael stared at the red-faced man and wondered what on earth he was talking about. Porter cleared his throat and continued.

"In the light of their recommendations and in spite of your hot-headed behavior in the past, I have decided to make you my official heir and the ultimate beneficiary of Porter's Clothing and Haberdashery Emporium. After I'm dead and gone, of course," he added hastily.

"But, I'm in the RAF."

Porter dismissed Michael's comment with a wave of his hand.

"Yes, yes, boy, I appreciate that. I'm talking about when the war is over. When it's over you will return to the shop, to take your proper place there. Ramsey is well above retirement age now. He's only staying on because of the war, don't you know. Most suitable replacements are away at war." His glance flickered to his sister before he concluded, "So you will take his place."

Michael was astonished; he didn't know what to say. He'd given up any idea of inheriting the shop or even having a civil relationship with Porter again. Yet suddenly, here he was, offering Michael the manager's position and ultimately store ownership!

"I'm not sure I understand, sir."

"Perfectly simple, boy. That's what families do. They look after each other. I think maybe you have lost sight of that a bit, lad. Family first, that's how it has to be. How it *should* be! So, now all you have to do is give me an assurance that you will give up this silly notion of marrying this chit, and you will be able to move forward and focus on your new career. As soon as the war is over, of course."

He sat back in his seat and gave a slight nod of satisfaction.

Michael stood again, more slowly this time. He looked from the large, balding man to the gray-haired old woman sitting in the rocking chair, her eyes fixed on her hands, which were clasped primly in her lap. He shook his head.

"I can't believe you would stoop to doing something like this." He spoke quietly, evenly, controlling his voice. Then he looked back at Porter and contempt overcame his control.

"You have no idea of the meaning of family. Families *care* for each other. *You* don't *really* care about me."

He turned back to Wyn, his voice rising in volume. "You talked him into this, though I don't know how. This is what *you* want, not me."

Michael bowed his head, unsure what to say next. His hands gripped the back of his chair. Anger choked him. He was afraid if he didn't control his temper he would hit something, or someone. He took a deep breath and regained control.

"I have lived here for as long as I can remember." He stared hard at his aunt, "I have tried to please you, tried to make you proud of me. I have always been grateful that you took me in and that you didn't send me to an orphanage. But you both lied to me, and you let me think my real family didn't care. And they did! You even stopped their letters to me, though I'm not sure why or how."

His aunt looked up in surprise.

"Yes, I know you did. Mary told me she wrote."

He turned and pointed a trembling finger at Porter, "And it was to *your* address, so I hold you both to blame."

Porter stood; his face red as a turkey's wattle. He, too, pointed his finger, "Don't you take that tone with me, young man."

"I'll speak to you however I like. And let me make this quite clear, to both of you. Beth Howard and I *will* marry, and it *will* be on May the second of next year."

He turned his back on Porter and addressed Wyn.

"I don't intend to stay in this house any longer. I'm going to pack my things. I'll be moving out today."

Wyn looked up at him, eyebrows arched and lips thin. "And where do you think you will go? Do you intend to live with that hussy even before you are married?"

"I'll get digs, not that it's any of your business anymore," he snapped, then took a deep breath. "I'm truly sorry it has come to this, Aunty Wyn." He looked at Porter, who was now fumbling with his pocket watch. "As for your offer, sir, I don't want your charity, or your business. I assume it was just an attempt to split up Beth and me anyway. You can keep your bloody shop and I wish you joy of it!"

He left the kitchen and took the stairs, two at a time, to his room. In only a few minutes his belongings were packed and, with a final look around the small sewing room that had been his home for seventeen years, he stepped out into the hall and closed the door. He glanced at the monkey knocker on the door and touched it, briefly, before hefting his kit bag onto his shoulder and descending the stairs. There had been no sound from the kitchen while he packed, and no one spoke now. Michael opened the front door and left the house without a backward glance.

Resolution

"You can stay in Paul's room. I'm sure Mum won't mind. I'm so sorry, Michael."

"It's been coming for a long time. I really did try, Beth. I tried to make excuses for her, tried to understand why she was so angry all the time. But I give up. Life's too short. I could be dead tomorrow."

"Don't say things like that. Don't worry. I'm sure she'll come round, wait and see."

"Yeah, well, I'm not going to waste time fighting with her anymore."

He hadn't told Beth everything that happened that morning. He was ashamed of the Porters; he didn't want her to know how they had tried to split up Beth and himself.

"Michael. I had an idea. I know it will probably sound silly, but it might be nice if it worked."

He smiled at her. "What are you scheming now?"

"Well, our wedding date is set for your birthday next year, right?"

He nodded.

"And Pierce and Maeve are engaged and going to get married too?"

"Yes, sometime. Why?"

"I just wondered ..."

"What is it, Beth? What's in your head?"

She took a deep breath.

"Well, I know you said you would like them to come to our wedding, and I'm *sure* they would like you to go to theirs, but that's probably not going to happen, as long as the war is on."
"So?"

"What if we had the *two* weddings, on the same day, at the same time? Then it would almost be like we were at each other's wedding,

287

wouldn't it? Well, almost. And Sheelagh and Colm could come to ours, and Mary and all the Irish relatives could go to theirs, so we would both have family there."

His smile had broadened to a grin. "How long have you been hatching this, Beth Howard?"

She shrugged and returned his smile. "What do you think? Do you think Pierce and Maeve would agree?"

"I think it's a beautiful idea, Beth, and I'm sure Mary and Maeve will convince Pierce. I'll write to them today and see what they say. Thank you, my love. It's a great idea."

Michael received Mary's letter soon after he returned to base. He kept it in his uniform pocket and read it over and over, whenever he got the chance. It made him smile every time. In her excitement his sister had forgotten to be careful about what she wrote, and he was grateful the censors hadn't opened this one.

Main Street.
Doonbeg,
Co. Galway.
July 8, 1942

Dear Michael and Beth,
    We think it is a great idea. That is, me and Maeve
think it is a great idea, and even Pierce smiled when we
told him. Of course he started making excuses, like it
was a busy market time and the lambing season would
be in full swing, and whatever other excuse he could
find. You know what he's like Michael, but to tell the
truth I think he likes the idea very much, and of course
Maeve is delighted to get him to agree to a date.
    It won't be the same as actually having you here,
but it will be the next best thing. Maeve has asked if our
Norah can be her bridesmaid, even though she's so young,
and the little one is beside herself with excitement.
Maeve says she will wear her mother's wedding dress,
which is trimmed with Carrickmacross lace, though I

*don't suppose that matters to you, Michael. You can tell
Beth, I'm sure she will appreciate it.*

*It has been a grand summer and now, after the
harvest, Pierce and Joe are busy taking grain to market.
The lorries make the work a sight easier, though Pierce
has gone back to using a horse and cart, when he can,
for local work, because of the petrol shortages.*

*Norah is growing taller everyday and still talks
about her uncle and 'his funny voice.' I think she means
your accent. Every time I think of your visit, I don't
know whether to laugh or cry. We were so happy to see
you, and so sorry it was for such a short time. Now we
worry about you constantly. We hear, on the wireless, all
about the aircraft that are missing, and the airmen lost
and of course we imagine the worst, so please write to us
as often as you can, so that we know you are well.*

*Well, Michael, I have to finish, the bell has gone in
the shop. If the two weddings are to happen on the same
day, I do hope, as you suggest, that they will be at the
same time; then I can close my eyes and imagine I'm at
yours as well. Write soon. Give our love to Beth and take
great care of yourself. We didn't find you just to lose you.*

Your loving sister,
Mary

Michael folded the letter. He knew Pierce would agree, especially
once the two women worked on him. He couldn't wait for the next
letter, confirming it, and he smiled again when he thought of the two
young women ganging up on his brother.

A knock on the door interrupted his thoughts. Michael looked up
as Frank stuck his head around the door.

"Are you busy? Ah, don't tell me you're reading that ould letter
again. You were reading it two hours ago."

"Come in. Yes I am, and I'll probably read it several more times
before I'm finished." Michael smiled and returned it to the envelope.

"What do you want, Frank? Come in and close the door for goodness sake. Stop hovering in the doorway, it's cold enough in here."

"Ah, yes. Well. … I have a little something for you, Mike. At least I have something for your Beth."

He stepped into the room and Michael saw that Frank was carrying a large canvas bag.

"What have you got there?"

"Well, Michael. First of all, I have to tell you my friend, that I'm very honored at you asking me to be your best man. It means a lot to me. And I didn't know what I could get you for a wedding gift. So I thought, what with the times that are in it, that your good lady might be having a little difficulty organizing her wedding dress. For the big day, like. So I had a word with the lads, to see what they could do, and it took a while, but they finally came up with the goods. I hope you don't mind."

He tipped the sack up with a flourish and a bundle of silky, white cloth tumbled out.

"What is it?"

"A parachute, man, a parachute! White silk, for to make the wedding dress."

Michael knew Mrs. Howard, Beth, and her sisters had been saving their clothing rations ever since the engagement.

"Wow, Frank. Where did you get it?"

"Never you mind, lad. I put out the feelers and I finally got hold of one. Like gold dust they are. I just hope she likes it."

"You're amazing, I'm sure she'll love it. I think they were talking about borrowing a dress if they couldn't save enough rations to buy material." Michael viewed the large heap with concern. "But how are we going to get it to her?"

"Don't you worry about that, Mikey; it's all organized, all part of my gift. I've spoken to the ladies in the parachute-packing department, and they say they will pack it tight as you like and we can arrange for it to go over to Bristol on one of the freighter flights. It's all organized. I just needed to know that it would be acceptable."

Michael was sure Beth would be delighted, and said so.

"Right then!" Frank bundled the fragile fabric back into the sack. "I've also taken the liberty of putting in a request for us to get leave at the same time again, Michael, if you don't mind. I thought perhaps I could go over to Bristol with you, maybe meet this lucky lady."

"That's a great idea, Frank. Of course I want you to meet everyone before the big day. I know you'll like her, Frank, and her family."

"Grand! Consider it done. Ops say it will probably not happen until the New Year, but that will be time enough, won't it?"

"Plenty of time," said Michael reflecting yet again on his friend's amazing ability to "fix" almost anything. He had been requesting leave for them both for some weeks, with no success.

"And I finally get to meet that Evelyn one you keep mentioning," Frank added, with a roguish grin.

It was three days before their leave that Frank's aircraft was declared missing. Michael's crew, along with several others, was scrambled immediately. Their aircraft took off into the sleeting rain and turbulent winds of a January morning to scout the area and help in the search, but the weather was foul, the visibility poor, and the search was abandoned long before Michael wanted them to give up.

On their reluctant return to base the aircraft shuddered and yawed through the heavy crosswinds. On descent, rain hammered at the fuselage, the engines sputtered, and a wing dipped dangerously. Michael peered through the sleet-battered cockpit window into the gray, impenetrable gloom, trying to identify the airfield, or *any* recognizable landmarks. He briefly wondered if they, too, would be listed among the day's casualties, then he thought of Beth and squinted more keenly into the storm. He finally saw the runway and indicated its location to the captain who struggled to keep the aircraft on a steady downward course. When the aircraft pounded its inelegant landing onto the airfield, Michael, along with the rest of the crew, breathed prayers of relief.

As he walked across the ramp he said a silent goodbye to his friend and was glad of the stinging rain that hid his tears.

Frank's was the second aircraft they had lost in the month. Schedules were tightened, all leave cancelled, and the atmosphere on the base was somber. Michael wrote to tell Beth what had happened.

*..... every time I think of him I find I'm smiling,
even though I'm sad. I keep thinking of all the crazy
things he did and the funny things he said. And I keep
remembering that journey in the cart. You know the one
I mean.*

*I know it's a war Beth, and I know that there has to
be casualties, but Frank was my friend and I'm going to
miss him so much. We've lost too many people.*

*I have written to his family. It was a hard letter
to write. I can picture them so clearly. They all seemed
so happy that time I met them and they had such fun
together.*

*I hope to see you soon my dear, sweet, Beth. I read
your letters over and over. I'm told I will definitely get
leave for the wedding, so even if you don't see me before
that, keep a space beside you at the altar, I can't wait to
fill it,*

*Yours, ever and always,
Michael*

Michael knew that Beth and Sheelagh had become good friends since their meeting the year before. They even went on bike rides together on their days off. Less than two weeks after Michael wrote to Beth about Frank he received an unexpected letter from his sister. Sheelagh's letters were usually few and far between. After Michael's argument with her father and Aunty Wyn, when Michael left home, Sheelagh tried to smooth things over. She wrote to Michael saying that her father was always a bit hasty, but he was generally fine when he calmed down. She said she was sure that if Michael wrote to him, that they could sort things out. Michael wrote back saying that he was very sorry, but he had no intention of writing to Porter and that the matter was closed as far as he was concerned. They didn't mention the argument again. Afterwards, when she wrote, it was usually about news, or gossip, from the shop. She occasionally mentioned boyfriends, whom she seemed to change regularly, and she also kept him up-to-date about Colm. Their brother was the subject of the letter Michael now read.

*Beth told me about your friend, Michael, and I'm so sorry. I know you were very close and had been through a great deal together. Beth said he was going to be your best man and she said she didn't know who you would have now. I'm sure you haven't even thought about it yet, but it occurred to me that you could always ask Colm. I know you and he are not very close, but he **is** your brother, and with all the family connections going on, on that day, perhaps it would be nice?*

Anyway, I just thought I would mention it. We are looking forward to seeing you, and to the wedding. My sympathies again,

love,
Sheelagh

He'd never thought of Colm. In fact he'd never been sure that he really even *liked* Colm, but Sheelagh was right. Colm *was* his brother and he knew that it would please Mary. It occurred to Michael that Sheelagh was very like Mary in some ways, the way they both worked to try and fix relationships. Two sisters, who were so very different, who were reared so differently and didn't look a bit alike, yet there were still ways they were the same. He'd noticed they even crinkled their eyes the same way when they smiled.

Yes, Colm was probably a good idea. It would connect the whole family, even if it was in an unusual way.

1943

Closing the Circle

Thirty guests were invited to the wedding, most of them from the Howard side of the family. Beth wrote to ask Michael who he wanted to invite. He listed all the men on his crew. They'd been together for a long time now and they were close. He said he would also like to invite the two ladies from the shop who had always been so nice to him, Mrs. Wall and Mrs. Williams. He also asked that she send invitations to the Porters. He said that, despite the argument, they were Sheelagh's parents and he didn't want to upset her.

> *....and you will send an invitation to Aunty Wyn too, won't you, Beth? I send her money regularly and always include a note, but she never replies. I just wonder if she will come. I hope so. It would be very sad, after all these years, if she was so bloody-minded she decided not to.*

His aunt did not come. Jim and Edith Porter did. Edith Porter wore a hat covered in feathers that Michael thought he remembered from a long time ago. She also wore a fox fur draped around her shoulders, despite the warm and sunny weather.

When Michael entered the church, he saw Sister Thomas sitting in the back row. She still had the same friendly smile he remembered from when he was in her class and she didn't look much older. She shook his hand and wished him well, then gave him a small prayer card with a picture of St. Christopher on the front. "To keep you safe," she whispered. He thanked her and slipped it into his uniform breast pocket. Colm walked beside him down the aisle, smartly dressed, as always, in a navy blue suit with a crisp white shirt and navy blue silk tie. They had spoken little, but Michael was glad he had asked his brother to stand with him. They stood at the altar and waited.

The organ played the Wedding March and Michael turned. His breath caught in his throat when he saw her; Beth looked so beautiful. It seemed to him that she almost floated down the aisle on Paul's arm. Her dress was elegantly simple. The top showed off her slim figure and narrow waist and the full-length skirt swished softly as she walked. Michael silently thanked Frank for his gift. The long white veil, fastened into her hair with a delicate coronet of white flowers, billowed around her like wisps of a cloud, he thought. He wanted to rush up the aisle, wrap his arms around her, and tell her how beautiful she was, but he smiled at her instead. She returned his smile and, as she came closer, he saw that her eyes seemed to sparkle.

When brother and sister reached the altar, he smiled at Paul and shook his hand. He knew his friend had been due to arrive that morning, but this was one time Michael was banned from staying in the Howard's house. Since his arrival two days before he'd stayed at a boarding house, along with the three of his crew members who had also managed to get leave. Paul, like Michael, was in full RAF dress uniform, shoes and buttons shined to perfection, with his uniform cap tucked under his arm.

The ceremony was brief. After the Mass the guests walked to the reception in the church hall. Neighbors of the Howards helped serve the wedding breakfast. One of Mrs. Howard's brothers set up a gramophone on a table in the corner and put one of his sons in charge of changing the records. During the meal the boy sometimes forgot to wind the handle, and the guests laughed when a Bing Crosby song slowed so much the famous crooner sounded drunk. Michael was surprised to see a superbly iced, three-tiered cake in the center of the head table. It was decorated with an intricate latticework of icing interwoven with delicate icing flowers and topped with small figures of a bride and groom.

"Where on earth did you get all the rations for that?" he asked Beth as they took their place at the top table.

"It's cardboard, silly, with plaster for the icing. It looks good though, doesn't it? That's what everyone has now. We just hold the knife over it and pretend to cut it for the photograph. The shop says we have to be careful. They said one couple forgot and stuck the knife into it. Don't worry, there's a small cake hiding underneath it; we've all been saving our sugar rations. We can eat that."

When the meal was over, Colm stood and made an eloquent and humorous speech before taking up the handful of telegrams to read aloud. There were a few from Beth's family who couldn't make the long journey to Bristol and one from Edith and May Sinclair, Colm's parents. There was also a telegram from flight ops at Michael's base.

When he had finished reading all the other cards and telegrams Colm took a buff envelope from his pocket and opened it. He turned to Michael and Beth and read;

TO MR. AND MRS. MICHAEL KELLY **STOP** EVERY HAPPINESS ON THIS AND EVERY DAY IN YOUR FUTURE **STOP** WITH LOVE AND BEST WISHES FROM MR. AND MRS. PIERCE KELLY **STOP** PS WE LOOK FORWARD TO SEEING YOU SOON **STOP**.

Michael felt tears stinging his eyes; Beth held his hand in hers.

Colm slipped the telegram back into his pocket and lifted his glass.

"Ladies and gentlemen, I would like you to raise your glasses and drink a toast. To the bride and groom."

All the guests stood. Some raised their glasses, others raised their teacups, but they all echoed the toast, "The bride and groom."

Michael stood, smiling and speechless, facing Beth as everyone applauded. She blushed and raised her face to his. He bowed his head and kissed her gently. The guests applauded again.

The End

Glossary

ALANNA: From the Gaelic a *leanbh* (lanav) meaning child

AMADAN: A fool.

BUGGER: Mildly abusive, sometimes an affectionately used term for a rogue.

BY-BLOW: Illegitimate child.

CRAYTHUR: Colloquial pronunciation of "creature," sometimes implying alcoholic drink.

HOOLEY: Party, Celebration

JAMMY: Term implying lucky.

LUCKY BAGS: Sealed paper bags that contained two or three small items, a balloon, plastic jewelry, sweets or a cheap toy.

MAVOURNEEN: My love.

SQUARE BASH: Marching practice.

TOSSER: Derogatory term, a wastrel.

WITTERING: Inconsequential chatter.

WVS: Women's Voluntary Service.

About the Author.

Ann O'Farrell lived most of her life in Dublin, Ireland, but her first job was as a laboratory technician in Bristol, England. Later, she returned to Dublin to work as a stewardess with Aer Lingus, Irish Airlines. After her marriage she was active in Community Theater for many years, particularly in Youth Theater. When her three sons were grown, she returned to university to study theater and sociology.

Ann's writing career began after her retirement to Florida in the late 1990s. Ann's letters home developed into humorous short stories, several of which have been published in newspapers, magazines, and short-story collections. Her first novel, *Norah's Children*, was published in 2006. She is currently working on her third novel, *Kitty's Hive*.

Breinigsville, PA USA
30 March 2010
235240BV00002B/29/P